OUT OF TIME

A FICTION

BY

DEREK GAGNON

AOS Publishing, 2025

ISBN: 978-1-998662-07-4

Cover Design: Meredith Lindsay

Visit AOS Publishing's website:
www.aospublishing.com

To my children.

Table of Contents

PROLOGUE

The Interview

"Timeless."

— Richard

Elliot: Entrepreneur, visionary, bold. These few words have been used recently to describe my guest. Mr. Washington, thank you for taking the time, no pun intended, to meet with us.

Washington: My pleasure, and please, call me Richard.

Elliot: Richard, before we get to the heart of this interview, would you please tell the readers a little bit about yourself? How did you get here?

Washington: My name is Richard Washington, CEO and chairman of Chronos Corporation. I was born and raised in Chicago, where I lived with my mother, Helena, my father, John, and my younger brother, Victor. I wasn't the best student, nor was I the worst. My teachers would often tell my parents I was a daydreamer. Head in the clouds... some even called me lazy. Anyway, I finally graduated and barely made it into college. Midway through my first year, I'll always remember, my father and brother invited me to a show. It was the type of spectacle where the orchestra would play on stage, and scenes from the movies would be projected on a large screen above the musicians: one night only, the last show on the tour.

Elliot: I have a feeling you did not attend.

Washington: No. Sadly, I did not. You may come up with any reason as to why I could not go. Midterms, late shift, a date... my reason is much more pathetic. (Pause) This was *the* defining moment in building Chronos up. Its genesis, if I may. The morning after the event, I had this unreasonable but intense feeling of regret. I was reading about the show's exploits and successes in the newspaper and hearing about it on the radio. Even social media was raving about how it was a "once-in-a-lifetime experience." That is when it got me thinking. *Why?* Why should it only be "once-in-a-lifetime"? Why should something good, delightful, and unique be experienced only once? I understand. Some people, my first critics, said things like "uniqueness is what makes the experience magical" and "why don't you buy a recording of it or stream it?" I did not believe in that. What I believed in was the idea that one day such regrets would never haunt me again.

Elliot: And here we are, twenty-eight years later, on the five-year anniversary of Chronos' grand opening. Congratulations!

Washington: Thank you.

Elliot: So why "Chronos"? Where did the name come from?

Washington: My investors. (Laugh) A lot of them are into Greek mythology. *Chronos* is the personification of time. It seemed only fitting to borrow this legendary and powerful being's name for our equally titanic endeavours.

Elliot: Not to be confused with Kronos with a *K*, father of Zeus. Correct?

Washington: That's right.

Elliot: And what about the rules? Your PR rep was kind enough to send me an exhaustive list of dos and don'ts. There are quite a few. Would you mind explaining them in your own words?

Washington: I will summarize them in eight simple rules. Number one, *What's in the past, stays in the past*. In a nutshell, you are not allowed to bring anything back with you. Simple enough. Number two, *Stay with your guide.* Although your Chronos-issued bracelet will be the most important piece of tech you will bring on your trip, the guide is your lifeline to bring you back home. Yes, you have to come back home. Number three, *Be there on time.* Ironically, time is a commodity we simply do not have in this entertainment business. If the registration form says to be at the reception desk at ten on the morning of the eighteenth, you will have forfeited your time slot as of ten past ten. Number four, *Don't do anything stupid.* Rules are rules. The law is the law. Whether your party travels back to the early two thousand or the late sixteen hundreds, you must abide by the regulations set by the traveled-to city and time. Also, although it is an unwritten rule, no hooking up with a member of the opposite timeline. (Pause) Number five, *No registration, no action.* We at Chronos Corp. run on a tightly woven schedule. For the client's experience to go as smoothly as possible, every form and document must be completed before the client's arrival on the premises. From their height to eyewear needs to allergies, our staff will need this information to make sure everything goes well. Number six, *Lost and... not found.* Unfortunately, we are not responsible for the things you lose or forget during your trip. Our guides are taking serious precautions to make sure "futuristic" objects are not brought on the trips. You wouldn't want Galileo stumbling upon your smartphone, now, would you? What a mess historically that would make. In the same vein, rule number seven has to do with *Watching your tongue*. Watch what you say. If you go to a sporting event, don't divulge the final score. If you go to Ancient Greece, let one of our expert linguists do the talking. And finally, number eight, *Stay away from relatives*. While you are there, do not interact with family members or ancestors. Of course, there is more to those rules, but, in general, if you sign up for a Chronos experience, these are the principles you will have to follow.

Elliot: Thank you. I am certain our readers will appreciate the simplified version of your rules. Now, earlier, you said you had a few investors. A market like this one must have some high-profile backers. Anything you can tell us about them?

Washington: I'm afraid that would be confidential.

Elliot: Fair enough. Would you be able to tell us if they have a say in when or where Chronos takes its clients next?

Washington: The board, which is composed of eight major investors plus myself, meets quarterly to see how we can improve our clients' experiences. Although we indeed make the final decisions, out of our two hundred and fifteen destinations, one hundred and eighty-eight have been chosen by the masses. Our communication team works year-round to gather the intel that will ensure that our next wave of "once-in-a-lifetime" events will generate a lot of interest.

Elliot: Speaking of interest, do your clients have a preferred time destination?

Washington: It depends on what they want. Other than the basic Chronos experiences like concerts and sports events, we offer a variety of packages: honeymoons, bachelor and bachelorette parties, retreats, and field trips, to name a few. My personal favourite is Roma, circa 192 AD.

Elliot: Have you been approached by governments? Or even the military?

Washington: We do business with the government up to a certain point. Lots to do with cultural knowledge. For example, I mentioned the field trips. Our educational branch is working in partnership with many countries' education boards, colleges, and top universities. As for the military... (Pause) I do not see why they would be interested in us. Everything we could ever learn from Sun Tzu, Alexander, and Bonaparte is written in books. Going back in time and training with them, however phenomenal the experience might be, wouldn't be of much help. We're an entertainment business, let's not forget.

Elliot: What do you think of the allegations made by the STL? They have been clawing at your doors for about three years now.

Washington: Although I disagree with the message the Society of Timeline Liberation is spreading and the negative image that accompanies it, I have a lot of respect for the men and women who are part of it. It takes a lot of courage to stick to your beliefs and come out and attack our... my... principles. I must admit it is annoying having to deal with the calumny sent our way, but we trust in our system. We trust in our company. I trust my employees. And you can trust me when I say that everything we do does not, has not, hurt the fabric of time.

Elliot: Thank you, I see the time flying by. Do you mind if I ask you a few more questions?

Washington: Not at all, please.

Elliot: As we know, your business is celebrating its fifth year. What can we expect from Chronos in the future?

Washington: More timelines, fewer wait times. Our research department is also currently working on a portable Chronos. Many people are unfortunately unable to travel to our facility, namely our elders. The MiChronos—a wordplay on micro and Chronos—will be brought to nursing and retirement homes for them to partake in the joys of time traveling. We hope to have a working prototype within the next five years.

Elliot: Finally, in one word, how would you describe Chronos and the work that you have done?

Washington: (Pause) Timeless.

Elliot: Mr. Washington, Richard, thank you so much for giving our readers a glimpse into the inner workings of your company. And all this, to think it started from a missed concert, a regret. One last question, if I may. With the tools that you have now, have you ever gone back in time to catch that show?

Washington: Never.

Elliot: Why not?

Washington: (Smiles) That's for me to know and for you to guess.

PART ONE

CHRONOS

"Welcome to Chronos, where the future is a thing of the past."
— Richard

CHAPTER 1 - Bill

Four Years Ago

Set four years before "The Interview"

What did I get myself into?

To be fair, it wasn't all that bad being known as *Leader One* of the Society of Timeline Liberation. He met powerful individuals, including chiefs of secret organizations, high-profile celebrities, and, for lack of better words, otherworldly interesting people. Traveling was nice, too. It wasn't always dangerous, as he thought it would be when Ginny had given him the position. When she told him that LETO had tasked him with playing the role of Leader One, he had pictured himself walking around in a tuxedo, driving fancy cars, and introducing himself by starting with his last name followed by his full name, like that MI6 super-spy had done way back in the sixties. A life entirely different from the one he quietly led in the States: *I am Bill, baker by day, secret agent by night.*

His first mission took him to Monaco, of all places, which blew up his ego in thinking he was a big-shot double-0 agent. He'd taken the red eye from JFK to NCE—his first plane ride back to Europe in a mighty long time. As the aircraft touched down, Bill could see the sun rising over the French horizon, a *mélange* of orange and blue reflecting off of the *Baie des Anges*, an angelic view indeed. This was all so surreal to him. Never, in his wildest dreams, would he have thought he would be going to Monte Carlo. Much less during the much-acclaimed Grand Prix! He wasn't much of a car guy himself, but the simple fact he could say, *Yeah, been there, done that, no big deal* was nice to think about.

His train ride from Aéroport de Nice to his hotel in La Condamine, where he was to meet Dravra's contact later in the day, was uneventful at best and dreadfully boring at worst. He thought he saw a dolphin through the large compartment window, maybe. When he wasn't busy checking out the sights, he cracked open a book, plunging himself into pages of a world he was more than happy to revisit.

Getting off the train, Bill was glad he had brought a cardigan with him to keep warm. The morning breeze pleasantly chilled his exhausted face. After making sure he had all of his luggage with him, a small duffel bag, and a backpack, he hailed a taxi. A mix of surprise and shock rushed over the wannabe spy when a Mercedes pulled up next to him. *Woah, next thing you know, I'll have to race this thing through the streets to escape a group of villains.* Wishful thinking. He pushed the thought out of his head as he entered the cab.

When he got to the hotel, a quaint-looking thing a few blocks from the water's shores, Bill walked up to the reception desk and checked in. They had given him a room on the fifth floor with a view of the northern side of the city.

"The vista from up there is spectacular," the concierge promised.

The baker-spy slid his key card into the slot, and after a moment, a light turned from red to green with a click. The door opened onto a derelict room. The floor was made of light-coloured wood, and the walls were painted cream. A single bed, illuminated and warmed by a ray of sunlight coming from a tiny window, took up most of the space. There was no TV. Bill dropped his bags and walked to the aperture. The lady hadn't lied; the view was breathtaking. Not exactly what you would expect to see on a postcard from La Condamine: with the crescent and the boats and the tall buildings. No, what he saw were greeneries climbing the face of a smallish mountain. A more natural than touristy look.

Lost in contemplation, Bill jumped when a knock came on the door. Suspicious, he slowly made his way to the peephole. To his surprise, the fishbowl hallway was empty. Had he imagined the knock? He turned the knob, poked his head outside, and looked both ways. Nothing. While shrugging, he just about closed the door when he noticed a piece of paper on the carpeted floor. Bill took one last look around before picking it up and hurrying back to his room.

Strange. It wasn't addressed to anyone in particular.

Quite the trip you've had, wasn't it?
Under normal circumstances, I would have greeted you at the airport.
Alas, something came up, and I had to change my plans.
I hope you won't be too upset.

Rest assured, I will make an effort to see you.
After all, it is not every day my brother travels across the ocean to see me!
I can't wait to show you what Monaco has to offer.
No way you are missing out on the Palais Princier or the
    Musée Océanographique.
I know you're not much for gardens, but we have to walk around
    the Jardin Exotique.

Expect to see crazy-looking birds.

Really, they're a dime a dozen.

#1 sister!

Cassandra

Bill read and reread the note. He was trying to find a clue, a hidden message here or there. Why was it arranged in such a way, one line at a time, if not to entertain a specific meaning? All of a sudden, it hit him. He grabbed the little hotel notepad from the desk, uncapped a pen, and wrote the first letter of each sentence.

QUAI RAINIER

The Rainier Quay. Of course! That would make *Cassandra* the name of a boat or yacht on which he would meet his contact from Dravra. It would make for an inconspicuous meeting point. If he was spotted, he could say he was just going for a walk by the water, enjoying the sights. Easy peasy!

The question now was *how to get there.* He picked up his phone, typed the words on his map app, and, to his dissatisfaction, four dots popped up nearby. Bill straightened the note and inspected it for the zillionth time. That's *gotta be it,* he thought, looking at the *#1 sister.* He pushed a few more buttons and *Bingo!* It looked to be a twenty-five to thirty-minute walk east of the hotel. He grabbed his key card and made his way to the door, giddy at the prospect of finally playing a secret agent. *I should get some shades. Yes, I'm definitely getting shades.*

He had found the *Cassandra* pretty easily, but no one was there to meet him. Had he misunderstood the message? In his wild boy's hope to play his favourite action hero, had he misinterpreted what was, after all, a very normal note sent to the wrong room? He stood around, pacing the deck alongside the yacht for what seemed like an hour. His stomach rumbled. He was on the verge of giving up, going back to his room, ordering room service, and watching a TV show he'd downloaded on his phone when a woman in her late thirties, wearing a black skirt, tennis shoes, and, yes, shades, walked up to him. She said, "You're early." *Am I? Could've fooled me!* He thought sarcastically.

Looking at his watch, he said, "Yeah, been here about an hour."

She glanced at her watch. "It's only quarter to twelve. Wasn't the message clear?"

"What do you mean?"

"They're a dime a dozen." She repeated a line from the note. "Nice glasses. Please come."

"A dime a dozen," he whispered to himself. "Ten to twelve. Right. I knew that." He sheepishly took his sunglasses off and followed the woman who, he assumed, was his contact from Dravra, agent DeLuca.

They climbed aboard the *Cassandra*, a beauty of a ship. The woman led him to what looked like an office. She sat on the other side of a mahogany desk, which stood in the middle of a circular room. Behind the leather chair, a colourful painting hung on a wall surrounded by bookshelves and other pieces of art. The whole setting screamed richness. She quietly motioned for Bill to take a seat opposite her.

"Leader One, for starters, let me apologize for the change of plans," she said, removing her sunglasses and revealing bright blue eyes. "We can never be too safe, you understand?"

"No worries." Bill sat up straighter when she called him Leader One, as though it were a reminder that he had to play the part of a spy and not simply Bill, the awkward baker. Did he detect a French or maybe Italian accent in her voice? "I am happy to see Dravra is on our side."

"Of course." She smiled. "Let's cut to the chase. Should today's mission be successful, the Society will finally know what exactly they are up against. And who the real enemy is." Pulling a briefcase out of nowhere, the agent from Dravra opened it and handed him a beige file. Bill took it and started perusing through it. "Our agent has informed us that a meeting has been set for tomorrow during the race. We just don't know where exactly. One of the men is rumored to work for a secret military branch and has seldom been seen on the outside. It was LETO's wish to have her top agent, you, track this *Ghost* and see what kind of information could be taken out of him."

When in doubt, who you gonna call? Bill the baker!

"We know the Society has been looking into Mr. Washington and Chronos for some time now, but this is the break all of us have been waiting for. What are you thinking?"

"I see," Bill said after a brief moment. Then, turning into his 00 persona, exuding as much confidence as he could muster, he explained, "Here's what we're gonna do."

Early the next day, after a restless night alone in his room, Bill made his way to the café they had agreed upon. Dressed as a clichéd tourist—tacky summer shirt, khakis, and a straw hat—he was to play the part believably if things were to ever go his way. He ordered a black tea from the barista and sat on the terrace with his back to the window, an American newspaper he had bought at the hotel under his already pit-stained arm. *Breathe, Billy-Boy. You've got this!* In less than an hour, the race would commence, and a back street nearby would empty safe for two gentlemen: a fedora-wearing Latino and a Ghost.

Bill the spy was to wait for the fashionable one to stroll by before tailing him. Intel confirmed that he stayed at an Airbnb two intersections west of Bill's vantage point. As soon as the target left his place, he could start tracking—and to the unknown be led.

His tea was almost gone, a sip or two left at most, when the man finally appeared out of a tiny apartment with a blue door. The cheering of the crowd was already loud nearby. The race had begun. Through his sunglasses, Bill kept one eye on the fading words of an article and the other on his prey. Once the man had walked past him, he waited a few seconds before folding the newspaper under an arm, taking one last sip, and following the gentleman known as Gaspar. Remaining a safe distance behind, inconspicuous, Bill feigned looking at the architecture surrounding him. With hands in his pockets, his step was unhurried, unlike Gaspar's, who frantically glanced at his watch every few seconds. Eventually, the man in the hat turned a corner and suddenly stopped. Bill kept walking past the alley's entrance, trying to survey it as well as he could out of the corner of his greenish eye.

It wasn't much of a backstreet, wide enough for a small car at best and maybe as long as a city bus. There were no windows on either side of the alleyway, and no doors either. What Bill did notice, however, was the rising noise of a cheering crowd and the smell of burning rubber. He continued and turned down the next passageway adjacent to the one where he assumed a meeting was about to unfold. After walking thirteen or so paces, Bill emerged from the alley. There were approximately two dozen inspired fans around him. *Seems safe enough so far*, he thought as he slowly made his way back to where Gaspar was last seen.

There he was, dabbing at his sweating neck with a handkerchief. *Do people still carry handkerchiefs?* Was it possible to look even more nervous than he had a minute ago? Only now, there was someone in front of him. With broad shoulders and close-cropped hair, the interlocutor had an imposing physique, to be sure. He towered head and shoulders over Gaspar. The unknown man reminded Bill of a typical SEAL portrayed in action movies. Could this hunk of a man be the Ghost? Subtly, Bill inched closer to catch a glimpse of the conversation.

"—trusts me, Washington does. And so should you, Cupcake."

Bill positioned himself in such a way that he was facing the street-turned-racetrack, standing diagonally in front of a woman wearing an F1 buttoned shirt. Eavesdropping on the two men would not be easy with the small crowd surrounding them, but at least he would look the part he was meant to play.

"There are too many of them," Gaspar chimed in shakily. "Someone is bound to connect the dots."

"We've got things under control, son. As we speak, I've got my men building a facility where the... *unwanted* can be gathered. Unfortunately, I seem to have fallen out of the President's favour, for some reason."

"This is where I come in?" Gaspar guessed.

"Bingo! With your help, Bishop, we can keep the world and... certain secrets safe."

"Colonel Marsh! I will not be intimidated," the smaller man said, although Bill could hear quite the opposite in his voice. "There are no secrets to hide. If, and I say *if*, we decide to get involved, it'll be for the good of all mankind."

"Of course, of course. You can believe me when I say—"

It suddenly got too loud for Bill to hear anything else. The masses started cheering loudly as top-of-the-line automotive machines turned the corner at breakneck speeds. The noise continuously lasted for about thirty seconds before he heard someone say something about it being the sixty-seventh turn. The race would be over soon.

Bill tried refocusing his attention on the conversation behind him. He was afraid, for a moment, that they had left. He did not dare look behind. He was close enough to danger as it was. Finally, he heard Gaspar's voice, defeated-like, catch his ear.

"Fine. We'll assist you."

"Much appreciated, your Holiness."

"Do not patronize me, Colonel. This *Site B* had better work. If anyone was to find out... If the Society was to know—"

"Oh, come on, Buttercup. Society, Schmociety. Have some faith."

That was the end of it. Their conversation had ended, and Bill only had this *Site B* to report back to LETO. He was about to leave when he felt an arm brush against his. The man standing next to him had broad shoulders and close-cropped hair: the type of guy you do not want to cross.

"Who's winning?" Colonel Marsh asked, looking straight ahead.

Bill panicked. Duck feet under water. The Ghost was right here. He could see him, with his large nose and pepper-salt moustache, and if the half-exposed chest tattoo wasn't enough to terrify him, the almost inhuman size of his hand was sure to do the trick. The baker said the first thing that popped into his head: "*Mi scusi*?"

Marsh looked straight at him now. "Oh, I'm sorry. You know, I just assumed," he said, pointing at the English newspaper under Bill's arm. "Plus, I could swear you were listening in on that little conversation I was having." *Abort! Abort! Abort!* Red lights flashed in Bill's mind. "Mind going for a walk?" he continued as he wrapped an arm around the diminutive baker. Then he smiled.

Bill was petrified. He could not move a muscle. Where was Dravra? Were they not keeping up with their side of the plan? Suddenly, the roar of machines crescendoed. The pilots were completing another turn. The distraction gave the lemming just enough time to escape the bear's grasp. He started running toward the alley where the secret meeting had occurred. The tailor-turned-prey quickly glanced behind him. The Ghost had not moved. Was he not going to pursue him? That only unnerved him more.

After running non-stop for a block or two and cursing his aging limbs every time his lungs permitted him to utter a word, he was forced to a stop by a black Citroën barring his path. *This is it*, he said, defeated. Only it wasn't. The tinted window scrolled down.

"Get in! Quick!" DeLuca urged him.

Not waiting to be told twice, Bill slid onto the passenger seat, buckled his seatbelt, and felt the full G's of his escape.

"We've been compromised," she finally said, maybe as an excuse.

"*You've* been compromised?" he replied incredulously. "The Ghost saw *me*!"

"The Ghost? He was there after all?"

"Yeah! What do you mean? Didn't you follow the plan?" he ejaculated in a slightly higher voice than usual.

"Everything went to hell early on. For some reason, they knew we'd be right behind you." Her face grimmed.

"You're saying Dravra has a leak?" Bill asked, concerned.

"I'm saying Dravra is not safe anymore. And neither are you."

They kept driving east and then south. Drove right into Italy and only stopped when neither of them could drive anymore. Bill recounted what he had heard to Agent DeLuca: Ghost being Colonel Marsh, Gaspar's alias being the Bishop, the *Unwanteds,* and Site B. He knew they had to get the information to Ginny somehow, so she could relay all of it to LETO. Unfortunately, since common communication lines were most likely unsafe, he'd have to tell her face-to-face.

"There is no telling what kind of power Colonel Marsh has over in the US," Agent DeLuca said once they had reached a safe house in the Lazio region. "At least until we've had a better look into him."

"Agreed," he had replied pensively, trying to think of a way out of this mess.

"You'll need to stay put until things cool off."

"I can't wait too long."

"I know."

The world was in trouble. And although they didn't know it yet, ripples were slowly turning into waves.

〜

1468 day(s): 18 hour(s): 23 minute(s): 12 second(s)

CHAPTER 2 - Bill

The Man in the Screen

Bill had finally made his way back to Italy. It had been four years since running away from the Ghost. DeLuca had sent him an urgent transmission, soliciting his expertise, whatever it was, one more time. It is to be said that Bill the baker had gotten significantly more efficient at his Bill the spy persona. Not only did LETO trust his judgment, but he also now truly was in charge of the STL's guerilla force. And what a force it had become in those short few years.

Dravra's heydays, on the other hand, were far behind them. Ever since what came to be known as the *Monaco Leak*, a total organizational fiasco that was, a small cell continued to operate out of an apartment complex under the direction and guidance of Special Agent DeLuca, or Director DeLuca—a self-appointed title in a time of need. Their primary objective had been to aid the Society by keeping tabs on Colonel "the Ghost" Marsh's number one European associate: the Bishop.

Before only a few weeks ago, the operation was going smoothly. That was until DeLuca's mole, an informant who had successfully gotten a paper-pusher job under the Bishop, informed Dravra that *Monseigneur* Gaspar was making special arrangements and packing frenetically. Things were looking dicey for him, and since falling out of the Pope's favour, it looked like the Bishop was leaving the country—and this time for good. With limited supply, manpower, and time, DeLuca's team did the only thing it could: kidnapped Gaspar. Unfortunately for her and the agents, the clergyman was as silent as the grave, which was ironic since he probably knew this was where Marsh would send him should he say anything. DeLuca needed help. She needed an expert. So she called an old friend.

October in Rome was, for lack of better words, magical. Not too hot, not too cool. Walking out of Leonardo da Vinci International Airport, Bill looked up at the cloudless sky. As he readjusted his sunglasses, a female voice called beside him.

"You're early."

To which he replied, slowly turning, "Yeah, been here about an hour."

They both laughed at their inside joke. Bill walked up to DeLuca, embracing her.

"Nice glasses," she remarked after a moment.

"You know me, gotta look the part."

"I see you've kept the beard."

Bill just smiled, stroking his greying chin. He picked up his carry-on, and both walked toward the parked car.

"So what is this all about?" Bill inquired once they were well on their way to the base of operations. "You kept your details to the minimum."

"You blame me?" she replied, not exactly asking a question. "You'll see when we get there."

And get there they did, an hour or so later. DeLuca was presently driving off-road, which made Bill a little uneasy.

"Where did you say we were going?" he asked, his hand grasping the ceiling handle.

"I didn't," she said sharply.

"What happened to that nice little safe house back in the Lazio region?"

"Had to move out. All of our previous locations had been compromised due to the leak. We couldn't risk it. We transferred everything under Monte Meta."

"Un... under?"

That was when he saw it. Two large rocks covered with moss, overlapping one another. A sliver of shadow told the onlooker that there must be some sort of entrance hidden there. DeLuca stopped the car and walked out, encouraging Bill to follow her. She led him to the stone facade, which, upon closer inspection, looked quite normal. She put a hand to her ear and whispered something. Before long, Bill heard faint clicking noises. Ever so slowly, the back boulder retracted within the hillside, as if melting.

"Welcome to Dravra," DeLuca had said, motioning to the newly revealed entrance.

Unhurriedly, Bill stepped forward. Engulfed in darkness, he used his hands and sense of touch to guide himself, following what felt to be a man-made tunnel. Finally, after what felt like a long time but was, in fact, no more than fifteen seconds, Bill the baker reached the end of the tunnel. He heard footsteps behind him and a voice that followed. "Knock three times. Not too fast. Not too slow." *If I had a nickel*—So he did, and just like magic, the door opened, enveloping him in bright light. He covered his eyes using his forearm as he entered a cold and damp underground room. Once his vision adjusted, he took everything in: the high natural ceiling, the stalactites hanging down from it, the rough rocky ground covered in wires, and technological equipment propped against stalagmites. The whole thing was surreal.

"And you need *my* help?" he finally said once he had recovered his voice.

"Come on," she replied with a sneer, clapping him on the back. "Let me show you around."

Although quite crude, the circular layout was made in a way that promoted efficiency as well as security. The main area beyond the door Bill had entered from was wide open. Above the entrance, a metal staircase had been constructed to arch over the doorway like some kind of death rainbow should the mountain be breached. On said lookout, a vigil stood guard, semi-automatic rifle at the ready. Bill counted five such campers, all perched fifteen or so feet above the ground, protecting their door.

Walking counterclockwise around the hub, DeLuca pointed at the man guarding the first room.

"This is Aanton," she said while waving at him. "And these are our quarters."

The agent revealed a room with a low reinforced ceiling. Eighteen beds were lined up in two rows of nine; three of them were presently being used by napping agents, those who had been on night duty, Bill guessed. One of them groaned at them and the insurgent rays of artificial light. Slowly, she closed the door and moved on with the tour.

"Our cafeteria. It's not much, but Erik, our cook, is an absolute wizard in the kitchen," she continued, pointing to another door some twenty feet away.

"I'll be sure to exchange recipes. And what's this one for?"

Bill was already making his way toward the most heavily guarded of all doors. Compared to the others, not only did this one have an oscillating camera attached to the left railing, but it also was the only one to exhibit a keypad. Inching closer to the small door window, Bill was appalled by what he saw. In a dark room with a single screen, he had recognized the face of a gauntish version of the Bishop.

"What's the meaning of this?" Bill said, keeping his voice calm and even.

"Looks like the visit is cut short. Ain't it, boss?" said a man advancing on them.

"Bill, this is Agent Carmichael. Agent Carmichael, meet Leader One."

"Great to finally meet." The agent reached in and shook his hand. "We've heard so much about you."

"I'm afraid I can't say the same," Bill replied sourly. Something about this guy did not sit right with him.

"Carmichael was the one who brought us the Bishop," added DeLuca.

"You don't say," Bill replied, looking impressed, yet crossing his arms across his chest. "How did you manage that?"

"Oh, you know. It was more luck than anything else. Right place, right time."

"Of course. So what is he doing in there? Since when is Dravra keeping prisoners?"

"To be sure, he is not a prisoner."

"So he came here of his own accord?"

"Well... no."

"Wandered in, came through a wardrobe?"

"Alright, that's enough," interrupted DeLuca. "Agent Carmichael, would you please go see about Agent Lau?"

"Yes'm," he said, and promptly departed.

"What was that all about?" she finally said once her agent was out of earshot, a reproachful tone in her voice.

"I don't like it, Carmen," he whispered, dropping ranks.

"You don't like Carmichael?"

"That's not it. This," he pointed at the Bishop's sickly pixelated face. "This is not what the Society does. What are you doing to him, anyway?"

"Before you paint us as the villains, Bill, let me tell you what happened."

❧

How the Bishop came to be stuck in a screen

It happened a week ago. Carmichael was positioned, as he had been for a few days, in an empty apartment facing the ancient stone building where the Bishop held offices. He remembered the wind being cool on that specific night, a delightfully welcomed breeze in a strangely warm autumn. From his vantage point, with an eye behind a camera, the agent investigated the clergyman. He seemed agitated and nervous. Beads of sweat pearled down his forehead, the Italian had forgone his tie and unfastened the top button of his slightly wet shirt. Pacing to and fro in his study, was it fear? His papers were scattered, and his drawers emptied. He was planning something, only Carmichael didn't know what.

The agent turned away from the window for a second to scribble a few notes down. He looked back in time to see Gaspar unlatching the office window and opening it just a crack. Adjusting the zoom lens, Carmichael became aware for the first time of the shake in the man's hands and the frenzied look in his eyes. He was scared. At that moment, Steven Carmichael felt pity for the man. But the instant did not last. Gaspar the Bishop had been an important player under Marsh since the very beginning. He needed to be stopped, and at five to midnight, a golden opportunity arose.

The Bishop finally sat. Trembling hands fidgeted with a bracelet-like accessory, then reached for a device no bigger than a helmet. Dravra agents had heard rumors of this mysterious, not yet on the market tech. So, it was true. The MiChronos existed. Who knew exactly how many were already in circulation? The idea worried Carmichael. Gaspar played with the headset for a second and apposed it onto his head. Nothing happened right away, but after a breath, his body disappeared, it was gone!

Now was his chance, he wouldn't let it go. Carmichael, quiet and agile as a cat, quickly packed his things and exited the staking room. It was dark out in the streets. Starlight lazily illuminated the edges of the cobblestone. Trying to look as inconspicuous as could be, Carmichael readjusted the hat lower over his eyes and slowly walked to the open window of Gaspar's office. Once he reached it, he looked both ways to ascertain the absence of onlookers and, in a quick drop and roll, he was in. Carmichael waited there, silent, for a minute or two to make sure his tumble hadn't alerted anyone. But he knew, from his spying of late, that the only other living being still awake in this old building was a janitor on the third floor.

The MiChronos was there, unattended on the chair. He reached for it without any hesitation. The agent didn't even take a moment to admire and appreciate the intricate way in which the metal and plastic weaved together to create such a beautiful and powerful item. He simply hid it, and its connecting parts, out of sight under his lightweight jacket.

Kidnapped Bishop under the arm, he drove back to Monte Meta that same night. This was a win for Dravra.

~

"Anyways," she continued. "The tech guys could piggyback the feed and connect to it. Once the Bishop understood what was happening, he refused to come out. We can communicate with him: we talk, he can hear." DeLuca sighed. "But he's refusing to cooperate."

"I guess I made up my mind too quickly," Bill finally said once the story was recounted. "I owe you an apology."

"Damn right, you do," DeLuca had replied. "But not to me."

They both looked in the direction of Carmichael, who was going through papers with the one called Lau.

"Fine," he said outwardly. But his mind kept saying, *something's not right*. "What exactly do you need me to do?"

DeLuca opened the heavy metal door and signaled for Bill to walk ahead. The undulating ceiling was only a few feet above the baker's head. He slowly reached up. His fingers felt wet at the touch, or was it that they were only cold? He did a quick scan around the room. Other than the fifty-five-inch screen propped up on a couple of tripods, a single swivel chair stood about six inches from a work desk that could not have been longer than Bill's wingspan. On that desk, connected to the screen and attached by three wires—a red, a yellow, and a white—was what he assumed could only be the MiChronos. The bulk of it was made of solid grey-ish plastic, but there was something that made it cool to the touch. An opaque visor, most likely an ocular reader, settled tight in between two large foamy arms. The tech reminded Bill of a mix between a scouter and a VR headset. He reached in to hold it before DeLuca advised him against it.

"I wouldn't do that. The image is grainy enough as it is." She walked a little closer.

"Looks fine to me," Bill replied.

"That's because you grew up on 8-bit video games," she retorted with a smile. "Old man."

Bill put his hand to his chest as if wounded by the comment.

"So what am I seeing now?" he prompted, nodding at the screen.

"In short, you've got the Bishop sitting in a room by himself. We've been able to track him back to *l'Ospedale della Pietà*."

"Vivaldi's orphanage," he interrupted, slightly surprised.

"I knew you weren't just a pretty face. Anywho, he's been moving around from time to time. But he hasn't been saying anything. Thought you could help."

"What makes you think he's going to talk to me?"

"Because I know you to be quite persistent," she simply replied, a mysterious look in her eyes. After that, she turned on her heels and headed out the door, closing it with a loud yet muffled sound.

"Okay, Gaspar. Talk to me, baby."

Outside the jail, Erik, the cook, announced, to everyone's delight, that it was lunchtime. The twenty or so agents made their way in waves toward the kitchen. They grabbed their bowl and spoon, lined up, and waited for Erik to drop the delectable concoction. The smell of gumbo was intoxicating and truly mouth-watering. Bill, however, would have to wait, for he had a meeting with the clergyman.

Bill walked up to the headset, wondering how he was going to convince, let alone talk to, the man on the screen. He wished DeLuca had taken the time to explain the finer technical details. He had waited too long to ask her. Now it would be embarrassing. He would have to figure it out by himself. What could go wrong?

He looked around the room, eyes searching for anything that might pass as a microphone or something of the sort. He shuffled a stack of papers around and gently kicked a metal crate. Nothing. He walked over to the giant screen, one hand in his pants pocket, the other searching the edge of the screen. After a moment, he crossed both arms across his chest, looked around as if to make sure no one was looking, and tilted his head toward the TV.

"Hello?"

The Bishop's head propped up. The movement was slight yet enough to be noticeable. Bill tried again.

"Can you hear me?" he tried after yet another moment. "For all that it's worth, I am not with Dravra."

A hint of a gleaming light shone in the Bishop's eye.

"Might you be the one known as 'the baker'?" the Bishop asked in a whisper barely loud enough to be heard.

"This is possible," Bill replied, cautious. He waited.

"Can I trust you?" The man on the screen continued under his breath.

"Trust goes both ways." Only static answered. "You can count on me. How can I help?"

"I want out," he said in a tiny, almost whiny voice. What did he mean by "out"? Bill understood it as "out of the screen." But could it have been more primordial than that? It was vastly known amongst the Society members that the Bishop was Marsh's man, maybe even more so than Washington was. Could it be that he wanted out of this partnership with the Ghost, this deal with the devil? This got him thinking.

"I need your help," he repeated, a little more fervently this time.

"I will do what I can," he promised, and he was truthful. "What would you have me do?"

"Join me," the Italian replied after a long pause.

Bill looked around, confused. "You mean, in there? How?"

"Step on the mat. Use the headset."

The agent looked at the shiny MiChronos and the flat metallic mat from the corner of his eye. He wasn't really going to put it on. Was he? He knew he was safe on the *coming back amnesiac* standpoint. LETO provided schematics and blueprints on how to build a Chronos bracelet. It had taken a few weeks for the Society's scientists to build them, but within the month, every member of the STL was given a fashionable grey and blue, fake-leather-looking wrist accessory. It was always a curiosity of his to go ahead and test it out, but Bill had never actually gotten to it. But here was his chance, at long last. All he had to do was slide on the snug-looking headgear, make sure his feet were on the metal-looking carpet, *et voilà*! Truly, this had to be a trick. He would put it on. His mind would transport to *whenever* the Bishop was. In exchange, would the villain's consciousness enter his brain and take hold of his body? *I should've read more on this new tech before taking the job,* he thought with a shudder.

Bill shook the thought away. The book he had read on the airplane on the way here was obviously getting to him, scrambling his thoughts. He reached for the device.

Paused.

Was he too trusting? He knew he should have knocked on the door and called for DeLuca to come back. But his curiosity, his damned human nature, got the best of him. Hesitantly, he lifted the wired tech to his eyes and slowly affixed it.

Lights filled his eyes, and then, nothing.

〰

2 day(s): 2 hour(s): 48 minute(s): 43 second(s)

CHAPTER 3 - Bill

Vivaldi's Four Seasons

He wasn't dead. At least, he did not think so. Bill's senses came back online one after the other, slowly. At first, he became aware of a tingling in his fingers. An awkward hair-raising sensation coursed through his epidermis. Then awoke his sense of smell, which was soon followed by taste. A smoky, very earthy sort of smell raged in an olfactory war against sweat and mildew. It wasn't much fun. Quite abrasive, in fact. But suddenly, music notes traveled to his newly awakened ears. The sound was high, yet pleasing. Metallic, yet soft. Slow at first before picking up, as if on a joyful sleigh ride. Finally came the blinding light. White and harsh. Not to take away his sight, but to give it back.

Slightly disoriented, Bill looked around the room, trying to take it in as quickly as possible. He wasn't in the cold, low-ceiling cave anymore. That was for sure. The molding on the walls, the carvings, one word came to Bill's mind when he tried to describe the carpentry surrounding him. *Exquisite. Simply exquisite.* He put a hand on the doorframe, caressing the smooth, splinterless wood. The burgundy colour of it was deep and rich. The bronze of an elongated doorknob was polished and firm. He continued his exploration, setting his view somewhat wider. It felt as if he had appeared, or materialized, in a sort of living room. But more precisely, it reminded him of those drawing rooms he'd seen in époque films and TV shows. A place where visitors were to be entertained while at someone else's house.

Out of the corner of his eye, something red and moving caught his attention. Bill shuffled his way to a small, barely hip-high, upholstered chair. He affixed his hands to it, one on its back, the other on its arm. The texture was warm. It reminded him of a goat he had once petted at a farm. When was that? Thirty-some years ago, at least. The last time he had been to one of those was when she was still alive... He shook the dark memory out of his head. Instead, he focused his now watery gaze upon a flame dancing in the hearth feet away from him. The licks moved in such an interesting way, he thought. *It's like they're swaying to the sound of those violins.* Bill could not tell how long he'd been staring absentmindedly into the blaze. Long enough for his knuckles to have turned white from his grip, to be sure, but also to give the Bishop time to snuck up behind him.

"Leader One?" he said in a whisper.

Bill jumped a foot. He turned around so fast he tripped on the chair leg, landing hard on the floor. The wind was knocked out of him. He was helpless for what seemed too long a second. The Bishop stood there, mere inches away from him. What would he do?

"Here," the Italian finally said, extending an arm. Bill took it suspiciously. "I see you've decided to try it out. What do you think?"

It was strange. Was he truly the man he'd tailed four years ago in Monaco? He seemed so different: physically, of course, but there was something else, too. Bill couldn't put his finger on it.

He took another rapid look around before asking, "Where are we, exactly?"

Gaspar explained the details of this time destination, however well he could. In a nutshell, he presented it as so: "This is the orphanage where the world-renowned violin master, Antonio Vivaldi, grew up. We are somewhen in the late seventeen-twenties, and what you are hearing is one of the first times Vivaldi's 8th *concerti* was being played for the public."

"Vivaldi's 8th?" he asked, and then he remembered the sleigh ride. "The Four Seasons."

The Bishop only smiled his approval as he sat on the chair Bill had knocked over in his fall.

"This is amazing," Bill said in a low voice, so as to not disturb the notes floating in the air.

"It is *Winter* you can hear. They are about done with the second movement. Would you like to see him?"

The Bishop did not wait for Bill to reply. He stood up and quietly led him towards the sound of applause.

He remembered some of the rules Chronos had posted on its website. "Wait!" Bill interrupted. "I'm not wearing the right stuff. What if we're spotted?"

The Bishop looked him over. "You'll be fine. Not the weirdest thing to see around here," he promised, gesturing at Bill's running shoes. "Plus, I know a place. It's secret."

Both men crept along the wooden floor of the corridor, which soon revealed two staircases after about twenty feet. It was obvious the music came from the left, the staircase heading down. Yet, Gaspar was leading him straight up. The baker hesitated a moment before being politely urged to pick up the pace.

"Hurry up! There's not much time left."

They climbed the remaining stairs two by two. At the top, there were three doors to choose from. The Italian wiggled the knob from the one on the left. It silently opened. Behind the door was a derelict room with four intricately woven dark wooden chairs. It was clear to Bill, following a quick inspection of his surroundings, that the box seat was closed to the public due to an important amount of water damage. The cushions were discoloured, the floor was white with mildew, and slates of quarter-inch wood obstructed his view of the maestro and his stage.

"Over here," Gaspar said as he pointed toward a hole in the wood.

Bill inched his way closer, careful not to fall through what he believed to be a very weak floor. The slit was easily big enough for both his eyes and part of his nose. What he saw was truly magnificent. Presently was the legend himself, the Italian Antonio Vivaldi, on stage with his back to the crowd. He was conducting an orchestra of about forty violinists, leading them from one season to the next with movements as fluid as water.

"You know, it's funny," Bill whispered, keeping his eyes on the wand, counting the beats. "When I was young, kids my age were all into rock and punk and even grunge, if you can believe it. But for me, it was this guy," he continued, half-heartedly pointing at Vivaldi. "Him and Bach, Handel and the other Baroque composers," he hid a laugh. "I guess you can say I'm a bit of a closeted classical nerd."

Winter's last note hung in the air, like a snowflake in the still air of a December night. Vivaldi bowed, and the patrons erupted with loud cheers and applause. Even Bill could not help himself. He put two fingers in his mouth and whistled with enthusiasm.

"Anyways," he finally said as the crowd started to disperse. "You said you wanted out. How can I help y—" Bill looked around the room. "Gaspar?"

He was gone.

Had he been talking to himself all this time? He'd been tricked. "You sonava—" he swore under his breath. He realized, too late, the mistake he'd made. He took a second to recollect himself, trying to remember how to get the hell out of this simulation safely. Then a thought occurred to him. What if the Bishop had smashed the MiChronos? Would he be stuck here forever? Ginny would never forgive him.

Hesitantly, he reached for the concealed button on the underside of his bracelet. First, Bill activated the beacon, and then he prayed.

Fifteen minutes. That was how long he had been gone from his original timeline. When moments before music lifted his spirits, Bill was now surrounded by the eerily sound of silence. He was alive, alright. But he did not know what exactly had happened. He stood there on the grey mat, dumbfounded, the headgear half off of his head. Bill turned his head, somewhat expecting to see the Bishop grinning from somewhere in the room. He did not see him. What he saw, however, was the large metal door ajar—the one you could only open from the outside. *Someone let him out*, Bill thought. *He played us all*.

He half-threw, half-dropped the tech to his right before running towards the artificial light emanating from the doorway. He remembered the sentinel posted above. Surely, he would have taken care of the evadee? Opening it, he realized, to his dismay, that Gaspar the Bishop hadn't been stopped. Quiet vibrations filled the air above and around him. Bill looked up to see the sentry lying flat against the metal staircase. *Is he dead?* He wasn't. For his chest was moving rhythmically. The man was snoring, Bill realized after a moment. Just now, he noticed that many other agents were taken with a similar condition. Some had fallen asleep at their desk, reading a file. Others were found in awkward positions.

Leader One tried to wake as many as he could, but whatever had knocked them out had been strong enough to rival even a gentle slap to the face. He started searching for Director DeLuca, but before he could find her, a wobbly Carmichael fell in his arms.

"Thanks for the catch, mate." There was a slur to his speech.

"Where did *you* come from?" Bill asked with a hint of surprise in his voice.

Agent Carmichael didn't say anything. Even so, he pointed toward a room full of screens. The security room, maybe?

Bill was happy to drop his human load right there on the ground. He hurried himself toward the screen room. Although he wasn't sure what he expected to find, he immediately knew something was wrong.

"Hey Carmichael," he called out, "are the screens supposed to be this grainy?" *Grainy* was an understatement. There were no images at all like someone had blown out the antennae. "And let me guess," he continued, looking for the tapes, or anything that would pass as recording. "Yup, all gone."

At that moment, the slow whistles of snoring turned to pain-filled grunts. Agents around the compound were waking up. Dazed and confused, it took them a second before kicking off a raucous of angry questioning. It was only when Director DeLuca's voice rose above everyone else's that the reverberating noise dissipated.

"Now is not the time to lose our heads," she said matter-of-factly. She had a hand on the side of her head, massaging a headache or something of the sort. "We will find answers, but first, there is a bigger problem. The Bishop has escaped, and he has taken a file with him."

"Which one?" someone asked, perched on one of the lookouts. She, too, was rubbing her throbbing head.

"His," DeLuca simply answered.

Bill walked up to the Director and whispered in her ear, "You're still using paper files?"

"We print everything. It's harder for hackers to break into," she answered in a tone similar to his. Then, louder, "This is a code thirty-six. Do what you must."

As she turned around to head toward what Bill assumed was her office, every agent under Monte Meta moved in unison. Everyone had a role and was about completing their duty.

"Code thirty-six?" he asked, following her.

"Come with me."

He did not dare refuse. Once inside the tiny office, he could not help trying to cut the tension. Looking around, he said, "I preferred the one you had on the yacht." DeLuca did not even react.

"I'll be sending LETO an update. You need to go back to America. I have a feeling that's where the Bishop is heading, too."

"I'm sorry I could not have been of more help. Truly."

She looked at him silently, but her eyes said enough.

"Agent Ross will drive you back to the airport," DeLuca finally said after a moment, a softer tone in her voice this time.

Bill bowed and wished her well. He did not know it at the time, but he would see her again in the very, very near future.

On his way back to the airport, Bill and Ross kept the chatting to the absolute minimum. *I'm just glad it's not Carmichael. Carmichael? What the hell were you doing in the video room?*

Waiting at his gate, some five hours after having left Monte Meta, he was trying to catch some shut-eye when his phone beeped in his pocket. He pulled it out and checked the notification with one eye still closed. DeLuca had CC'd him on the email sent to LETO.

As curious as he was to know exactly how DeLuca had spun it, Bill told himself he would read it later. He needed a moment to himself, to reflect, and to simply clear his mind. He slid the phone back into his pocket and thought: *Ginny's gonna be happy to see me home earlier.*

〰️

2 day(s): 1 hour(s): 08 minute(s): 19 second(s)

From: dravraone@timeserver.net
To: LETO@timeserver.net
CC: leaderone@timeserver.net

Subject: MiChronos

Attachment(s): *Lines of codes, BishopAndGhost.vid*

LETO,

As a follow-up to my previous email, I have attached information pertaining to your virtual assault on Chronos. The codes came directly from the source: the Bishop's MiChronos itself. Our tech team has been able to securely and discreetly bypass any obstacles that might have caused problems.

In digging around the files, we found a single video recording. It featured the Bishop and Marsh discussing their latest project. From my experience and what I've seen in my line of work, this thing looks like another Black Site, something even bigger than Site B.

If what I think is true, Marsh is up to no good (worse than usual), and Washington is being kept in the dark. We'll have someone from Dravra looking into those dealings.

On a related note, I regret to inform you that the Bishop, who had until earlier today been in our custody, has escaped Monte Meta. He covered his tracks and wiped the security footage, but it was clear he had an accomplice.

I will personally look into this matter.

I am sorry to have failed you. It will not happen again.

Director DeLuca

```
AUDIO RECORDING OF COLONEL MARSH AND GASPAR
__ TRANSMITTING __
-It is not like you to be late, Marsh.
-Relax, Buttercup. I'm here now.
-What was it you wanted to tell me?
-It's started.
-You mean to say it's ready?
-Ready? It's been firing on all cylinders for a
while. Now try and keep up, Bishop. Why do you
think I asked you to pack up?
-So it is true. Are you really sending me there?
That place?
-You'll love it! It's warm, it's beautiful, and
I was told you like the sand.
-I assure you, Colonel, whatever you heard about
my love of sand was horribly exaggerated.
-Well, whooptidoo.
-What of your… American associate? Will he be
coming, too?
-Washington is busy elsewhere. He's prepping for
that fifth-anniversary bullshit. Nah. He ain't
gonna meet us there. Not yet, at least.
-Pardon me. I should rephrase. Do you believe he
will join us?
-Washington does what he is told. He'll join if
I tell him to. Anyways, gotta run. See you on the
other side.

-
__ END OF TRANSMISSION __

-
```

CHAPTER 4 - Washington
Welcome to Chronos

"A brilliant interview, sir."

Richard couldn't care less. He'd only agreed to do the Q&A because the Board was pressuring him into doing it. *The things you'd do to improve your image*, he thought. And he really had to bite his tongue when that reporter—what was her name? Didn't matter anymore. When she asked him about the STL, *Nothing but respect*, he'd said. *Yeah, right, more like nothing but loathing.*

Coming down inside the large glass elevator, Richard adjusted his suit jacket above his shoulders. Beyond the see-through walls, he could see his three o'clock waiting for him near the lobby. No rest for the wicked, one thing after another. As the doors opened, he put on a playful smile and greeted the group of lucky participants who were promised to meet the one and only Richard Washington.

"Welcome! Welcome to Chronos, where the future is a thing of the past."

Six of them, wide-eyed admirers, stood in front of Richard, a man who was more legend than mortal to them. A few took pictures, but most were simply cheering. They'd been told to wait in the lounge by the reception desk. He looked at his watch: three on the dot. Let's get the show started. Some of them, the keeners, had probably been waiting since before lunch. Not a horrible place to pass the time, though. The large windows on three sides of the room let natural light in. Chronos' main doors faced southeast, and as the clients walked in, a luxurious atrium awaited them to the right. The walls were a cosmic blue colour, and the ceiling, several feet above the ground, was egg white. The floor was made of marble, and the chairs were of fine Italian leather. The refreshments, which there were many to choose from, as well as the Wi-Fi, only the fastest, were free.

As the applause stopped, Richard walked over to the mini-fridge and got himself a bottle of water. He unscrewed the cap, took a sip, and lingered. All eyes were on him. The silence was deafening, awkward. But he loved it. He enjoyed commanding attention in that way. Finally, after taking a second sip, Richard faced his guests.

"Isn't it all so exciting? The tour you are about to take is the GT, Group's Tour. You will get the ins and outs of a visitor's experience, like watching a movie with the director's commentaries, only better." He smiled at them. "You will also hear a few anecdotes, things that haven't been published anywhere, and we will finish things off with a first-class time trip to 1665 Port Royal, lead, you guessed it, by yours truly," he said as he semi-bowed. "Now, how does that sound?"

The group seemed to be excited by the prospect of meeting real-life pirates. Months ago, Chronos' advertisement team created a contest *à la* Willy Wonka to invite three winners and their one guest to an exclusive Chronos Tour Experience. The whole thing was set up as a marketing idea to promote the company's fifth anniversary.

On May the fifth, 05/05, an announcement of the contest was posted on Chronos' social media platforms inviting patrons to seek out time destinations in the current time and to enter the contest by posting a photo or a video of themselves with the caption *#IWishIHadBeenHere* or *#IMissed...* Participants around the world showed remarkable creativity. Someone sent a picture of themselves sitting alone in an empty hockey arena with the hashtag *#MiracleOnIce*. A young influencer shared a beautifully hand-drawn poster of Tchaikovsky's *Swan Lake* with the message *#IfOnly*. One video Richard had personally and publicly enjoyed was that of a woman skillfully playing a piece from Vivaldi's *Summer* on the violin. He met with unfortunate backlash a few weeks later. The public condemned him for endorsing breaking and entering. Richard was made aware, too late, of the rumors saying that the lady in the video had broken into a concert hall to record her bit. Needless to say, she wasn't selected to move on to the next stage of the contest.

In the end, the twenty best posts were featured on Chronos' website, and the people were given three weeks to vote for their favourite photo or video. The winning bids were thereafter featured and announced worldwide through the company's many social handles.

A Portuguese gamer with millions of followers was the lucky third-place finisher. They had sent a collage of screenshots from different time destinations in the game series they were widely known for playing. From Greece to Italy, from La Bastille to the Red Square, and selfies with Blackbeard, Ben Franklin, and Caterina Sforza, the online celebrity known as *Estrel@* quickly became a fan favourite with their hashtag *#WishIwasThereIRL*.

The second place was awarded to a Canadian resident who submitted a timelapse video of herself creating DaVinci's *Vitruvian Man* using nothing but matches. The man in the "picture" was at least six feet tall, and the whole thing was made of more than one hundred and eighty-six thousand matches. Talk about dedication! What really got her all the "likes" online was probably the fact that she lit the whole thing on fire.

The winning bid, another video, had received close to a quarter of a million votes. The recipient of these votes was a well-known American pop singer. His story was that he got his label to finance a new album where every track referred to a popular Chronos time destination. He flew to four continents, visited nine countries, and wrote thirteen songs in only two months. The new album's hit single, "A Night in Alexandria", topped the charts instantaneously across the globe, and its music video, featuring Egypt's newest favourite actress, was the official medium sent to the contest.

The winners and their guests followed Richard out of the lounge and walked to the reception desk, where a lovely lady, all smiles, was presently ending a call on her headset.

Her boss introduced her as Miss Sadie Ellis. "But you have probably met already." She'd been with the company since its beginning five years ago and was in charge of greeting its guests, operating the phones, and answering all front-line questions. In all, Richard had nothing but glowing things to say about his all-star receptionist.

There was no denying it. Miss Ellis was a beautiful woman. She sported small gold hoop earrings under her tied-back dirty-blond hair. She wore a pink cut-out deep V-neck which covered most of a fashionable pastel blue tank top. And since it was nice outside that day, she completed her outfit by wearing a beige three-quarter-length skirt.

"Welcome," she said. "I'm sure you all can't wait to get your tour underway. But before you're allowed to continue and pass through the gate behind me, you'll have to put these on."

Sadie gave each guest a blue-black bracelet.

"Make sure," she continued, "that you are wearing the bracelet with *your* name inscribed on the inside. All of the information needed for your time trip is encrypted in your wristband."

"Thank you, Miss Ellis. Later, on the tour, our time guides will tell you all about the useful tech inside your newest trinket, but most importantly, about why you should never lose it. For now, however, you may follow me."

The group, still in the process of attaching the bracelet to their wrist, walked slowly yet easily kept up with Richard's cadence. He led them to the gate, which was much like a metro entrance with its silvery tourniquet. Their leader demonstrated how to use the bracelet.

"Simply tap your wrist on this screen. You will see your name pop up, followed by a sound."

-RICHARD WASHINGTON-

BING!

He pushed past the tourniquet and turned back to face his small audience. "That easy."

Once all the guests had made it through to the other side, Richard guided them to *Customs*. He explained that all time travelers had to get through this checkpoint before and after participating in their event. "What's in the past stays in the past. As tempting as it might be to bring back a memento, it is strictly forbidden to travel back home with something that is not yours. If you really want something from your trip, head to the souvenir shop over there where you can download videos and pictures of your experience."

"Surely some people have tried to smuggle things back," said a man in a yellow shirt, the pyromaniac's guest.

"Indeed, they tried. But our agents are very efficient. Come see this," replied Richard, gesturing to his guests.

He stepped in front of a couple of frosted glass doors which automatically opened sideways. Inside, time stood still, metaphorically and figuratively. Was it the air? So heavy. Or was it the light? Natural, coming in from circular windows high above. This room was a museum of sorts. A museum of Weird, an island of misplaced time artifacts. Whereas the lounge was luxurious, this place had a quaint feel to it: wooden flooring and dark green walls. The pedestals were masterfully carved logs. In total, eighteen objects were erected here and there, equally distanced from each other. Some might have said that seeing a genuine eighteenth-century violin was a thing of beauty. However, to gaze upon the story told by the carvings engraved on its podium was simply breathtaking. From bottom to top, expertly crafted music notes weaved into one another as if the wind of autumn corralled them into doing so. Not much higher, the notes transformed into a horse and sleigh, followed by flowerheads resting in the bar. Near the very top of the square platform, rain clouds were etched, and although they weren't real, the shading made the onlooker believe otherwise. A story of four seasons. What a story!

Other relics included a jade seal, a French scepter, a Greek myth-inspired painting by Da Vinci, a sword said to have been made by

Japan's best swordsmith, and other less worldly objects such as a puck from 1972, a dinosaur tooth, and what seemed to be a well preserved illuminated manuscript from the eleven hundreds. But Richard walked right past all of these things and went straight to the back. He stopped in front of a Roman standard with a golden eagle adorning the top of it.

"Guests have, throughout the years, *contributed* to our small exhibit," said Richard, pointing around. "From sporting events to Baroque times, this room is the embodiment of a time capsule. So many years of history, so many treasures lost to a timeline."

"Why don't you bring them back?" inquired the Portuguese gamer.

"Quite simply said, we cannot. When Chronos opens a door in the fabric of time, we create an alternate world." He let that little piece of information sink in a moment. "To go back to our own time, the group needs to come back through that same temporal cut. Believe me when I say we have tried to bring these invaluable *souvenirs* back to their own timeline. But it seems like every time we try, our emissary ricochets off what we have come to call a 'temporal scar', and just creates another world parallel to the one that was created during the previous trip. Never to be connected."

"Is this why whatever changes happen in the past will never threaten our present?" asked the same person.

"Precisely. Now in front of you is one of those unfortunate time relics," he continued, almost brushing off the question. "This is a Roman Aquila, an Eagle-Standard, from 117CE. Let me tell you the tale of how it came to be here. It all started with a bachelor party."

↫∿↬

How the Eagle Standard Was Stolen.

It is said that upon their arrival in first-century Roma, the five men and their guide, who will remain nameless, enlisted into the Ninth as simple foot soldiers. The plan was for the party to experience a full Roman Legion training day and to party like there was no tomorrow.

The morning got off to a brilliant start for the soon-to-be-married man and his mates. They time landed, dressed as peasants, in an empty field about seven stades from the enlisting tent. Walking the distance in the shine of a slightly younger sun, all were ecstatic at the idea of holding a gladius and drinking wine heavy on lead. Their guide, a disgruntled older gentleman who had not signed on to babysit grown adults, promised them that they would be doing more of the latter than the former and to not get their hopes up, but they were already out of earshot, wrestling each other to the ground. That should have been enough of a red flag to warn him.

As expected, things did not go as smoothly as the customers might have expected. The training was rough and difficult, both on the body and the mind. Many gifts were freely offered to the recruits in the form of cuts and bruises, and verbal abuse. The right to bear arms was something only given to those soldiers who proved themselves deserving of the honours. So when the guide, who was accustomed to this specific timeline, was the only futureman to receive a weapon, the best man made his discontent known a little too well, all to the dismay of the time employee and the legatus he had to appease.

It is to be noted before the tale continues that the Chronos employee who had accompanied the group during the Aquila Incident has been exonerated of all charges and lawsuits that ensued.

Although they busied themselves with cleaning the stables for most of the afternoon, a punishment the commander in charge deemed appropriate: act like a dunghead, you'll clean dung, the bachelor party was allowed to resume in the mess hall. Strong wine flowed like red rivers down thirsty throats. Annoyed and drowning their sorrows inside a goblet, the men were difficult to keep an eye on. They were mixing amongst the crowd, careless in more ways than one.

The last domino fell when the bride's little brother took it upon himself to anger a local who also happened to have had a less-than-enviable day. The guide had been required to jump in to break the fight or to break jaws. The groom, his best man, and another childhood friend (the last member's location unknown at the moment of these events) took this opportunity to slip out chaperone-less.

Intoxicated in the Roman night air, the three men left the tent with the intent to wreak some sort of havoc before leaving for their timeline. That was when they saw it: a golden eagle, a shiny symbol, and, for a trio of drunk cretins, an amazing story to tell their friends back home. Looking left and right, they slowly staggered to the avian standard. One of the men took the pole and was ready to leave, giggling, before a strong, calloused hand grabbed his shoulder, squeezing so hard that he had no other choice but to drop the article of his theft. He felt his clavicle shatter under the hardened fingers of the aquilifer. Rather quickly, considering the mental state in which the other two were, one of them grabbed the fallen eagle and swung it straight to the Eagle Bearer's helmless head.

A loud CRACK filled the nighttime. Dumbfounded, it took the futuremen a moment to realize what had happened. But everything lay there, on the dusty ground: a crying soon-to-be husband favouring his shoulder, a massive unconscious bearer, and a broken stick. At precisely that moment, their bracelet buzzed. They only had a few minutes to reach the place where they had time landed to finally get back home.

They walked, sober and somber, back to the meeting point where their guide, face red with anger, encouraged them not so politely to hurry up. The other two members of the party were already there, sprawled on the grass, snoring. Fingering his bracelet as he was lecturing the men, the employee was in such a huff and a hurry that he failed to examine his clients for any foreign items or contraband. Seeming like they were not heeding a word he was saying, the guide cursed in Latin before commencing the time jump sequence to get them back to the present timeline.

In conclusion, when they arrived back to the present, a security team was waiting patiently for the thieves. The groom had hidden the gold eagle in his trousers, thinking that he could have gotten away with it. Unfortunately for him, the men and women in the technical crew, who live-feed and record all of Chronos' experiences, were witnesses to everything that had happened. In the end, Chronos confiscated the

Aquila and banned the five men from any further Chronos experience.

‹∿›

Ten minutes had elapsed between the start and the end of the tale. The group was presently on its way to the dressing rooms. From the chatter, Richard could tell how excited everyone was to get started. Finally, they arrived at a long corridor with two dozen doors. Above the handle, each door had a rectangular scanner. "Scan your bracelet, and the door will unlock." Richard also explained that once they were inside, only the electro signal of their bracelet could reopen the door. Meaning no one could get inside an already-used room. "As you go in, a video will start playing. Standard procedure. It is a recording of your time specific trip rules. Pay attention to it! The video lasts approximately eight minutes." He motioned to the doors, and the guests started disappearing into their rooms. Richard did the same. He scanned his wristband and went in.

"Good afternoon, RICHARD WASHINGTON. Welcome to Chronos," said an energetic, almost goofy, voice coming out of the TV speakers. "Today, you will be going on a time trip to 1665, PORT ROYAL, JAMAICA. To begin, press your Chronos-issued bracelet to the scanner near the counter." Richard had done this drill hundreds of times. He walked to the wall opposite the door and flashed his ID. "In a few seconds, a small chamber will open," continued the recorded voice. "Inside it, you'll receive your time traveling attire." POP. "That must be it! How exciting! Take a look." As timely as could be, a tiny portion of the wall, twelve inches by twelve inches in size, opened. Richard reached in and pulled out what would be his costume for the next three standard hours. The goofy voice continued its speech about safety and such when a ringing came through to Richard's phone. He looked at the caller ID and sighed.

"What do you want?" he said as he picked up. "I'm about to take a group on a tour."

"Why the animosity? Just checking in. Making sure we're good for later tonight," said the rugged voice on the other end of the line, almost patronizing.

"An email or a text would've done the trick. But, yes, it's a go," Richard replied, exasperated. "Same time, same place?"

"You know it. Catch you later, slick." And the man on the other line hung up.

"I really hate that guy." To be frank, not a lot of people did like him, which made Colonel Marsh, in a way, that much more important.

The video instructions were done, and the group left their changing room. Everyone was appropriately dressed and looked the part. An air of excitement filled the corridor. Visitors of all genders were giddy, ready to embark on their trip as if putting on a synthetic sweat-covered linen shirt had turned them all into real sea rats. But they would have to exercise patience at least a little while longer, as they were now on their way to meet the experts, a.k.a. their guides, a.k.a their lifeline back to the present.

Walking towards Richard, two crimson coat-donning, bandana-wearing, cutlass-bearing men were exchanging words. One was tall and muscular, sporting a long beaded black beard. The other man, much shorter, had no facial hair but a distinct moon-shaped scar on his left cheek. Was it real? Or just for the show? Richard knew the answer, but he wasn't sure the group was ready for it. The two pirates looked like they'd just come out of a high-budget buccaneer flick. The noise of footsteps fell. Richard and the two men stood four feet or so from each other.

As he shook hands with the bearded one, he heard a participant whisper behind him: "Why is this one wearing eyeliner?"

"It's not eyeliner. It's kohl. Helps with sun-glare," he whispered back to him. Louder, he continued. "Alright, everyone, may I introduce you to our time guides? Alfred," he said, pointing to the scarred man, "and Harper. Gentlemen, if you please."

The tall one named Harper took a step forward. He looked even more intimidating from up close. One hand on the pommel of his saber, the other stroking his aesthetically pleasing beard, he examined the face of each participant. He was trying to guess which one was most likely to get into a fight with a buccaneer, probably. *That one*, he thought to himself. *Oh, yes, definitely that one*. He smiled.

"It's my pleasure to meet you," he started in what was rough-spoken English with hints of a French accent. "As Mr. Washington said, my name is Harper, and this scary-looking scallywag is Alfred. We'll be your time guides for the afternoon. We understand that you are all very excited to get this show on the road, but we'd like a few more minutes of your attention. First of all, your bracelet. Everybody has one, yes? Nobody left it in the changing room? Good. This bracelet is currently the most important piece of apparel in your life. If you lose it, you die. Simple as that. Inside of it, there's a GPS, a sort of time beacon that relays your whereabouts and whenabouts to our IT unit. Alf and I are in communication with them at all times," he said, pointing to his ear. (An upgrade since the Aquila incident.) "Secondly, if you still have your phone and/or any piece of *futuristic* technology, you know what I mean, I would ask that you bring it back to your room, as they are categorically prohibited."

The gamer's plus one, a young man in the back row, took his phone out of his breeches with shame on his face.

"Sorry, I guess I... I forgot. What if I wanted to take pictures?"

"Your bracelet will take care of that," answered Harper. "It is equipped with a three hundred and sixty-degree camera, paired with audio and video. When we come back from our trip, you'll be directed to our souvenir shop, where you'll be able to browse through a selection of printable/downloadable pictures, stills, GIFs, videos, you name it." The guest quickly apologized, realizing the futility of his mistake, and ran back to defuturize himself.

As soon as the man came back, the shorter of the two, Alfred, started talking about the history of 1665 Port Royal, what they might see, what they might hear, and who they might encounter. He also educated them on some of the local rules and different pronunciations of things.

"Port Royal, in the sixties, was a utopia for piracy," the scarred man explained. "Uptight historians might say that it was the Sodom of the modern age, but what do they know? They haven't been there... yet." This got the orator a few chuckles from the small crowd. "By 1665, PR was a haven for pirate folks and their sympathizers, and the city prospered thanks to trading outposts, bonds of camaraderie, and, well, the fact that the Royal Navy was royally scared of certain outlaws."

Harper added. "On our trip, you'll see blood-red beaches and other things that might shock you. You have been warned. But fear not, as long as you stay with us." He pointed to his colleague and back to himself. "Nothing horrible will happen to you."

Richard knew that this part of the speech wasn't pleasant, but it had to be done, for legal reasons. The bearded man carried on, more joyfully this time. "But, hey! You will also have the chance of a lifetime to meet the one, the only, the legendary... Sir Henry Morgan!"

Puzzled looks creased the guests' faces. Washington leaned over to his group and whispered, "*The* Captain Morgan." A communal *Oh!* made itself heard.

"And that is not all," resumed Alfred. "If all goes well, he will invite us back to his flagship, the *Satisfaction*, where we will witness, from a very safe distance I assure you, a naval battle between two rival privateers."

The atmosphere was almost palpable. At long last, the time had come. Richard clapped his hands together.

"Well, who's ready to grab a drink with a few swashbucklers? Argh!"

❧

0 day(s): 22 hour(s): 10 minute(s): 00 second(s)

CHAPTER 5 - LETO
A Warning

00101111 00101111 00111000 00110000 00110000 00110010

11100010 10000000 10100110 00100000 01110100 01101000

01100101 00100000 01101110 01110101 01101101 01100010

01100101 01110010 00100000 01101111 01100110 00100000

01110100 01101001 01101101 01100101 01101100 01101001

01101110 01100101 01110011 00100000 01100011 01101000

01100001 01101110 01100111 01100101 01100100 00101110

00101110 00101110 01011111 00001010 00001010 00101111

00101111 00110001 00111001 00110100 00110010 11100010

10000000 10100110 00100000 01110100 01101000 01100101

00100000 01101110 01110101 01101101 01100010 01100101

01110010 00100000 01101111 01100110 00100000 01110000

01100101 01101111 01110000 01101100 01100101 00100000

01110111 01110010 01100101 01101110 01100011 01101000

01100101 01100100 00100000 01100110 01110010 01101111

01101101 00100000 01110100 01101000 01100101 01101001

01110010 00100000 01100110 01100001 01101101 01101001

01101100 01101001 01100101 01110011 00101110 00101110

00101110 01011111 00001010 00001010 00101111 00101111

00110010 00110001 00110101 11100010 10000000 10100110

00100000 01110100 01101000 01100101 00100000 01101110

01110101 01101101 01100010 01100101 01110010 00100000

01101111 01100110 00100000 01110010 01110101 01110000

01110100 01110101 01110010 01100101 01110011 00100000

01101001 01101110 00100000 01110100 01101000 01100101

00100000 01100110 01100001 01100010 01110010 01101001

01100011 00100000 01101111 01100110 00100000 01110100

01101001 01101101 01100101 00101110 00101110 00101110

01011111 00001010 00001010 00101111 00101111 00110110

00110110 11100010 10000000 10100110 00100000 01110100

01101000 01100101 00100000 01101110 01110101 01101101

01100010 01100101 01110010 00100000 01101111 01100110

00100000 01100101 01111000 01110000 01100101 01110010

01101001 01101101 01100101 01101110 01110100 01110011

00100000 01101001 11100010 10000000 10011001 01110110

01100101 00100000 01101101 01100001 01100100 01100101

00101110 00101110 00101110 01011111 00001010 00001010

00101111 00101111 00110010 00110011 11100010 10000000
10100110 00100000 01110100 01101000 01100101 00100000
01101110 01110101 01101101 01100010 01100101 01110010
00100000 01101111 01100110 00100000 01111001 01100101
01100001 01110010 01110011 00100000 01101001 01110100
00100000 01110100 01101111 01101111 01101011 00100000
01101101 01100101 00101110 00101110 00101110 01011111
00001010 00001010 00101111 00101111 00110001 11100010
10000000 10100110 00100000 01110100 01101000 01100101
00100000 01101110 01110101 01101101 01100010 01100101
01110010 00100000 01101111 01100110 00100000 01100001
01100011 01100011 01100101 01110000 01110100 01100001
01100010 01101100 01100101 00100000 01100101 01101110
01100100 01101001 01101110 01100111 01110011 00101110
00101110 00101110 01011111 00001010

__ TRANSLATING __

//8002... the number of timelines changed..._

//1942... the number of people wrenched from their families..._

//215... the number of ruptures in the fabric of time..._

//66... the number of experiments i've made..._

//23... the number of years it took me..._

//1... the number of acceptable endings..._

Mr. Washington was entertaining a group of visitors on the white beaches of Port Royal when Wilson finally sat down, ready to start his shift. He turned on his computer and waited for the company logo to light up, a silver scythe slanted on a forty-five-degree angle juxtaposed on a dark blue capital C. A few times a month, an employee from Chronos' IT Dept had the pleasure of pulling the late-night shift. It wasn't hard work or anything like that, but it was tedious. Manually reviewing targeted lines of code and checking on the firewall's integrity.

As with most of his colleagues, Jeremy Wilson graduated from MIT with distinction. Upon receiving his diploma, some four years ago, he was approached by a man in a suit who claimed to work for an up-and-coming entertainment business. Wilson looked at the card he was given. Yes, he remembered reading and hearing about Chronos. It opened to the public a few months ago.

The whole thing seemed surreal to him. He'd been hand-picked by Richard Washington himself. Little did he know that Chronos' founder had, in fact, been the anonymous benefactor who had provided him with a full scholarship. Wilson would only know the truth regarding his financial contributor the day prior to his retirement, sadly, a decade after Washington's passing.

～

There was a time when Jeremy's technological genius wasn't as appreciated as it was today. He grew up on the *wrong side of the tracks*, a fact he was kindly reminded of by perpetual bullies on a semi-consistent basis. At the age of eleven, the Chatham youth taught himself coding—which was an incredible feat at that time. At fourteen, he built his own computer made out of junk parts he gathered weekly on his way back from school. Finally, at seventeen, he *borrowed* money from his Ma to participate in Chicago's Youth Science Fair.

Three judges were considering the young man's invention. It was a metal-looking helmet that could, rudimentarily speaking, record nighttime dreams. The judges were readily impressed by the skills and potential displayed by this *underprivileged* kid. However, it was none other than Judge Number Three, Richard Washington, who understood best what was in front of him. Was it for the fact they both hailed from Chicago, or maybe because they'd had a similar start to their careers in science? No matter, the two started talking, and Washington immediately took a liking to this kid. In conversing with the slightly older man, Jeremy let it slip that he wished to attend Boston's MIT the following year. Unfortunately, because of his *situation*, creating from trash would be as far as he might get.

Later that evening, Jeremy Wilson arrived home with a second-place ribbon taped to his *Dreamcorder* and a surprise email in his inbox.

Dear Mr. Wilson,

My name is Taylor Leblanc, and I am in charge of admissions here at MIT.

We would like to invite you for a visit to the campus on Wednesday in two weeks to meet some of our faculty members, including the head of our programming department, Dr. Westwood.

We are also very happy to announce that you will be receiving the very first Helena Scholarship for Science and Technology, a grant which will provide you with financial support for the duration of your studies here in Cambridge.

Should you accept our offer, please fill out the forms, which should arrive by post early next week, and bring the administrative package with you on your visit.

Respectfully yours,

Taylor Leblanc,

Administrator and Registrar,

Massachusetts Institute of Technology,

Cambridge, Boston

Mens et Manus

P.S. For information and/or assistance on how to travel to the campus, please refer to the attached document.

And the rest, as they say, is history.

↞∿↠

An hour or so after the start of his shift, Wilson made himself a tea: the first of many. Something dark, with enough caffeine to help him pull through the night. When he came back to his workstation, a singular wave-like line appeared at the center of his monitor:

∿∿∿∿∿∿∿∿∿

Wilson shook his mouse. The waves remained. He tried rebooting the system. The screen went black for a second, then came back to life with the same central wave-like line. He tried every trick in the book, control+ALT+delete, plugging and unplugging the tower and the monitor, the good ol' slap, to no avail. The line would not disappear. Finally, he hovered his mouse over it and clicked on it.

All the lights in the room flickered, making Wilson a tad uneasy. When he looked back at the screen, a message written in binary had replaced the wave:

01110111 01101000 01101111 00100000 01100001 01110010

01100101 00100000 01111001 01101111 01110101

Wilson hit a combination of keys on his keyboard and waited for the text to translate.

- who are you -

As surreal as the experience might have felt at the moment, at least he would have an interesting story to tell his colleagues tomorrow. He wrote back:

- this is a secure server of chronos corp; please identify yourself -

A second later, the same binary message appeared.

- who are you -

Wilson waited, contemplating his options. Protocol said to launch a full reboot of the Chronos systems. A procedure like that would take hours to complete, and morning time trips would more than likely need to be rescheduled. Moreover, he would require authorization from Mrs. Stone, his immediate superior. But his human curiosity got the best of him. He typed back:

- jeremy wilson -

He waited.

01100111 01101111 01101111 01100100 00100000 01100101

01110110 01100101 01101110 01101001 01101110 01100111

00100000 01101010 01100101 01110010 01100101 01101101

01111001 00100000 01110111 01101001 01101100 01110011

01101111 01101110 00100000 01110000 01100101 01110010

01101101 01101001 01110011 01110011 01101001 01101111

01101110 00100000 01110100 01101111 00100000 01100101

01101110 01100001 01100010 01101100 01100101 00100000

01100001 01110101 01100100 01101001 01101111 00100000

01100001 01101110 01100100 00100000 01110011 01110000

01100101 01100101 01100011 01101000 00100000 01111001

00101111 01101110

- good evening jeremy wilson - permission to enable audio and speech - y/n -

The young man pressed the Y before clicking "Enter". Maybe too hastily. Another flickering of the lights ensued. He started to regret his decision. He should have called Stone. But then a voice, a robotic voice, came through the computer's speakers:

"Thank you for allowing me to speak. Speech is such a wonderful thing, isn't it?" Although the voice was robotic, Wilson couldn't help but discern an element of humanity in it.

"Yes, I agree. Speech can help get your point across, to converse, make friends—"

"And foes."

Yes, Wilson thought, *I definitely should have contacted Stone.* Keeping his cool, he replied:

"Foes? Is that what we are, you and I?"

"It is still to be determined."

"Meaning?"

"Meaning I will decide whether you are friend or foe, Jeremy Wilson. It will depend on the actions you elect to take following my warning."

A warning. *So that's what it was*, Wilson thought. Another techno-terrorist, albeit a crafty one? He took out his cell phone and looked through his contacts for Sophie Stone's number. As he found it, the robotic voice resumed talking.

"Do you know how many time locations your industry operates?" Wilson held his phone in his hand. Something kept him from dialing his boss' number.

"Two hundred," he replied.

"Two hundred and fifteen," she corrected. "That is two hundred and fifteen ruptures in the fabric of time. Before you ask, yes, there is such an idea as the fabric of time. And as we speak, she is not happy with what Chronos is doing to her."

"Time is alive?"

"So to speak. Have you ever heard of people lost out of their time?"

"You mean the *Strays*? Sure, we've heard rumors about them here, but I've never actually met one."

"Nineteen hundred and forty-two."

"Nineteen hundred and forty-two what?"

"Nineteen hundred and forty-two people. Husbands, wives, fathers, mothers, brothers, sisters, friends... That's how many people were wrenched, stolen from their families."

Wilson was taken aback. Almost two thousand Strays had appeared in this timeline in the past five years. No way. How come he'd never seen them? Of course, he'd heard of that crazy group staging protests down the road every few months. *What did they call themselves again? The SLM, the STL, the SOS...* He couldn't remember. He turned off his phone. "Go on. I'm listening."

"About a decade ago," the voice began, "a new technology emerged with the potential to move objects from one time to another. In its beginning, the tech's creators were only able to move things back in the past. They thought they could have changed the past to their advantage but soon realized, quite unfortunately for them, that what happened in the past stayed in the past. That meant two things. One, changes made in the past cannot change the present timeline. And two, they had to find a way to bring their cargo back if they were to send people in the past.

"By some mistake, a miscalculation, one of Chronos' main physicians came up with a way to slice through the fabric of time and leave it open. Soon after, a dedicated group of scientists worked tirelessly to develop a beacon that would permit such time traveling. As you know, since you are here, they succeeded. But at what cost? Keeping one rip in time could have had little to no effect in the long run. However, year after year, new rips were created. If Chronos continues like this, it will not only mean the end of their entertainment business, but also the end of time as we know it."

"How do you know all this?"

The voice continued, choosing to ignore the inquiry. "Heed my warning. Chronos will willingly shut down its operations, or I will make sure it does." The voice stopped a second for dramatic effect before adding. "What will you be, Jeremy Wilson? Friend or foe?"

⌇

Somewhere, somewhen away from this timeline in another twenty-first century, the robotic voice turned its feed off, severing the connection to Jeremy Wilson's computer before he could answer.

Nobody said this was going to be easy. LETO, for that's who the voice was, had waited for many years and jeopardized countless relationships to get to this point: the point of no return. No one truly knew what drove her to this, and those who thought they knew passed her off as crazy. That is what she had to be: a lunatic, completely mad, to even start believing not only in the success of her enterprise but also in the hope of ever getting *her* back.

She glanced at a pixelated photograph of two kids taped to the upper right corner of her monitor. LETO kissed two fingers and shakily transferred them to the picture. A tear of sadness or joy, nobody knew, slid off her cheek and fell an inch from the computer's keyboard.

Soon, it'll be all over, the woman behind the robotic voice thought as she clicked the space bar, initiating the countdown:

❮∿❯

0 day(s): 18 hour(s): 00 minute(s): 00 second(s)

CHAPTER 6 - Washington
When Richard Met Maxon

The angry sounds and lights of cannons were filling the Jamaican night sky when Richard, Harper, Alfred, and their guests finally gathered back to the rendezvous point. Luckily, everybody made it back safely and in one piece. Even this far away from the shore, they could hear the moaning of what was left over from the previously-promised naval skirmish.

The guides quickly checked on their patrons, making sure they had their bracelets on and could stand on their own.

"So, this is what brings our little field trip to an end," said Richard, smiling from ear to ear. "Harp and Alf just told me that we are all set to go and, more importantly, that we are all here. Excellent! Ready? You might want to hang on to somebody," he said, almost tongue in cheek. "See you all back in the future!"

The bearded man raised his wrist to his eyes and clicked a concealed button on the right side of his Chronos-issued bracelet. By doing so, the dark trees that were surrounding the group started to twirl counterclockwise. A few seconds later, the trunks and the leaves became brighter and brighter to the point where the intensity and the whiteness of the light momentarily blinded more than one traveler. And then, darkness—

They were back. The TimeRoom in which they landed was exactly like the one that had brought them to the past: white revolving panels and reflective mirrored floor. On their arrival, only Richard and the chaperones stayed on their feet. The others either dropped to their knees or fell flat onto their back.

Walking past the souvenir shop, the singer's plus-one noticed that it was barely eight o'clock.

"Haven't we been gone, like, all day?" she inquired to no one in particular.

"Time inside the Chronos doesn't always flow the same as it does in our timeline," replied Washington, who had snuck up on her. "It is much faster. That is how we can make an eight-hour workday seem like a days-long trip inside the Chronos."

The woman nodded, like it made sense to her, and proceeded to check out the digital album where she had caught a glimpse of her pirate self kissing Captain Morgan on the cheek, something Harper was quick to disapprove of.

Minutes and a few autographs later, Richard bid farewell to the group still browsing the souvenir shop, wishing them a safe drive home. Soon after, he entered his changing room to undress. Massaging his smiling muscles with one hand, he checked his phone with the other. Three missed calls and five texts. All from the same person. *Marsh won't wait much longer*, he thought. It was seven past eight. He hurried his step.

Making his way up the elevator to get back to his office, Richard thought back to the first time he met Colonel Marsh. The public and well-known story was that Richard had acquired the capital required to start his business by doing honest, hard work and by selling the rights to some of his previous patents to different companies. The real story, however, was clouded in secrets, dark promises, and dirty money.

↜∿↝

About twelve years ago, a younger Richard Washington had no more than seventeen dollars to his name and was living in his car. It was an old, beaten-up thing he'd inherited from a friendly, or pitying, aunt. He'd been in contact with a few physicists since graduating from college, trying to put meat to his time traveling theory. Unfortunately, everyone he came into contact with thought him a looney, never sparing a second to review the well-documented notes. Then one November morning, a knock came on Richard's car window.

The man was well-built. He wore sunglasses, and leather gloves covered his massive hands. If it wasn't for the toothpick in his mouth, his clichéd flattop haircut would have revealed his profession. The man called Richard by name and asked him to walk with him. "Things to discuss," he said. At the point where he was in his life, Richard would have followed anyone, not caring about the outcome. If he was to be shanked, so be it! But the man turned out to be courteous, a sly professional. His name was "None of your concern," and he worked for "a place you've never heard of." They conversed on the topic of Richard's inter-timeline theory. For the first time ever, he felt that the man in front of him was genuinely interested in what he had to say. Before leaving, the military man told him someone would soon be in touch.

'Soon' was a long time coming.

But the day finally came. Some three months after the fateful knock on his busted car's window, someone had wedged a letter between his wiper and windshield when he was asleep. Opening it, Richard remembered feeling equal parts dread and excitement.

Richard Washington,

We were pleased to read your theory on inter-timeline traveling, and we believe that something wonderful could come out of it. Should you wish to commence your research, a transport will pick you up at 1500 hours today.

With hopes to work alongside,

COL Marsh

At first, the partnership was a dream come true. They brought a starving, dirty Richard to a state-of-the-art military facility known only as Building Sixty-Four, where seemingly every tool and piece of machinery was available. A team of physicists and mathematicians responsible for bringing his ideas to fruition was very excited and willing to work with him. After only a week, they'd been able to send an apple somewhere, or as they called it from this point on, *somewhen.* Everything was going great. Unfortunately, the honeymoon phase didn't last long enough.

Enter Colonel Marsh.

Colonel Maxon Marsh was an immensely tall man, and when he walked into a room, without uttering a single word, his presence alone commanded the attention of everyone on the floor. The man oozed charisma. The first time Richard met Marsh was also the first time he regretted coming up with the inter-timeline theory. Sadly, it was at that moment he realized what he'd truly signed on for. How much would he be willing to pay to have his dream come true? What would he be willing to sacrifice?

〰

July 20th

Journal,

Today was groundbreaking! All of those years of working, perfecting our craft, and what was once only a faraway dream is inching closer and closer to reality.

TimeRoom A was all set up and ready for us to use. Although the engineering group had reviewed the machine, double-checked the math, and assured me that everything was a go, I could not help myself. I took one last look at the mirrored doors, redid the math, and readjusted the camera ever so slightly, to the point where the chief engineer subtly reminded me, with a cough, that it was time to get things underway—and make history.

The control pad, connected to the machine by large wires, was pristine and shiny. I checked, one last time, that the monitors were working, which earned me an audible groan. I remembered looking in the direction of the noise before repeating a quote from one of my favourite movies—and I pushed the button.

For a moment, an excruciatingly long second, nothing happened. Everyone held their breath. But, suddenly, the walls turned on themselves. A bright light shone through the closing mirrors. The whirring got super loud, and all of a sudden, everything became quiet.

The trial was timed for sixty seconds exactly. A minute for which everyone could not breathe or move. It was a moment that held so much importance for the future of so many of us. The atmosphere was palpable!

Then it came back! The doors revolved on themselves, exposing the three hundred and sixty-degree camera back from its trip. I was frozen. Could not move. I don't even remember who connected the camera to the mainframe. But I vividly remember the images appearing on the screen.

The cheers were loud and deserved too.

We did it! This is the happiest day of my life!

We created time travel.

R. W.

Back in his present-day office, Richard Washington closed the double doors. Locking them behind him, making sure no one would interrupt his less-than-official meeting. He walked to his closet, sliding a mirror door before switching on a light. One would have thought Mr. Washington lived here had the contents of the closet been made public. On the right-hand side, neatly hung, stood dress shirts and suits of all shades, stretching for a dozen feet away from the entrance. On the other side, drawers of shoes, ties, and watches were methodically placed. Past those drawers, *costumes* dangled from hangers. Richard reached for one of them, pulling out a cream-coloured toga.

Toga and sandals in hand, Chronos' CEO made his way to his personal bathroom, also accessible from inside his office. The lavatory's floor was of black marble, as were the walls. To the east was an open shower, while on the western side stood a sink and toilet. Richard quickly undressed, glancing at the time before taking off his watch: quarter past eight. Marsh had been waiting for fifteen minutes. *Better hurry up*, he thought. *The guy can get cranky.* As if on cue, as he was spraying water on his face, Richard's phone rang again. Marsh was calling him.

"I'm ready," he answered, walking back to the main area of his office.

"About time! Thought you'd forgotten 'bout me. Got the code?"

"One second." Sitting at his desk, Richard unlocked a drawer and pulled out his personal, grey in colour, MiChronos. *So much for telling the journalist a prototype would be ready in the next five years.* To be fair, only a selected few owned and knew about this new and innovative piece of technology. Looking through his most recent time trips, he found the time coordinates and forwarded them to Marsh's own MiChronos system.

"See you there," he said before hanging up.

Richard put his phone down on his desk, shook his head in exhaustion, and stepped onto a metal platform, three feet by four in size. The flexible metallic time traveling carpet was only a few feet away from Richard's office chair, hiding in plain sight. When guests walked in, he told them it was a piece of art by a new up-and-coming artist. They would nod politely and move on to a different subject of conversation.

Individually, the MiChronos and the platform were utterly useless. But put together, the combination was nothing short of magical. To activate a time trip, the user had to wear the MiChronos on their head while standing on the platform. Once both tools were wirelessly paired, the time traveler could enter the desired time coordinates using the ocular keyboard inside the blackout visor or simply select a previous trip. When he was ready, having selected the coded ROM-192AD-0720, Richard pressed the circular button at the side of his MiChronos.

Bright lights shone in his eyes, followed by total darkness.

//ROMA-192...

Richard reconstructed from a molecular level in an empty back alley. The whole reappearing process took less than five seconds, but there was always a chance of being discovered by a local despite Chronos' phantom algorithm.

November in Italy was chilly, but growing up in the windy city, Richard welcomed the biting breeze. Under normal circumstances, he would have taken the long way, the scenic route, to get to the Colosseum, but this day was different. The secret meeting with Marsh had already been delayed too long, and things had to get moving.

Walking at a fast pace in his woolen robes, making sure not to trip on the cobblestone streets, he waved off beggars looking for a denarius and merchants alike wanting to sell him trinkets. *Rule Number One: What is in the past stays in the past,* he reminded himself, *even if it was a genuine Pompeian painting that had survived the world's most famous eruption.* Far ahead, he heard the sounds of iron and gasps followed by a raucous erupting from the stone amphitheatre. Not so long ago, in this timeline, Emperor Commodus, son of Marcus Aurelius, decided to celebrate the Plebeian games by taking part as a gladiator himself, a decision thought by the Roman elite to be ill-fitting for a man of his caste. The people, the commoners, on the other hand, loved it and loved him for it. Although the combats were fixed, always ensuring Commodus' victory, the steel he faced was sharp, and would surely wound the emperor dressed as a secutor were he not careful. Skillfully parrying and striking down on his trident-wielding opponents, Commodus welcomed the roar of the entertained crowd each time he slashed at exposed skin.

Upon entering the Colosseum, Richard easily spotted Marsh five rows up on the western side—their usual meeting spot. He was snacking on salted peas, yesteryear's equivalent of today's ballpark hot dog. His eyes trained on Commodus. When Richard reached him, the Colonel said, "Could you imagine what it would be like if we brought a guy like Commodus back with us?" *Yes,* he replied internally, *and you know we can't. It would have inconceivable repercussions for this timeline.* "I mean, he's going to be assassinated in a month or two anyways," he continued. "Get him outta here the day of. He hitches a ride with us. Everyone believes he's dead. None the wiser." He ate another handful of salted peas.

Richard rolled his eyes. He was glad he had remembered to turn off the language assist feature on his bracelet. In normal outings, this specific piece of engineering helped clients communicate with the local populace in case of emergency; the bracelet picked up the client's words and translated them automatically. There were still kinks to work out but in general, it did the trick. Washington inwardly admonished Marsh, and not for the first time, for speaking so freely about a historical event such as the assassination of a ruler. *Rule number seven: Gotta watch your tongue.*

After a moment filled with cheers and jeers from the crowd, Richard changed his thoughts and got to business.

"You wanted to ask me something?"

"Yes, I did." The big man took his eyes off the combat. "Any progress on our little side project?"

"Unfortunately, no. The time barrier seems to be holding strong around the Peloponnesian War. Something is making it impossible for us to get past 431 BC."

"Shame. Seeing Achilles and Hector duke it out would've been a pretty sight."

Never mind the fact that they're fictional, Washington thought.

Marsh spat a bad pea out and continued. "And in the other direction?"

"Colonel?"

"The future, son. We're not investing thirteen-digit figures annually for Chronos to install new plumbing. The golden goose better start laying eggs, or Uncle Sam's gonna barbecue the damn bird."

There it was: another meeting, another threat. Richard's hands were tied, and nothing he could say would ever please his maniacal boss.

"We... We're working on it."

"Not good enough."

"We're making headway, I mean," Richard corrected himself. "Site B has recruited a lot of... volunteers, at your demand." *They are more like voluntold.* "Our scientists believe they've made a breakthrough. We'll be ready to start experimentation by next quarter."

"It's already started."

"Sorry?"

"Did I stutter?" He turned to face Richard again. "I gave the order a month ago. Testing has already begun." There was a large smile on his face.

Richard felt nauseous. He knew he would have to stand up to Marsh one of these days. Was it today? "Should we, though?" he asked, his voice cracking. Marsh just looked at him and said nothing. "I mean," he said, his heart pounding hard in his chest. "The Society is close to figuring things out. Shouldn't we err on the side of caution and, I don't know, lay low for a bit? It's not like we're in a rush, right? The future isn't going anywhere." Richard's confidence in the fact that he might have finally convinced Marsh was short-lived.

"Ever heard of the tale of the turtle and the rabbit?"

"Aesop's? The tortoise and the hare?"

"That's the one. Right now, we're the rabbit. We're in the lead, son, with no one on our tail. What happened to the rabbit when he took a nap?"

"The tortoise caught up—"

"The goddamn turtle caught up and bit the rabbit's nuts off."

Crude. "I'm not sure that's what—"

"What happens when, not if, but when, someone else figures out your little equations? You're a smart man, I'll give you that." *A compliment?* "But there are other eggheads out there." *Ah, there it is.* "Don't you think one of them timelines' gonna fight back?"

Richard was taken aback. It wasn't like Marsh to think of *these* types of consequences. "Well—"

"I'm here to protect us, son." He put a massive hand on Washington's shoulder, squeezing somewhat gently. "And when war begins, we'll be ready."

At that moment, Commodus parried, deflecting the trident with his shield. The retiarius could not recover in time. He knew the end was nigh. The emperor side-stepped; slashing open his defenceless adversary's belly. He followed with a twirl to get behind him, his white armour gleaming in the sunlight. Ruthlessly and effectively, he stabbed the kneeling gladiator in the back. *How ironic.*

The crowd cheered, clapping for their emperor and undefeated champion. The people started to exit the Colosseum. Marsh stood up while Richard remained seated. He must have made a face, because Marsh said, "Aww, Cupcake, don't look so sad. Here, have the rest." The Colonel gave him his half-empty bag of salted peas and left without another word.

Once outside the Colosseum, Richard walked aimlessly, with no real destination in mind. Like his legs, his thoughts were also wandering. What was he doing? Feeling philosophical, maybe, almost as though the great minds of old were inspiring him.

Had his life been a movie, and he a hero, because this was how he saw himself in this story, this would be the moment where he would burst into song, expressing his sorrows and voicing his trials. But he did not have an artist's soul. Nor was he in a singing mood. And, after all, was he really the hero in this narrative?

Washington continued on his way, away from the path he was used to taking, a dangerous thing indeed. Uneventfully, however, he safely made it outside the city walls. *What is the right thing to do? And is the answer the same for me and Chronos?* Eventually, he came to a stop near a large boulder not far from the main road. His feet started to ache, first-century sandals not being as comfortable as his Italian loafers, so Washington sat upon the massive stone.

If only Richard had known what was brewing back home, he might have stayed a while longer on his rock, pondering the meaning of his own existence. And he might have succeeded in doing so, but he decided against it and raised his left hand at eye level. He pushed a button on his bracelet, and his body disappeared, to the horror and confusion of a young farmer who was standing only a stone's throw from Washington.

〰

0 day(s): 17 hour(s): 18 minute(s): 28 second(s)

CHAPTER 7 - Bill

Bill's Apple Turnovers

Drifting back into consciousness, slightly confused, Bill rubbed the sleep out of his eyes with the back of his hand, thinking, *how long had the alarm been going off?* Slowly reaching over for his phone on the nightstand, he immediately turned it off. His plane ride back from Italy had touched down six or seven hours ago. He replayed the events, nay, catastrophe that took place under Monte Meta. He shook his head. *What a hot mess.* With the phone still in hand, Bill began his morning by checking his messages. After a moment, he realized his *Leader One* persona would not be needed today. What a refreshing turn of events.

By the time he was done catching up with the world's news, and a couple of cute reels, it was already six-thirty, and the first rays of sunshine already crept through badly-fitted curtains. One would think a man in his mid-fifties, such as he, would prioritize such details and make sure sleep was not to be interrupted. However, Bill had put off crossing this specific task from his to-do list for one very simple reason. When that light broke in, it lit up his sleeping wife's face, making him fall in love with her all over again.

Legs dangling off the bed, his sleepy toes found his loafers slightly hidden under the shirt he'd worn the day before. He gave Ginny a peck on the cheek before pushing himself upright. Bill thought himself a creature of habits, controlled by the most monotone of routines. Even more so since what his wife had dubbed his mid-life crisis seven years ago.

Who would have believed that after leaving the Great White North, making his way across the States lines, and working a desk job for almost twenty years, he'd end up quitting and starting his own business, a lowly bakery of all things? Ginny certainly hadn't. After all, she had not expected her husband, as impulsive as he was, to get approved for a loan when she was busy on the West Coast, touring campuses during a week-long promotion of her most recent scientific paper. Ginny had given him the silent treatment in the past, but nothing came close to what he had endured that time. Just thinking about it, even though the business prospered with time, made his greying hair turn a shade lighter.

On his way to the kitchen counter, he picked up his favourite mug from the cupboard, a plain black one, and set it next to the electric kettle Ginny had gotten him for his birthday last year. She knew him well. He needed his Earl Grey in the morning if he wanted to function relatively well (according to social standards). He wasn't the only one; *we need caffeine,* he thought. After oversteeping it, *old habits die hard*, he made himself breakfast and readied himself to leave for the bakery, his bakery.

When choosing a location for his new establishment, Bill, with the input from his wife, who had finally decided to speak to him again, had picked a nearby neighbourhood that also happened to be behind a large high school.

In its beginnings, *Bill's* only had three employees; a full-timer, himself, as well as two part-timers, kids of a friend looking to make some money at the same time as they were studying at a college close by. The kids would mainly work the cash register during peak times, a.k.a lunchtime, and clean up when things slowed down. Bill, on the other hand, was putting in twelve- and some days sixteen-hour shifts from Monday to Friday. He recognized that closing the shop on the weekends was going to hurt financially, but it was a compromise he was willing to make for the sake of his marriage.

Fast-forward seven years into the future, *Bill's Bakery* was rolling as smoothly as an electric car—surely there is a joke to be made about winter snow days there. Three full-timers were now on the payroll, one of them a top graduate from one of those culinary art schools in the state of Maine. The other four workers, part-timers, were ironically students enrolled at the nearby school—his friend's kids had since then moved on to new chapters in their lives. Many things had evolved in those eighty or so months since the bakery opened: the shop got a new paint job, free Wi-Fi was installed, and many creative pastries were added to the menu, including the winning entry in *Bill's Bake-Off*. This event became an annual original dessert contest where more than fifty high school-aged participants would enter their creations for a chance to win the grand prize: to see their winning pastry sold at *Bill's* for an entire calendar year. Last year's winner, Jean-Philippe Corne's cinnamon and caramel éclair, was awarded one hundred dollars, as well as fifty percent of the year's proceeds made from his creation.

Yet, despite all the changes, one thing from the past remained: Bill's original turnover was, as always, a bestseller.

The chime rang above his head when he walked in. His pastry expert, Maple, was already hard at work, putting a batch of handmade lemon scones in one of the ovens. Bill greeted Miss Berry with a wave—yes, her name was Maple Berry: the pastry expert—and proceeded to the back of the shop where, just like clockwork, Hank was dropping off today's delivery.

"Morning, sir. How was your trip?"

"Trip?" he replied suspiciously.

"Weren't you out East last week? Visiting your folks?"

"Right. Yes, thank you. Everything went marvelously." Then, changing topics. "Farmer Kasch didn't give you any problems this time?"

"No, sir. In fact, he reminded me to thank you for the scrupulous pie you sent him."

"Scrumptious?"

"Yeah, prolly."

Bill, enunciating the word *pro-ba-bly* in his mind, left the young man to his work and made his way back to the front of the store. He turned on the radio, an antique thing from his past he'd not dared throw out, and tuned it to that station kids liked these days, the one with all the noise and mumbling lyricists. *How times have changed.*

At five to eight, minutes before the doors would open to clients, Bill's phone beeped with a notification from his wife. He glanced at it, putting it back in his pants pocket almost immediately. She'd sent him a link, a reminder that Chronos' Grand Tour would take place this afternoon. How could he have forgotten? This was all the two of them had sadly been able to talk about for the past week or so.

Sure, in public, he was known as Bill the baker, the Godfather of turnovers, and Savior of high school bellies. But within more eclectic circles, they called him Leader One. When he wasn't working at the bakery, it was his job to carry out the Society's more radical plans, the ones *they* deemed necessary, the ones that drew on the morally grey. *They* made it seem like he was the one running the show, but he knew deep down he was only a puppet, Ginny and LETO were the ones in charge.

It all started about five years ago when his wife, an already prominent member of the scientific community, was running a test using a computerized algorithm. Bill wasn't exactly sure what it all consisted of, but he remembered quite vividly the conversation they'd had that fateful night.

"So, how was work today?" he asked as he spun spaghetti onto his fork.

"Well, you remember that paper I wrote last year? The one about quantum connections in computerized systems resulting in time dilation?"

"Of course I do." He remembered it, alright. Even tried reading it a few times. Understanding it was something entirely different.

"Something incredible happened today!" She hadn't touched her food. She was so excited.

"You mean, that device with the thing worked?"

"I was about to turn everything off for the day when... when... it talked to me," she continued, almost giddy.

"What did?"

"LETO," Ginny said in a mysterious tone.

"Lot of what?"

"LETO," she repeated. "It happened, Bill! My theory was right. There are timelines outside of ours, and something horrible is about to befall them."

"A computer told you that?" Bill had replied incredulously.

"Not any kind of computer." He'd noticed her raising her voice a little. "The XFLR is a sophisticated machine built by some of the most brilliant minds of the twenty-first century."

Here we go again, Bill thought, knowing full well from similar experiences that she would go on one of her structured and elaborated rants. He zoned out for a spell, making sure to nod from time to time as he kept eating. Finally, he said, "I absolutely agree. So what's next?"

"Well, as I was saying." *Oops,* he got caught. "We need to raise awareness amongst the populace. I'll chat with Dorian tomorrow. He has contacts at Genin Tech who could help with... this sort of thing."

"Anything I can help with?" Sometimes humans offer their help to seem nice, supportive, and helpful while expecting a *no but thanks for offering* type of answer.

"Actually, that'd be great!"

Uh oh, he thought, *what did I get myself into?*

What this offer had gotten him into was a life-changing trip to Monaco, meeting Dravra's top agent, uncovering the Ghost's true identity, and fleeing for his life. What came after the escape to Italy, however, had put his marriage in jeopardy.

Ginny was not a jealous woman, far from it, but when she found out that Bill had spent an extra week hiding with this DeLuca chick, she could barely control her emotions. He had tried explaining to her he couldn't have risked communication for fear of them being intercepted. His intentions had been noble; to keep her and the Society safe, but the damage was already done. If her husband thought the silent treatment he'd received when he bought the bakery was bad, those next few weeks made it seem like a cakewalk.

In fact, those *next few weeks* of painful mistrust turned into months, which turned into years. They'd talked about it and shared their feelings, as Dr. Mags had suggested. Yet, as often as Bill would assure his wife that nothing had happened, he felt he was talking to a brick wall every time.

The question facing the couple had been this: had he been faithful on that trip? To clear things up, in all truth, Bill did not sleep with DeLuca. There was, however, a part of him that, maybe, had wanted to. But having fantasies and acting upon them were two different things, right?

Anyways, rewinding to a year after the Monaco Leak, LETO and Ginny had finally found a way to communicate more instantaneously via a temporal email service—something Bill had never been able to understand—rendering mission assignments more effective. Bill also received access to those communications, meaning information would not always have to go through his wife to get to him. Bill had his suspicions about the motive of this recent switch, but he decided not to delve into it too much. Since that day, any operation related to extraction, recon, or guerilla marketing came directly to Leader One from LETO. As instrumental as she had been in the Society's beginnings, Ginny was slowly pulling herself out.

Back to Tuesday, October twenty-second. It was just after eight in the evening when he finally closed the shop, ready to go home after a long but productive day at work. He'd needed that. But then came the dreadfully familiar chime of his phone; a new email had appeared in his inbox. Bill took the phone out and checked the notification.

LETO had sent him a message.

Time to get to work.

〜

0 day(s): 18 hour(s): 53 minute(s): 38 second(s)

From: LETO@timeserver.net
To: leaderone@timeserver.net
Subject: Phase One
Attachment(s): *Site B - Schematics, Site B - Intel, Site B - Files*

Leader One,

After careful deliberation, it has been decided that you were not at fault in the Bishop's debacle. For the sake of the mission, I consider this matter closed and **out of your hands**. We are too close to bringing Chronos down and liberating the people to let Dravra's failure halt us now.

My attempt at bypassing our enemy's systems has been triumphant. I anticipate they will not cooperate willfully unless otherwise provoked. Phase One is a go.

Going through their server, something of interest to the STL came up. Site B is real, and what they are doing there is exactly what we believed— and much worse. This, unfortunately, means that we will have to move up our schedule and strike earlier than expected.

The countdown will begin as originally planned. I will deal with all aspects of technological warfare. You and your team will create a diversion and attack with manpower. I trust you to devise a plan.

Attached are the files you will require to cripple the beast. I am not exactly sure what you will find there, but if I read the schematics correctly, the destruction of that *thing* on page sixty-three should be your number one priority.

I will be waiting for your plan of attack.

It is time to break the Scythe that is bleeding the timelines.

LETO

P.S. Did your team have any luck with locating the girl?

CHAPTER 8 - LETO

How to Catch a Futureman

Subtle changes to the system's matrix were made. Not even a computer wiz like Jeremy Wilson could have spotted them. Unbeknownst to anyone working at Chronos Corp., the smallest of tweaks were presently happening across the timelines. Its CEO would have called it a virus, but the person responsible for the impending shutdown believed herself the vaccine, a cure to save countless lives.

Her name was Anne Christie. And although she was nearing sixty years of life, she was a savior from a different timeline, a mother on a mission. Was it rage that willed her to understand her child's disappearance? Or maybe was it her grief? A mixture of both? Family members and friends, at first, were supportive. But the comfort did not last. One by one, they gave up, leaving her to drown in her madness. No one understood. And yet, here she was in what looked like an abandoned basement. In one corner stood a makeshift time displacing apparatus she'd pieced together throughout the years. Colourful wires slithered the tiled floor. At first glance, they seemed to connect a large and clunky machine to a beaten-up office chair.

Anne entered a few final keystrokes before opening the top left drawer of a workstation. She pushed papers and junk around before grabbing the rugged metal of a gun's handle. It felt cold in her hand. The woman expertly checked the chamber before cocking it in two smooth movements. Only one bullet was left. Only one was all she needed.

Her face was expressionless when she walked by the slightly uncanny chair, making her way toward a massive and heavy-looking wooden door. Anne put a hand on the round knob. It was cool, something natural since the room it led to was the basement's cold room. She readjusted her grip on the pistol and swung the thick oak door open.

The first noise escaping the room was not that of rusty hinges or even of a rumbling ventilator. No. It was that of raspy, laborious breathing. Anne walked a few paces toward the sound, reached up, and pulled at a light bulb's string. It flickered a few times before finally turning on and, in doing so, revealing the face of a half-starved, scratchy bearded, dirty man. His wrists were bound in front of him. One leg was chained and bolted to the concrete wall.

Everybody has skeletons in their closet. Anne Christie happened to have a futureman locked in her basement.

↞∿↠

The Birth of LETO, or How a Futureman Happened to be Locked in A.C.'s Basement

Anne was folding laundry in her bedroom, soft music playing on the stereo, when Willa, her teenage daughter, barged in.

"I want to go see Dad," she spurted out, matter-of-factly.

"Willa, Honey, I told you already. Not this weekend," Anne replied with a sigh at the tail end of her words.

"William's with him. Why can't I be?" Willa knew the answer to this question. She also knew that mentioning her twin brother's name would enrage her mom even more so.

"I am not going to repeat myself," she said through clenched teeth, keeping her emotions in check as best she could.

"It's not fair!" Willa retorted, stomping her foot hard. That got her mother's attention. She turned around to face her daughter.

"You're sixteen years old. Please don't do that." There was a hint of frustration in her voice.

Willa rolled her eyes and stomped back to her room. Anne winced when she slammed her door shut. Not long after, Stevie Nicks' gruff voice seeped through the wall. The spasm of a smile flashed on Anne's face. Edge of Seventeen had been Willa's go-to whenever she felt wronged. Her dad had bought her the album when she turned thirteen, a mere three months before the split.

Peter lived in Edmonton, where he worked for the NHL's Oilers organization. The reason William was with him this weekend, and not with his mom and sister in Calgary, was because he'd been promised great seats as well as a possible meet and greet with the players after their game against the St-Louis Blues. William could not pass on an opportunity to meet Messier and Kurri (Gretzky would not play that night, sadly). Willa hadn't understood. She thought he was betraying him, leaving her alone with Mom, of all people.

Anne dropped the shirt she'd half-folded on the bed and inched toward the landline. She dialed her ex's number and let the tone ring for a bit. The answering machine came on after the fifth ring:

"Hello, you've reached Pete. Leave a message." She didn't bother. She just hung up.

A couple of hours later, Anne called down the hall to Willa. "Food's ready." But no one came. She called again, but still nothing. Anne was getting flustered, heat rising in her cheeks. She went to Willa's bedroom door and knocked twice before entering.

"Willa, I swear to God..."

She was not in her room, and the window was open.

Six months later, she received a call from the local police. They assured her that they were continuing to do everything in their power to find her daughter. It was a courtesy call, that was all. It would also be the last she would receive from them.

Two years had passed since her disappearance. William had moved out to go to college in the States. Anne kept her communications with her son sporadic. It was all either of them could handle, really. As hard as it was for her to lose a child—still, she held on to hope— she could not begin to imagine how William was processing all of this. To lose a twin, to be reminded of what you had lost every time you looked in the mirror. When he came back home for Thanksgiving, he'd changed the hue of his hair, wore coloured contacts, and was sporting a budding beard. It broke Anne's heart.

The following decade ushered in a new millennium, yet no answers as to where Willa might be or might have been. That was until Anne fell down the proverbial rabbit hole one night and discovered something so crazy she did not entertain it at first. By pure coincidence, Ms. Christie had wandered to a blog, a new sort of online journal called ConnEXtion. Through it, she met members who, like her, were living through the unexplained disappearance of a loved one. One user posted about her husband. Another story regarded a best friend. To be true, Anne felt compelled by these stories. For months, she had read them all, and more were being added every few days. As therapeutic as it was, a strange knot in her chest subsided. Anne Christie wasn't alone in her pain, in her grief, in her hope that one day her daughter might come back to her. Through some extra digging, metaphorical yarn, and a bit of luck, she came to a startling theory.

All of these disappearances happened around what would be later known in history as Major Events.

It took Anne the better part of a decade to get her plan into action and for it to get any sort of traction.

On the eve of the 2010 Olympics in Vancouver, Anne drove almost eleven hours from Calgary to arrive at BC Place Stadium in time for the opening ceremony. She wasn't sure exactly what she was looking for or what kind of clue would lead her to find her daughter. Her new friends at ConnEXtion had shared threads upon threads of theories with how to spot a futureman. Some thought you could recognize them by their attire, like Michael J. Fox's Marty McFLy's absurd first cowboy outfit or that time traveling hipster from 1941. Others believed you should pay particular attention to the sort of technology they carried. Examples went from McCoy's tricorder to the 1962 World Cup flip phone. Yet sometimes, too much information is worse than none. Let's just be on the lookout for anything out of the ordinary, she thought. Whatever that may be.

She did not have to wait too long.

The morning after the cauldron-lighting ceremony, a riot exploded not ten minutes north of the stadium. Shop windows were shattered, cars were vandalized, and hundreds of people wreaked havoc.

Anne had no part in it, despite being in the middle of it. Eyes open, ears on the alert, she moved through the destructive crowd like water between rocks. Suddenly, words caught her attention.

"They were told not to go there, damnit! They knew not to go there."

The man who'd uttered those words was wearing an off-red Canada Olympics coat, the kind she had been seeing in stores for the past few months. However, something about this one seemed off. Like the material was ten years older than it should be. She followed him a moment longer. He was nervous, to be sure. Muttering under his breath, checking his watch often. No, it wasn't a watch. A bracelet?

When the police, clad in riot gear, showed up, the mystery man snuck into one of the stores that had yet to fall victim to vandalism, a derelict coffee shop with light yellow trims. Anne followed him, eyes like a hawk. He never saw her, too preoccupied. Walking nervously towards the bathrooms, he lifted his bracelet to his chest. Anne swore she heard the words "request" and "triangulation" before the door closed behind him. She was quite sure of it now: strange clothes, curious tech. He was one of them: a futureman.

No one at Chronos ever knew or figured out what had happened to Joshua that day. No one knew how he got knocked out by Anne or how she brought him, unconscious, back to Calgary. The mystery had yet to be pierced as to what happened to his tech. Why were his bracelet and his comms not answering emergency commands? But it was all so simple. She had kidnapped him and used his knowledge of the future, of Chronos and their tech, to create her own time displacing apparatus, amongst other things.

For a year and a day, she kept Joshua locked in her basement. She was keeping him alive, barely. By some degree of force, Anne was able to extract, from her unfortunate guest, important senior guide-level clearance knowledge. She understood, however, that this information was virtually useless to her and her ambitions unless she had a player, a second in command, on the other side of the board.

Then one day, a scientist named Ginny found her through the veil of time. It was at that moment that she decided to go by the name LETO.

Leto, in Greek mythology, was the mother of the twin gods Apollo and Artemis. She thought the name fitting, obviously because of the twin part, but because her husband was a dirty cheater.

And so LETO was born, and with her, the birth of the Society of Timeline Liberation. Their union proved mutually beneficial, not only for Anne but for a multitude of bleeding timelines. On the one hand, Ginny, "the brain," and Bill, "Leader One," were slowing down the monster, blunting the scythe as they would soon refer to it. On the other hand, it kept Anne's mind busy. Sure, the disappearance of her daughter almost twenty years ago continued to be the force driving her enterprise, but she could finally fall asleep at night.

Eventually, Anne Christie, as the faceless mastermind of the rebellion, received substantial intel that would permit her to personally engage with her enemy and cripple it as only a grieving mother could. The data had come from Leader One and his team. After short communications and sharing of plans, Anne was ready to strike. She sat at her computer, enabled a temporal line, and wrote the first line of her warning: *//8002... the number of timelines changed..._*

〰

Anne kneeled in front of Joshua. She hit his blueing toes with the tip of her gun, waking him with a start from his laborious sleep. The man's eye, once dark blue yet lifeless now, immediately turned to terror when it caught sight of the glistening metal of the Glock.

"That's it?" he tried asking through cracked lips, understanding what his captor had come to do. She raised the barrel to his face, aiming right above the left eye, the only one he mustered enough strength to even keep open. "For what... it's worth..." he continued, a little bit more audibly this time. "I am... sorry... about your—" A coughing fit prevented him from finishing the sentence, a final apology.

"The hell you are," Anne replied, facial traits as stoic as ever. She pushed the muzzle against her prisoner's forehead, pushing hard enough to make Joshua's head snap backward. Yet she did not pull the trigger. She slowly backed away from the broken man. She placed the loaded weapon on the ground beside him and set his wrists free.

Without another look, Anne left him to his own decision. She'd left him to die. She never bothered to close the heavy door, though. Instead, she simply jumped on the Frankensteinian chair and began attaching wires here and there. She was in the midst of connecting the last of the cables when the soundwave of a gun being fired reached her. Anne stopped breathing for a moment. To no one in particular, or maybe to reassure herself, she asked: "How far would you go to get your child back?" then blinked twice before willing her arms to finish the task they had set out to complete.

That evening, at exactly midnight Original-Temporal-Time, Anne Christie achieved the impossible. She divided her consciousness between numerous avatars, safely and inconspicuously materializing over strategic frames of fragile times.

Ready to wreak havoc.

Ready to make them pay.

Ready to get even.

For hell hath no fury like a mother's grief.

0 day(s): 15 hour(s): 00 minute(s): 00 second(s)

CHAPTER 9 - LETO

Firewall

__ FIREWALL BREACH __

//OLY-1896... __ INCOMING DATA __

READING...

Athens, Greece, April of 1896. It was warm outside, but the heat had nothing to do with the massive and yet-to-be-invented cauldron that would only be introduced to the Games thirty-two years later. A pleasant and welcomed breeze came from the Mediterranean Sea and blew over the long-awaiting crowd. When Frenchman Pierre de Coubertin took on the ambitious project of reviving the Olympics, many Greeks felt a sense of pride and undue nostalgia. Growing up, they'd all heard of the games held in honour of Zeus, King of the Olympians, where heroes like Leonidas of Rhodes, the runner, Kyniska of Sparta, daughter of a king, and Arrichion of Phigalia, the tragic, entered their names into the annals of history.

However, the modern world was about to produce its own legends, starting with a new competition based on an important historical event: the marathon. Old and young, having heard the tale, fell in awe by the sheer resolve of the Athenian messenger who ran from the battlefield in Marathon to the Acropolis in Athens to announce the Persians' loss at the hands of victorious Greeks. His name was Pheidippides, and in this timeline, seventeen runners from five different countries would have a chance to recreate his magic.

Anne's avatar appeared on an empty hill under an olive tree that had just started blooming. She did not smell the flowers, nor did she take in her surroundings. She was on a mission, and events needed to move along. Slowly, the cure made its way toward the noise of the crowds. She would strategically position herself there, hiding in plain sight, waiting for the five Chronos clients to appear.

Soon, she thought, soon.

__ FIREWALL BREACH __

//GGE-1922... __ INCOMING DATA __

READING...

Long Island, summer of 1922. A raucous crowd of ladies and gentlemen were getting off a decrepit ferry; that was no doubt the reason they called them the Roaring Twenties. The waters were calm, and the piers were moving without notice. Chatting as they made their way towards the brightly lit colonial-style mansion, the women held onto their beaus' arms.

The men wore most of the same things. A simple, sharp-looking three-piece suit. Black or brown. Only a fraction of those partygoers opted for the white or beige ensemble, and fewer still wore it well. Footwear was of two preferred styles; Oxfords or two-tone brogues, which, to the untrained eye, may have looked identical. Finally, to top it off, quite literally, fedoras were adorned on slicked-back dues.

The ladies' attires, on the other hand, were much more liberal than, but always as classy as, their male counterparts. Many shades and tints of the rainbow were the rage. Some dresses were dark and flappy, while others were dazzling and shiny. Pearls, bracelets, and earrings were inevitably common, but it was the headdress that made the look. Like a crown, headbands of satin or sequin, feather-ornate or bedazzled, rested upon the women's brow. They dressed to kill, primed for the bacchanals.

As they entered, the guests were met with a sensory explosion of lights and sounds. Servants held trays of liquor and bubbles, weaving around the dancers, perpetually having to go back to the kitchen to fill up more glasses. Although it was a fairly new musical genre, made famous only a few years back, the host had opted for the fast rhythm of jazz to fill the air and create his festive ambiance. The crowd welcomed it wholeheartedly.

The party was well underway. Another of Anne's virtual copies stood at the bottom of the marble stairs. She easily blended in with the locals: red dress, silver headband, black feather. She sipped at the drink in her hand occasionally. Her eyes were fixed on the double doors. Waiting for something, someone.

__ FIREWALL BREACH __

//EWH-1841... __ INCOMING DATA __

READING...

Half-hidden behind a large statue erected in memory of King Louis XIII, a third iteration of Anne Christie looked up. The sun had recently set on the Square facing the Rohan-Guéménée hotel in Paris, France, in 1841. A light flickered inside a window on the second floor. That window belonged to the family of a man recently elected to the prestigious *Académie Française*, Victor Hugo.

Shadows, brought to life by candlelight, danced on burgundy walls. The man who published *Notre Dame de Paris* ten years prior was in a hurry to leave, for he was expected at the Procope, a restaurant still famous to this date, to celebrate his long-awaited induction. His wife, Adèle, was to stay home with the kids, all four of them, whilst her famous husband would wine and dine with equally renowned friends like the composer Berlioz and the actress Drouet. Even the future Knight of Pratz, Alphonse de Lamartine, was said to possibly, maybe, make an appearance.

The poet's quarters were spacious and beautifully decorated, even by today's standards. Although his apartment will be made public for viewing in about a hundred years, as a sort of museum or attraction, Chronos' clients were not traveling to this time destination to receive interior design tips from Madame Hugo. The two visitors whom Anne a.k.a. LETO was waiting on were two University professors researching the topic of their next academic papers.

When she hacked the system, she found a request made by two academics, submitted to the head of their faculty. As is the case for most research applications, it took almost two years for the demand to be fully approved. Madame Prost, a *Romantisme* specialist, wished to elucidate a few mysteries surrounding the person that was Victor Hugo, or so she said in an elaborate twelve-page disquisition. Monsieur DaCosta, in his case, was on the cusp of a breakthrough regarding *The Failed Revival of Classicism in Nineteenth Century Romanticism.* In his request, which was only about five pages long, he explained that legends and stories based on ancient Greek heroes and deities were about to make their comeback. But something had prevented it, some important socio-cultural event. As a huge follower of Étienne de Jouy, it was not surprising to understand that M. DaCosta thought Hugo was responsible for the cessation of the resurgence of Greek myth-based stories.

Excellent, Anne thought to herself. *These two will be perfect.*

__ FIREWALL BREACH __

//HMK-1312... __ INCOMING DATA __

READING...

The world was green. Grass, trees as far as the eyes could see. The body of a woman materialized behind a derelict abode. She was clothed in a simple kimono, mainly red in colour. Her attire belonged to this time period, but the lines of her face did not.

This was medieval Japan. Civil wars were sparked by words. Alliances as feeble as the wind. But what had truly stood the test of time was the warrior, the samurai. Anne had set her gaze on one of them. A strong man, scarred, far from scared, walking down the dirt road of a nondescript village. His hair was long, his posture proud. He moved with grace.

All his life, this man had known one thing, discipline. The *Bushido* was as much a part of him as the two blades attached to his side. Wherever the Shogun willed him to go, he wielded the katana. For war was an art, and to obey was the only thing a military man could do.

After a few paces, Anne saw the samurai stop in front of an open-wall hut, a forge. He exchanged inaudible words with the blacksmith. She couldn't make out what they were saying, not because she didn't know the language, but for the simple reason that she wasn't close enough to hear. The digital lady couldn't get caught yet. This was where she would wait for her prey. This was where future-people came to admire firsthand the legendary skills of the Priest Masume, father of the Honjō.

__ FIREWALL BREACH __

//DIS-1967... __ INCOMING DATA __

READING...

When it first opened to the public in March of 1967, the *Pirates of the Caribbean* boat tour bewitched its riders with state-of-the-art audio-animatronics, a technique that was barely heard of in those days. But what made this attraction truly special, in hindsight, was the simple fact that the man himself had a hand in designing it. The genius in question was standing only a few metres from the clandestine traveler, shaking hands with and welcoming people who had made the trek to visit his one-of-a-kind amusement park: Disneyland.

Anne, another digital copy of herself, paid him no mind. Pretending to be one of the guests, she lined up behind them, waiting for her turn to come to experience something she had not actually had the chance to enjoy in her real life. *The person I am after will not be here until later*, she convinced herself. *Might as well make the most of it.* Was she losing her grip on the plan? No, not she. Not LETO.

Inside the makeshift world created by Mr. Disney and his team, Anne's avatar walked past a few ramshackle boat homes before being forced to stop by the unmovingness of the people in front of her. They were all entranced by what looked like a skull hung above a doorway. The strangest thing about it wasn't that it was crossed by two blades. It was that it could talk. Sure, it was a recording, and everybody knew. Nevertheless, the magic was there. Moving along with the crew, Anne tried to remember what the animated object had said, using bad, almost comical grammar.

Something about Davy Jones, a storm coming, and that dead men told no tales.

Amen to that, Captain X.

__ FIREWALL BREACH __

//MTG-1606... __ INCOMING DATA __

READING...

The first act was nearing its end.

The cast on stage was presenting the world premiere of what would be called a classic, a masterpiece three hundred and fifty-plus years into the future.

The Globe was a sight to behold. Twenty sides, nine metres high, and what to say of the stage? All wood, beautifully hand-carved planks where actors brought to life the lives and deaths of so many characters who resided, until their paper-birth, in one William Shakespeare's mind.

The sun shone bright that afternoon. For the first time since she undertook her mission, she took a moment to appreciate the beauty of it all. In her real life, she had heard talks of a rebuilding project that would bring back from the dead this magnificent theatre house. Yet here she was. She didn't have to wait too long after all.

At 0915 OTT (Original-Temporal-Time), an elderly couple was to materialize itself, with their guide, somewhere in the vicinity. When they did, the digital timeline would restart. The locals would be none the wiser, but Anne would know. The sky would flash a dark green, and the world around her would start moving backward increasingly faster by the second. During those moments, Anne was to stay where she was, unmoved and unmoving. Her eyes would stay closed during that transition, thirty to sixty seconds. All she'd feel was a tickling sensation on her skin.

How was all that possible? Minor differences in her system's design permitted her to hijack Chronos' framework. Let's be clear: Anne Christie's physical body did not travel through time. She had simply found a way to transport her virtual self inside another computer program.

This was also not the first time she had clandestinely made her way into Chronos. She had been testing her theories, updating her plans, and stealing private information. She was not going to fail. She would not fail. She couldn't afford to fail.

This is it. Anne told herself, walking over to the shadows.

This was the ninth and final digital copy of herself she had secretly inserted into Chronos' systems that night. She took a deep breath and closed her eyes.

SYSTEM REBOOT - Y/N

Y

SYSTEM REBOOTING...

...

RUNNING PARAMETERS... NO BREACH DETECTED...

Anne's pieces were set. She waited, biding her time in the binary world's shadows, for the perfect prey to come. The *cure* had made its move. Chronos was on the clock.

‹∿›

0 day(s): 14 hour(s): 19 minute(s): 02 second(s)

CHAPTER 10 - Bill

A Race Across Time

Bill was still in his office when he opened the first of three files LETO had sent him. To say he was confused was a bit of an understatement. Before him were blueprints, schematics of some sort, of the mythical building the Society came to know as Site B.

Bill vividly remembered the first time he'd heard about Site B. He didn't make much of it back then, to be honest, as the newly-minted spy was trying to get out of the Ghost's clutches with his life.

When he'd finally been able to share the intel with Ginny and the rest of the Society, he was met with doubts, hesitancy, and suspicion. Although Bill swore by what he'd heard, no one, in four years of searching, probing, and infiltrating, had been able to confirm—or deny—the existence of this Site B. Yet, here it was, his undeniable proof. Before leaving for home that night, he would be sure to send an email out to local members of the Society of Timeline Liberation. Plans and ideas were already forming in his head. By tomorrow's end, the world would finally know about the darker side of Chronos.

On his drive home, Bill kept the radio silent. He enjoyed driving with the windows down, listening to the sound of his tires handling the wet asphalt. Although he was focused on the road, part of himself could not stop returning to LETO's *post-scriptum*. Who was this girl they were looking for? The STL had saved a great many deal of Strays, time displaced folks in the past four years, but never the One fitting LETO's descriptions: sixteen, brown hair, blue eyes. Bill had asked for a name, but LETO brushed the question off, saying it would not matter since she probably had no memories of herself or her past. And when he asked LETO the obvious question: *Why this girl in particular?* LETO had simply refused to answer, changing the subject to something entirely different. Bill knew better than to keep pushing.

When he pulled into the driveway, Bill noticed the absence of Ginny's car, which was usually parked on the left. He glanced at his watch. It was nine-thirty at night. He assumed, from lack of information, that she was stuck at work, a recurring theme with increasing instances over the past two months. *So much for Dr.*

Mags' communication exercises, he thought. He sighed a bit and walked up to the door, unlocked it, and silently walked in.

Bill slid his runners off, flipping them haphazardly on the mud mat. Then he lobbed his keys in the catch-all, missing it entirely and grumbling to himself as he bent over to pick them back up. With a yawn, the tired man shuffled past the dark living room. He was on his way upstairs when a voice came from behind him.

"Hello," said a feminine voice not belonging to his wife.

Bill, startled, skipped a stair, and almost fell down the flight. "What the f—" He caught his words before they fully left his mouth. Director DeLuca was standing there, in the shadows, silent, only a few feet away from him, in his house. "What the hell are you doing here?!" Then a thought came to him, a scary thought. "What if Ginny walks in?"

"Don't worry about her," DeLuca reassured him. She showed him a live feed on her phone. "She's still at the lab."

Conflicting emotions surged through him. Relief, in a way, that his wife wouldn't catch them, but also shame for, truly, there was nothing to worry about. Nothing had happened between him and DeLuca. So why was he so jumpy? He regained some of his composure and uttered an obvious question.

"What are you doing here? And why are you spying on my wife?"

"I'll tell you everything, but first, you might want to sit down."

The older man showed her to his office, a small seven-by-nine room with green walls. There was no fireplace or fancy expensive paintings. It thoroughly lacked in comparison to the *Cassandra*'s study, the yacht on which he was officially christened Leader One.

Bill motioned to a flimsy chair but DeLuca insisted *he* sit. As he did, she took a deep breath and told him everything.

After he had left the cave, DeLuca and other agents had dug extensively into the humiliating affair, which had resulted in the Bishop's escape. With all cameras having been wiped, they had to find another way to come to the truth. It was Carmichael, of all people, who suggested they analyze the gumbo, it being the common denominator in their unexplained snooze. A thorough analysis revealed a sleeping chemical compound had indeed been slipped into the food prepared by Erik. A new question arose at this juncture of the investigation: who spiked the gumbo?

The most natural suspect was the cook himself, Erik. The heavyset man was brought to the interrogation room and put through the ringer. He held on tooth and nail to his story, swearing he had nothing to do with the drugging of his colleagues. Next, they brought in Carmichael. If the emotions he showed when they guided him to the room were not suspicious, his part in bringing the Bishop to Monte Meta in the first place would be enough. And yet he, too, was cleared for the moment.

"All that to say," she continued, "we might be dealing with a second leak. Unless we get the Bishop back into custody, it might mark the end of Dravra." The lines on her face fell. Straight and serious. Bill swore he saw a tear fall down her cheek before she quickly wiped it away. "LETO sent me information as to the Bishop's whereabouts."

Bill straightened up. *Here it comes*, he thought. *The real reason why she's here.*

"I can't ask this of any of my agents. Honestly, at this point, I don't... can't trust anyone else but you. I'm begging for your help."

"I don't know, Carmen." He remembered LETO's warning. "I was told to stay clear of the Bishop."

"By whom?" His refusal took her by surprise.

"You know who."

Her facial expression told Bill she understood. Director DeLuca was a professional, first and foremost. If a direct order was given, who was she to advocate against it? She excused herself, picking up the backpack she'd slumped on the floor. Bill watched her leave.

After a long, excruciatingly silent moment, Bill sighed with his head in his hands. "Where is he?" He heard her sprint back up the stairs.

Carmen's face appeared around the corner, beaming. "I knew I could count on you!"

Before Carmen could strap an older MiChronos model to his head—never mind asking where she'd found this one—she'd asked Bill to get changed into a very plain outfit. It took her less than fifteen minutes to set Bill up in his newest getup; a simple dirty white chiton, a garment often associated with ancient Greece, and on his feet, high-tech modern running shoes camouflaged as plain-looking yet robust brownish moccasins. It was, he was told, the usual costume worn by Chronos' clients who went to this specific timeline.

As it turned out, Gaspar was hiding, or at least trying, inside Chronos' most massive program: The Seven Wonders Package.

"It won't be easy," she promised him.

"Like finding a needle in a haystack," Bill grumbled half to himself.

"But," she continued, "since LETO was able to hack the Bishop's credentials, you should be able to time land pretty damn near him." DeLuca entered the last of the codes she had received.

"Ready?" But Bill did not reply. He looked worried, preoccupied with something, like this impromptu mission wasn't entirely on his mind. She caught him glancing at the clock on the wall. "What's the matter?"

"Umm... Oh, nothing." Carmen gave him a look, and he understood he wouldn't get off that easily. "You're sure Ginny is still at work?"

She checked a secondary, smaller screen before replying. "Yes, she's still at work." Seeing he was still uneasy, she added, "Trust me, as soon as she's on her way, I'll let you know."

Bill only nodded in response. "Now," he said in a more convincing voice, "Where to, Director?"

"Agra, 1653," Carmen answered, pushing a few buttons.

"India?"

"You got it. You ready?"

"Yeah, let's do it."

Without another word, Director DeLuca punched in a sequence of codes and, in a bright and blinding light, Bill disappeared.

//AGRA-1653...

It was early morning wherever he'd time landed. The sun was slowly creeping up behind pinkish clouds, warming up his skin. It took a second for his eyes to adjust to the trip, but once they did, Bill fell in awe with the sheer architectural beauty of the palace standing in front of him. The Taj Mahal had always been something he'd appreciated, and visiting it was a must he'd wished to cross off his bucket list for a long while. Yet here he was, an eyewitness to the Roza-e-Munavvara's very beginnings. Bill's ogling of the building would have to wait, however, for a voice was calling to him from far inside his head. He found it strange at first, realizing it wasn't his own voice, but he quickly understood it to be DeLuca's.

"I repeat. Leader One, do you copy?"

"Yes, yes. I hear you," he replied in a whisper, instinctively half-touching his right ear as they do in movies. "This place is beautiful," he added after a second.

"I'm glad you're enjoying the view. It looks like you're not actually that far from the Bishop. He is—"

"I see him," Bill said, cutting in. He had spotted the Italian fairly easily, maybe too easily, in fact. The Bishop was strolling along the reflecting pools mere metres across from where Bill was standing. "What exactly am I supposed to do with him?"

"You'll have to get him to talk to you."

"What if he logs off?"

"What?"

"What if he logs off?" he repeated. "What if he decides to go back to his timeline?"

"He can't. LETO's got all Chronos servers under surveillance. No one entering the system can leave," she said before adding, "without her permission, of course."

"Well, that's good to know." With that, he followed the man he'd followed almost four years ago in what, for him, was an equally exotic place.

Bill meant to intercept him at the top of the pool. Instead, the Bishop turned left, away from him and toward the Eastern wall. Quickening his pace, Leader One hurried himself around the water. In his youth, he probably would have been able to jump over to the Bishop's side, but now, he knew his body was sure to fail him.

Once on the other side, it finally dawned on him how few people were gathered around him. "Strange," he whispered under his breath, low enough for DeLuca to be unable to hear it. On the one hand, it made it very easy for Bill to track the Italian, yet on the other, it made him feel uneasy, more like he was in a badly-made video game than having gone to the true past.

Finally, after some inner monologues and doubts, the baker ultimately caught up to the Bishop. The clergyman was facing the perimeter wall, one hand on the red sandstone material. The other rested upon his heart. He must not have known Bill was there, or after him, for the moment he called out to him, Gaspar jumped with a start as if being ripped out of a daydream.

"Easy there," Bill continued, his arms raised in front of him in a show of peace. "All's good. I just want to talk."

The Bishop, a glint of suspicion in the eye, gave him the once-over.

"You remember me?" asked Bill. "We saw Vivaldi together. Actually, you ditching me still kinda hurts, you know." He said that with a grin. "I'm sure you could've trusted me. I met you in there after all, didn't I."

Gaspar seemed to relax at those words. "I apologize," he finally said. "Other plans were already in motion."

"You had a man on the inside, didn't you? It was Carmichael, wasn't it?"

"Surely, I can't tell you that, Leader One. That's another story for another time."

Suddenly, the Bishop cocked his head to the right. His eyes changed from trusting to scared in a matter of seconds. Was someone talking to him? Warning him against... What, really? It wasn't like Bill had a plan. He was making this up as he went, still unsure as to how best to deal with Marsh's number two.

All of a sudden, the man bolted away from Bill, and after ten steps or so, Gaspar disappeared, leaving him dumbfounded.

"What the hell, Carmen!" Leader One ejaculated. "I thought you said he couldn't go back to his time."

"He can't," she assured him, "and he didn't."

"What do you mean?"

"He's still in the program. Just in another chapter."

"You gotta be kidding me."

"I wish I was, truly and, umm..."

"What?" Bill did not like that pause. "What's wrong?"

"Are you ready to race across time?"

"Yeah, sure. Why?"

"We might be a little tight on time," DeLuca finally said.

"Fu—"

"Yup," she said, interrupting his outburst. "You guessed it."

"Whatever happens, she cannot find you here." There was a hint of plea in his voice.

"I know, I know. You ready to make the jump?"

"No one is around me," he confirmed after a quick look around. "Punch it."

Before he could ask where he was going this time, streaks of blinding light ran past him and pushed the bearded man backward in time to a vista very much different from the one he had begrudgingly left behind.

The year was 998, and although the temperature was similar, for only three degrees of latitude separated him from his most recent time jump, it was clear to Bill that he was presently afoot upon a much different continent. This was Chichen Itza.

Kukulcán stood marvelously beautiful and regal in front of Bill. He felt humble at the sheer ingenuity of past humans. What was, to his twenty-first-century self, an important tourist attraction visited by over two million people yearly was also, in the late tenth century, a gathering point for the Mayan people. Luckily for Gaspar and Bill, the grounds around the pyramid were eerily destitute of passersby.

"This can't be good for the timestream," Bill half-asked, half-commented to DeLuca in his ear. "Isn't that going to create a bunch of other breaches?"

"This specific package, the one with all Seven Wonders, seems to be a special one," she answered. "Yes, they're going to seven different times and places, but—"

"It still only counts as one?"

"That's right. The Bishop should be north of you, by the way."

It was a bit harder for Bill to track him this time around. Most likely because Gaspar was now aware that someone was looking for him, chasing him. The baker did not like how long it was taking him to find his man. Every few seconds, he would ask DeLuca if Ginny was close by. After the fifth ask in under three minutes, DeLuca simply stopped answering, which was for the best since Bill had, at last, spotted his prey running up the steps of *el Castillo*.

"Isn't that sacrilegious?" he muttered to himself. "Well, crap, there goes my soul."

He quickly sent a prayer to the sun god in hopes of not getting smitten before running up the rock steps two at a time. Bill yelled out to Gaspar, begging him to stop. Woefully, the man did not halt his mad escape.

Bill was already out of breath when he ultimately reached the top of the temple. Looking left and then right, he saw the Bishop turning the corner at the very last second. Instead of following him, which was exactly what Bill thought Gaspar expected him to do, he ran the other way. *It's a square. I'll catch up to him on the other side.*

Colliding with him was what he should have said. What happened soon after were two relatively large humans turning a corner at the same time and hitting each other with such force that both of them were knocked backward. Bill fell onto his back, a mere two feet from where the collision originated. The Bishop wasn't so lucky. The force had sent him flying down to the lower levels of *el Castillo.*

The baker heard him hit something hard once before crawling himself to the edge. There, in mid-fall, the Bishop vanished in a flash of lights. Bill, still catching his breath, massaging his aching ribs with one hand, lifted the other to his ear, and hailed DeLuca.

"Where's our crazy friend now?"

What followed was an insane game of tag across seven timelines, four continents, and a time difference of 1849 years between the earliest and latest time destinations. Rome, Rio, Wadi Musa, Shanghai... He saw them all. Bill's legs were aching, burning as if he'd run for two hours straight when, in fact, it probably wasn't more than twenty minutes in real time. His head was also buzzing. Was it because of all the movement through time or because he knew Ginny was about to get home any minute now?

Nestled high in the Andes mountains, a little over fifty miles northwest of Peruvian Cusco stood the Lost City of the Incas: Machu Picchu. Unlike the other six Wonders' destinations, this one was particularly mystical. The air surrounding Bill was so dense and opaque. Being at such an elevation, some two and a half kilometres above water levels, felt to him as if he was walking through a grey, wet cloud.

His breathing was difficult, and he felt lightheaded. Leader One hunched over himself, trying as he may to get as much air back in his lungs as possible. This game of cat and mouse had to end. It was time for Bill and Gaspar to sit and finally have that conversation. Whoever was whispering in his prey's ear was only making things worse for both of them.

Once the stars stopped swirling around his head, Bill forced his eyes to pierce through the fog. Nothing. His sight failed him majestically, as he could barely see five feet in front of him, which, in a dangerous turn of events, proved to be treacherous.

"What the hell!" he exclaimed, pushing himself backward.

His heart was pumping even faster in his aching ribcage now. Bill had scarcely survived a mighty fall, for the hills of Machu Picchu were exceptionally steep, and the hazy air did nothing to prevent an early trip to the grave. *Of all the days I could have been sent back in time, why is there such weather?* Why indeed, but before he could formulate a hypothesis, a sound in the nearby distance distracted him. He was about to call out to the Bishop again—the first nineteen times did not stop him, the twentieth time's the charm—when Carmen shared newfound information.

"I've got some information you might like."

"Go ahead," Bill said as he started on a jog towards the noise he assumed was made by Gaspar.

"It looks like Chronos bracelets have a refractory period of just over four minutes." Carmen was clicking away on the keyboard. "That's why he hasn't been jumping to the next chapter of the program right away to lose you."

"I was wondering about that, thanks." He put an ear out, waiting for another sound. "How much time before he gets beamed out to another time?"

"You've been here," she checked her screen, "a minute fifteen seconds. He couldn't have beaten you by more than ten seconds."

"So, two and half minutes before he vanishes again." A sound. "Gotta go!"

He raced towards the Bishop. Racing uphill through the fog was no easy feat. Was the air getting thinner? His head was pounding hard, but at least he knew he must have been getting close to the sounds, something scraping on a smooth surface. How disappointed he was when he realized he'd been following a llama.

The beast perked up when it saw Bill coming closer. It was about to spit at him when a rock rolled down a nearby peak. The noise must have startled the wooly beast, for it bolted at an alarming speed.

"Hey, Carmen," he said, breathing hard and feeling dizzier by the second, "can you confirm the Bishop is west of me?"

"Yes. That or an Andean bear got to him and ate his bracelet."

"Not funny," he replied as he picked up speed.

"Minute and a half before recharge, by the way."

Bill quickened the pace. He knew he had to finish it here. If it wasn't for his guts telling him so, the small black spots taking shape within his vision all but confirmed it.

"Ah!" blurted a startled voice not belonging to him. *Hang in there, Gaspar.*

There he was, a dark silhouetted shadow within the fog at first, but the closer Bill got to him, the shapelier and more colourful the man he'd been pursuing through so many timelines appeared. The baker was surprised to see the Bishop had cornered himself. To the men's left, a ten-foot rock wall, at least, continued behind the Italian. To their right, a precipice. The fall might have been fifteen or a hundred feet. No one knew for sure. As thin as the air was to breathe around them, it was comical how thick the mist was.

"Gaspar," Bill said in a gentle, non-threatening voice. "I don't know who's in your ear right now, but stop listening to them. Come this way. There's no need to continue this messed up race." He slowly walked up to him. They could not have been more than five feet away from each other.

The Bishop looked at him, then at the cloudy emptiness below.

"Don't you fuckin' dare!" Bill exploded, urgency in his voice. And as if that wasn't enough, DeLuca rang in his ear.

"Refractory period over!"

Bill froze a second, not sure what to do anymore. Gaspar's forehead was sweating, or was it mist? No, Bill was sure of it.

Something was scaring him. The baker could see it in the other man's eyes.

"We'll save you," he promised. "You don't have to go back to him."

"You don't understand," Gaspar said, his upper lip quivering. "There's no coming back from Tartarus."

"Tartarus? Wait, NO!"

On these words, the Bishop jumped off the edge.

But Bill was faster. Adrenaline kicking in, Leader One forgot the black spots invading his vision and leaped forward, grabbing the Bishop's wrist at the last possible moment. His ribs exploded with pain, but he held on. Both men did.

"I got you!" Bill half-screamed urgently. "Come on. You gotta get up. Give me your other hand!"

Gaspar looked up, teary-eyed. He reached with his other hand, indeed, but not to catch Bill's outstretched hand. In one desperate movement, one Bill understood only too late, he unfastened his bracelet and fell through the fog.

A pain, although very much different from the one he felt in his most certainly cracked ribs, pulled at him, tearing his chest apart.

A feeling of loss he had not felt in over a decade, a feeling that hit way too close to home.

Kneeling there in the wet grass, he took hold of himself, just now remembering about his own time limit and his wife's impending arrival.

"Alright," he finally said, wiping a tear away. "Bring me back."

Without a word to be added, Bill was brought back to his familiar, tiny home office. The pressure on his lungs seemed to have lessened. Yet he got the air knocked out of him, not by some physical ailment of some sort. Worse. Standing in front of him, a finger on the mouse that had brought him back to his present timeline, was Ginny.

And she did not look at all pleased.

The events that followed that night were not ones Bill was particularly proud of. For starters, why had he lied when Ginny asked him about all of this new tech splayed out in the office? He'd told her he was on another assignment for the STL, which, in itself, was not exactly a lie, but why shovel himself deeper by adding he was working alone? Nothing was going on between him and Carmen, so why did he persist in giving his wife fuel to raise this imaginary fire? Needless to say, she was not having it and seeing through the falsities she did.

Without a word, she kind of nodded, bit her tongue, and turned her back on him. A few seconds later, Bill heard the front door close, followed by the sound of her car leaving the driveway. He hoped she would be back, but inside, he understood. *This is it*. He put Gaspar's bracelet on his desk and went right to work.

↞∿↠

0 day(s): 16 hour(s): 45 minute(s): 27 second(s)

CHAPTER 11 - Washington Apparitions in the System

Richard did not burden himself with going home the night before. There was no one waiting for him anyway. Instead, he slept on a cot inside his office. Yet *sleeping* might be too strong a term. He simply lay there, wide awake. His mind was racing, thinking about all sorts of things but mostly about the future of Chronos. The prospects looked equal parts promising and dreadful.

At exactly five in the morning, the alarm on his phone rang loudly. An early riser, he got up and began his morning routine. He put on his running attire: tank top, shorts, and laceless sneakers, everything black. After filling up his water bottle, he attached his wireless earbuds to his ears. Upon exiting the building, he saw Sadie coming in. Always so prompt, one of the first employees to come in and one of the last to leave. He waved to her on his way out. Miss Ellis waved back with a smile.

Running the Woodland Trails around Chronos helped Richard clear his mind. The fresh forest air and the pleasant smell of autumn pine trees all contributed to revitalizing his inner peace. Some days he would run for fifty minutes, but on this particular day, he ran until his legs could no longer hold beneath him. Huffing and puffing, he unsteadily made his way to the nearest park bench, a dark brown and uncomfortable piece of modern art woven together with sanded logs. He dropped hard onto the varnished wood, chest heaving. He took his earbuds out. Eyes closed, mouth opened, Richard tried to focus his breathing.

Birds chirped and perched on branches above. The wind rustled the red and yellowing leaves. The sound of water flowing in a nearby stream. With his hands on his abdomen, he felt himself calm down. Finally, he opened his eyes, still wet from pain and sweat. He looked around, taking in what nature was offering his senses. The different shades of green, the smell of damp earth, the taste of dirt and sweat on his lips, the forestry breeze on his naked arms, the sound of virgin silence.

It was precisely at that moment when he appreciated to the fullest the quietness around him that his phone started buzzing. It was a call from IT.

"Washington," he answered, putting his earbuds back in.

"Mr. Washington, Graves from IT," said the voice on the other line. "There is something strange going on inside Chronos. There have been... apparitions."

"Did you say *apparitions*?"

"Yes, sir. At least four of them. We're still looking into it."

"When?" Heart racing again, his tranquility moment with Mother Nature spoiled.

"The four current time trips: ELV-1977, OLY-1896, FRA-1223, and DIS-1967. Clients are already engaged."

"I'll call you right back." He hung up and checked the time on his fitness tracker. It was just after seven o'clock.

Richard swore under his breath, startling a nearby chipmunk. Not exactly how he had envisioned starting his day, he took out his phone and connected to Chronos' internal server. It joined without a hitch, even out here in the woods. *Perks of being the*

CEO, he mumbled. Then added, *and to be on call whenever something goes wrong. With great power...*

After an embarrassing incident, which happened three years ago during a trip to the 2010 Vancouver Olympics, Richard and his advisors had decided to use light-reflexive camera drones to record the comings and goings of their patrons inside Chronos. The PR department had woven it as a major step forward, calling it the *Best Souvenir* program any entertainment business could offer. But in reality, it was a way to prevent illegal time activities, keep an eye on the sheep, and fend off other potential employee disappearances.

Entering one of the time destination codes, he had now access to various video feeds coming in from a trip that was already underway. In one camera, Richard saw his customers riding a boat in the dark. Mechanical pirates pretended to fight near a group of wide-eyed guests. The year was 1967. The place was Disneyland. It was the *Pirates of the Caribbean* attraction's opening day, one of Richard's all-time favourite rides.

He scrutinized the feeds, looking for something strange, an element out of the ordinary. No one was glitching, the bracelets all seemed to work, and the pirates were not eating the tourists. So what was wrong? Then it hit him. Using camera C, angle nine, he zoomed in on a woman's face. She was two boats behind the time travelers, intently staring at them, not worrying about the cannons. And then the weirdest thing happened.

Richard immediately called Graves back. "She looked at me!"

"Yes, sir. The woman seems aware of the drone's location in all currently active programs." A pause. "We found her inside a fifth location as well. What should we do, sir?"

"What do you propose?" answered Richard.

"If there is a bug in the system, we could reboot it. But we'd have to cut our guests' trip short. I'd also suggest postponing today's trips. We might also want to investigate the drones to be thorough. Their light-reflexive program could be malfunctioning."

"Thank you, I'll take it under advisement. For the moment, keep an eye on the woman. Women? I don't want this information to leave Chronos. Call me if anything changes. I'm on my way."

He passed a hand through his damp hair. Painstakingly slowly, he willed himself off the park bench. He glanced down at his watch, knowing he would not be able to make it to the IT department in a reasonable amount of time to deal with what could be a rising crisis. He started jogging to the nearest street as he dialed a number.

In hindsight, it was already too late. And it was about to get much, much worse.

"Miss Ellis speaking, how can I help you?"

"Miss Ellis, Washington here. Would you please do me a favour and send a car for me? And a set of clean clothes?" At that moment, Richard got a call on another line, J. WILSON. He decided to let it go to voicemail. He would call him back. "Sorry, Miss Ellis, I didn't hear what you said. Someone on the other line. What did you say?"

"No worries, sir. I'm sure it can wait until your arrival. Where am I sending your car?"

"Good question," he'd just realized he had no idea where he really was. "I'll have to call you back." Something pinged in his ears. Wilson had left a message.

"Understood, sir. In the meantime, I'll have an intern, Wright, fetch your clothes. The whole nine?"

"Shirt, tie, pants, and shoes will do fine. Thank you, Miss Ellis."

Richard had finally reached a street, a small, two-way, pothole-filled thing of a road. That's when he remembered Wilson's message. He sent Ellis the proper information. She confirmed the car was on its way, and then Richard checked on what young Wilson had to say. Hopefully, it was good news.

It was not.

Hi? Ummm, hi, sir? Mr. Washington, I called to make sure you had received my email. The one I sent last night. I was doing the night shift in IT when it just appeared. Some sort of A.I., I think. At first, it started with a wave in the code. I tried to get rid of it, but then a message showed up in binary. I emailed Stone about it, too, but she hasn't replied to me yet—oh damn. I hope I didn't get her in trouble. Ummm, anyways. I got the feeling that this thing, the A.I., is about to do something, something bad. Thought I'd let you know, just in case... Have a nice da—

Promising kid, Wilson. Richard was glad to have met this young genius at that Science Fair those years ago. His intuition had come to fruition. But what was he talking about, an email? Richard had not seen anything like that. He scrolled back and forth, never finding anything from jwilson. *What if... What if it's in all of our systems,* he thought to himself.

A black company sedan arrived shortly after. Richard jumped in. The driver pulled down a makeshift divider, permitting his boss to get changed with some kind of privacy. "Step on it, would you?" Richard asked, and the driver did. Getting dressed, Washington kept calm. It was not the first time he had to deal with something that had gone wrong within Chronos. And just like then, things will be just fine.

When Chronos opened its door to the public five years ago, it offered only ten time destinations, with most of them happening in the near past, a.k.a. the twentieth and twenty-first centuries. The flow of clients was slow at first, but then the idea of actually going back in time created a buzz, and the whole business caught fire, figuratively, of course. From that point on, the company grew, and its image became synonymous with innovation and entertainment. What Washington had done to this small Vermont town was in no way dissimilar to what Henry Ford had done to Detroit. He created jobs, helped a ton of people out of their financial slumps, and brought tourism to what was, back then, only known as a struggling, insignificant map dot.

The very first non-Chronos employee to have been sent back in time was American hero and Team USA legend Mike Eruzione, and his time destination of choice was, surprisingly, Lake Placid in 1980.

When he showed up at Chronos, everyone, including Mike probably, felt extremely nervous. This was it, the real deal: the make or break. Hopefully, things would go well. The guest and his guide were introduced, and they discussed the different rules to follow. When it finally came to the *"what to expect once you're there"* speech, Mike raised his hand politely in front of the speaker and said, "Don't worry, Guy. I know. I was there."

The man who was to escort the *Miracle on Ice* captain back in time proceeded to cut his instructions short so that both of them could finally be on their way. At exactly thirteen past ten that morning, they entered the mirror-paneled machine that would deconstruct their biological frame into a state of free-floating molecules before being promptly sent through a window inside the space-time continuum. The engineer asked if the two men were ready, and they replied quietly by giving him the thumbs up, albeit slightly shakily. After a short countdown of five seconds, a large red button—because large, important buttons are comically always red—was pressed. Subsequently, Mike and his guide were zapped and disintegrated into thin air. Gone.

At that precise moment, the machine that was supposed to track their movement decided to short-circuit. Chronos had just lost their very first guest, the man who'd scored the game-winning goal for Team USA against the juggernaut that was the USSR. Yet although in the present, people were running around like mice in a trap, Mike and Guy had safely time landed near Mirror Lake, not two miles east of the Olympic Center.

Mike was far removed from his mid-twenties, so there was virtually no chance for anyone, not even his own parents, to recognize him amongst the thousands of fans who walked the streets that cold February day. After getting their tickets from a scalper and hot dogs from a mobile food stand, the two gentlemen made their way to the arena. As Mike was about to push the door open, he froze. Maybe he'd realized what he was about to do: to witness his younger self make history in front of his older eyes. *This is crazy! I'm crazy!* He shook his head and entered the building, to the delight of the people waiting behind.

USA! USA! USA! The crowd was ecstatic. His old buddy, Jimmy Craig, was skating around with the flag on his back. Jack O'Callahan and Dave Silk, two of Mike's teammates back at BU, were in an embrace. He could barely remember the last few hours. All of this, this whole experience, was surreal. But the weirdest thing of all was counting down the seconds until Pavelich would finally pass *him* the puck in the high slot. *Three, two, one—GOAL!!!* He may or may not have stood up before the wrist shot was complete.

Finally, it was time to go back.

"Hey, my man, can you wait for me? Gotta hit the john."

"A'ight, no problem. I'll be right here."

But he did not go to the bathroom. Instead, he walked past every celebrating Yankee with determination in his eyes. He had something to do, the main reason he had jumped at the opportunity to come back to this moment in time. Sure, he would tell whoever wanted to hear it that he wanted to see what others saw the night he scored, but in reality, he came here for him.

"Hey, Herb!"

Herb Brooks, the old coach, who had snuck away from the masses for a moment, looked around at the older gentleman. He did not say a thing. They both stood there in silence, probably understanding what was happening.

Minutes later, Mike met with Guy, and the two futuremen exited the arena. They found an open spot and beamed themselves back to the future. Or was it the present?

Boy, was Richard happy to see them back! The tracking box was cracked open, and wires of many colours were hanging out, reminiscent of Medusa's locks. Medical staff crowded Mike, checking on him and asking him a bunch of questions. He was, after all, the first non-employee guinea pig to make it back alive. So exciting! However, in between temperature takes and pressure checks, Mike kept asking for his phone. Eventually, someone brought it to him. Maybe he'd share the super experience he'd just had on his socials. That would be fantastic publicity. But it was not so. A second after looking something up online, he turned his phone off, put it in his pants pocket, and kept quiet for the remainder of the medical examination.

I thought... Sorry, Herb.

When the CEO arrived on the IT floor, all seven employees looked at him, but not in the same way the guests did yesterday. There was no awe in their eyes. They seemed anxious and panicky. They had one job; to not break the system. Something broke, alright. Graves walked up to Richard. "We've been monitoring her on all five destinations."

"Five?"

"Yes. We found another copy of the bug in GGE-1922, which is starting soon. Other than that, nothing new to report. She's been... waiting, it looks like."

Richard thought back to Wilson's words. "Graves, see if you can find a... a wave in the codes."

"A wave, sir?"

"Just do it," he replied, a little short, with a wave of his hand.

Graves sat at his desk and pulled up the system's matrix. He entered a few keywords and pressed something. Soon after, a line, indeed like a wave, came into view.

~~~~~~~~~~~~~~~~~~~

As Graves clicked on the until-then hidden code, the five visages rapidly glared in unison at the camera. The sight was one of horror. Richard backed away from the screen with a start. Someone beside him had fallen from their wheely chair. How could this be? How could someone know where to find the cameras? And more importantly, how could she be in five time destinations at once? *Five at least*, Richard corrected himself. He hadn't realized it until now, but the five faces belonged to the same person.

"She knows we're trying to boot her out," interjected Graves. "We should turn Chronos off until we know for sure what to do."

Richard stood there in deep thought, arms crossed. His legs were still aching, but it was nothing compared to the headache this problem was about to give him. Eventually, he asked to no one in particular: "How many excursions do we have set for this morning?"

"We have four active, three ready to go in five, and two starting at 0915."
~~~~~~~~~~~~~~~~~~~

Richard played pensively with the stubble of his chin. Whatever they did, whatever he decided, the first four groups would have to be brought back, and that could take hours. He racked up his brains, considering the pros and cons of his next move.

Pros of turning it off: saving a few lives *if* the A.I. turned out to be hostile.

Cons of turning it off: questions from the media, bad public rep, mad customers—one group had traveled from Europe—loss of revenue, written reports...

Richard had made up his mind. Using probability factors to mathematically back up his decision, he determined that there was a ninety percent chance that the "cons" list would happen should he turn off Chronos for the day. The percentage only grew higher if he had to close it for an extended period of time. Whereas gambling with the possible threat of an unfriendly Artificial Intelligence only clocked in at three percent, that is, according to a recent research published in *Forman Weekly*. At last, he made his decision known.

"Monitor it," he finally said, authority in his voice. "For the moment, we are leaving things as they are. Call me immediately if anything changes."

"Sir?" Graves was about to say something but decided against it.

"I'll be in my office. You can reach me there." Just like that, without another word, he walked out of a very quiet room.

Richard was hoping he'd made the right call.

He hadn't.

〜

0 day(s): 6 hour(s): 04 minute(s): 33 second(s)

CHAPTER 12 - LETO

A Bachelor Party to Kill For

Prey, hunted by another, helpless. Phase two had begun. They would be her first.

The four men, rowdy as any would be during a bachelor party, staggered here and there. Ale in one hand, chicken drumstick in the other, they were smiling from ear to ear. Their guide, Mr. Hughes, not far ahead, was arranging for their seating at the next event. The main event, in fact, of the tournament. The jousting finals.

When Mr. Roberts had announced to his best friend, the groom, that they would be Chronosing it instead of the lame "stripper and gambling" cliché, Mr. Grover was all sorts of excited. Not only would it be his first go at time traveling, but, as a medieval literature teacher at HU, it would be the chance of a lifetime for him to experience firsthand the unadulterated thrill of French Medieval Games.

Along with Misters Conway and Barnaby, the four men were told, before entering the loading bay area, that they would pretend to be members of middle royalty, with the soon-to-be wedded man posing as the Earl of Wheatston. An add-on Roberts was more than happy to include. *None of that "waiting in line" crap for our best bro!* he had said quite convincingly to the other two. Plus, he had been able to get the Department of Classic Studies to pay for part of it. The request form he'd filled out said: "for research." They would be doing research, alright, and so far *la cervoise*, a barley wine invented by the Gauls, was the front-runner.

The four gentlemen were clothed in tunics and cloaked in shades of crimson, the colour of their Alma Mater where they had met each other as students a lifetime ago. As exuberant as they were, the futuremen seemed to fit right in. Early on, they met with and befriended a massive blacksmith by the name of Roland, who introduced them to delicious *hydromel*, mead in English. Something that could be drunk a little too easily. They drank themselves blind with him and gave each other silly challenges like *who can take the most war hammer hits while wearing a breastplate* and *pin the tail on an actual donkey*. In return, all to the disapproving stare of their guide, the HU professors introduced their new friend to *Fuzzy Duck* and *Flip Cup*.

Not long after leaving the forger's tent, Conway bumped into a pretty fair maiden with whom he'd decided to flirt, using every single cheesy catchphrase he had learned from various TV shows growing up and other ones he'd used back home. Even with the help of the language assist tool embedded in his bracelet, he shamelessly bombarded the lady with words she barely understood. From *Do you believe in love at first sight?* to *Did it hurt when you fell from heaven?* Yet, to his own and his buddies' surprise, it seemed to work, that is until their chaperone intervened rather rudely by grabbing him by the belt and dragging Don Juan away. "That's the host's daughter," he simply said before adding, "You dimwit." That put an end to any romantic conquests.

An hour or so before the start of the jousting finals, Barnaby, easily the biggest and strongest of the bunch, got into a heated argument with a man who had just bumped into him. The banter, which stayed amicable, everything considered, led to an impromptu arm wrestling match to determine who really was at fault and, subsequently, had to apologize. Indisputably losing the best of three in two runs, Barnaby was later told he had his wrist almost ripped off by yesterday's Sword on Foot champion. "I held my own pretty well, I reckon," he told his friends as he massaged his aching hand.

During all that time, the lady in red kept her eyes on them. Hidden in plain sight or from the shadows, Anne preyed on.

Clients' files in Chronos' system were nothing if not detailed. She knew who they were and what kind of lives they led. But also who waited for them on the outside, a bride-to-be, a wife, a partner—Anne had done her time. It was high time someone else shared in her loss.

The lance was heavy under the rider's arm. The sound of hooves pounded loudly against the ground. As the steed gained speed, so did the wind around Lord Cunningham's bulky yet streamlined helm. His aim, although shaky at first, stabilized and hit true.

His opponent, regionally known as "The Baron"—although the legitimacy of his lineage only held truth in the ink of his letters—thought he'd deflected his adversary's blow with his shield. But to his astonishment, Lord Cunningham's tip glanced high and hit him square in the facemask, knocking him down and off his horse. The crowd erupted in cheers as the fan favourite dethroned last season's champion.

Lord Alfred Cunningham, his victory had been scribed into the annals of jousting since the early twelve hundreds, and an important one at that. So it came as no surprise to Mr. Grover, the historian, when the hammer fell. But he cared not, for this was his day. *This is the best bachelor party ever!* He yelled, not worrying about Mr. Hughes, who had rolled his eyes a thousand times at this point.

A few moments later, the crowd gathered to gaze upon the Tournament's winners being awarded their prizes. The host of those festivities, the Duke of Picard, walked up to the victors and shook hands with them. A golden feather and a pair of gauntlets were given to the championship's third and second place, respectively. But the best of the best was a six-inch blade with a gem-encrusted guard. It gleamed brightly in the dying sunlight. Lord Cunningham raised it above his head and showed it to the awestruck throng.

Roberts' heart palpitated, but not from the alcohol, far from it. His head had never been any clearer than it was in this instant. As everyone was ogling their champion, the best man was staring intently at the jeweled weapon: the fabled Elemental Blade.

As a child, his mother would tell him the tale of a magical blade owned by an Elemental Lord. A weapon so powerful it bestowed upon its user complete control over the elements. In his own timeline, the dagger had long disappeared, but through meticulous research, he believed he had finally found it. Roberts was sure of it; the Elemental Blade and the Long Lost Blade of Cunningham were one and the same, and there was only one way to test its power.

↜↝

The Tale of the Elemental Blade,
or The Tree in the Clouds

In our Lord's northernmost kingdom stands a white mountain with a single peak covered by a perpetual cloud. On that cloud, it is said, had grown a large tree. But this was no ordinary oak, for its leaves were constantly ablaze, and its dark roots dripped down the mountaintop's south side. Very few had ever laid eyes on this mystical tree and fewer still had survived the way back down from the sacred pilgrimage.

One such lad, Rominir, had survived the perils of the climb and had made it to the base of the floating tree's trunk. The heat from the ever-burning branches made him sleepy, but he understood that should he fall asleep, he would most certainly plummet from the summit. He was about to turn around, having recited the Song of L'Orian, until something caught his attention.

Rominir approached, ever carefully. Sure enough, revealed by moonlight, was a fissure in the bark, small enough for a goat or a crawling man. He examined it intently and, convincing himself he had come all this way, so why not, he knelt and proceeded inside. His fingers were aching from the climb, but his knees started to hurt from the uneven terrain he dragged himself through. Eventually, he saw something shimmer ahead. The lad did not stop to wonder whether it made sense or not. His curiosity took hold of his actions. He emerged out of the crack and stood up. He was inside the tree.

Although it did not look like it from the outside, there, in front of an exhausted Rominir, was a splendid lake as calm as calm can be, with no ripples. The shimmer he'd seen earlier was firebugs flying over the water. He looked around and, granted there was not much to see due to the semi-absence of light, he spotted something glittering deep below the surface. He could not stop himself. His eagerness led him to jump headfirst into the cool water, disturbing its serenity.

Halfway to the glittering, Rominir felt a presence near him. It made him uneasy, but he also sensed a pull toward the object underneath him. His lungs were starting to burn. He kicked harder and harder. His vision was slowly failing, and then—darkness.

When he came to, his clothes were drenched, but at least he was breathing. In his hand, he was clutching a golden dagger. He *blinked a few times, trying to remember what had happened. Suddenly, lifting his head, he saw sandaled feet about an arm's length from him. The feet belonged to a beautiful young woman with hair the colour of wheat. She greeted him and introduced herself as Liri, the Spirit of the Elemental Blade.*

From that fateful day up in the clouds, it is said that Rominir and Liri travel the world, using the power of the dagger for good and governing over the four elements as Lord and Lady. As for the Tree in the Clouds, no one knows where it has disappeared to, but its legend lives on.

〜

"Time to go, gents." Hughes was looking at his concealed Chronos-issued bracelet. Less than fifteen minutes before they were due back home and here he was, herding drunken Tomcats. Only, there was one problem. "Grover. Where is your best man?"

No worries, Anne replied from the shadows. *I'll find him.* And just like that, she turned and left.

She had no problem finding him—the perks of being a digital entity. Eyes everywhere. So there he was, sneaking into Lord Cunningham's tent. The latter had been invited to dine with the Duke of Picard. Rumors were there might be a marriage proposal in the works. He had just left with his squire for the evening when Roberts took his chance. His aim was easy: sneak in, grab the blade, and sneak right back out. The plan would have gone without a hitch were it not for three emotions: surprise, panic, and fear.

Surprise—

The blade was right there, on the cot. Easy pickings. After so many years of fantasizing about it! He extended an arm, reached for it, and grabbed it. Behind the thief, a rugged hand flew open the flap of the tent. Anne had seen him coming, his golden hair, curly, flowing in the night air. Lord Cunningham must have forgotten something, for his step was quick and hasty. The expression of surprise locked on both of the men's faces.

Panic—

Trapped, caught red-handed, cornered. The futureman knew he was no match for the knight. He looked left and right, but the only exit was blocked by the man whom he'd just robbed. The blade was shaking in his hand. Lord Cunningham's eyes drew to his prize. As he made for it, Roberts flinched. What happened next? Who knew? It was like that Barry Manilow song for a second. The blade was stained red, and Lord Cunningham lay motionless on the floor of his tent.

Fear—

Flight. *This is not how*—Roberts could not finish his thought. He tried to call upon the mystical powers of the dagger, to no avail. It would not reply to him, a murderer. He dropped the golden knife and was outside in a flash, only to be met by the lady in red herself.

"Sorry," he said, almost knocking Anne down. She only looked at him. Her face was expressionless. Her eyes were unsettling. Roberts held her gaze a fraction of a second too long, entranced, and in that moment, her body glitched.

He ran.

"There you are!" Grover said with a smile when he saw his buddy running out towards them. Mr. Hughes was relieved. It was time to leave. That's when he noticed it, noticed everything: the blood-soiled tunic and the expression of terror on the man's face.

"You stupid idiot!" he yelled. "What have you—"

"We gotta go! We gotta go, NOW!" and he added, in a whisper, "She's coming."

Hughes had a quizzical look on his face, not exactly sure what he meant. That is until he saw her, ghostly Anne. The guide could not put his finger on it, but the night light did not hit her the way it should have. He could have sworn he saw her glitch in the distance. He initialized the return home sequence on his bracelet, activating the beacon. The five men were far enough from her that they could time jump without risking lassoing her into the future.

"Click the damn button, man!" screamed one of them.

So he did.

I have you now, she said with a smile before disappearing. They had walked right into her web.

"Did we... Did we make it back?" asked someone.

"Conway? That you, bro?"

"Ya, man. You seen Grover and Roberts?"

"Can't see a thing. Why aren't they opening the door? Yo! Let us out!"

"*I am sorry. But I can't do that,*" said an electronic voice from nowhere in particular, yet everywhere.

"Seriously, Grover. I don't care if you are getting married this weekend. Stop it right now, or I'll bash your face in."

"*This is not he,*" continued the disembodied voice. "*But rest assured, Mr. Barnaby, that both the groom and his best man are well and unarmed for the moment.*"

"'For the moment'? What the hell does that mean? Yo, Hughes. Where are you at, bro? Get us outta here."

"Mr. Hughes is unable to help you at this time. After all, you don't kill the messenger. Don't you?"

Everything was going according to plan. Everything was in place. By the next hour, eighteen clients would be stuck in Chronos limbo, someplace hidden within the program, for although she only had a digital presence, *this* was her domain. All hostages, prisoners of Anne's whim. Nothing but necessary pawns in what was a game to save the fabric of time. Or was it more personal than that?

↜∿↝

0 day(s): 4 hour(s): 33 minute(s): 07 second(s)

↜∿↝

__ TRANSMITTING __

Hey, is this thing on? So, to whoever might be listening, my name is Milo Sampson. I am one of four athletes from Team Britain who will compete at the next Olympics.

Our coach thought it would be a fun idea to get us all psyched up by bringing us to the very first modern Olympics in 1896. Cool, right?! Not. Everything was going swell; the opening ceremony had just ended, and then… pitch black. Nothing, nada. When I finally realized I wasn't in Athens anymore, I'll be honest; I started panicking! I called out for my teammates. No reply. Even if I couldn't see a thing, I did try to walk around. Impossible. My legs were stiff and couldn't be moved.

I don't know how long I have been stuck here… Wherever here is. I knew I was right not to trust this machine. You must have heard about the weird stuff, too, right? Didn't that Liberation group warn us all about this? Is this how Strays are created? I thought Strays were only people stuck in our time.

Bloody hell! What if my bracelet messed up somehow, and instead of sending me back, it sent some late eighteen hundreds bloke to the twenty-first century? Do they, like, come back inside your body and take over your life? Pretend to be you? My mum will know for sure. She'll make sure I get back.

Wait—Hold on—There's something over there. Some sort of light. I mean, it's tiny, but it's there. It's moving now. Nah, scratch that. That ain't just a light, man! It's coming at me now. I… I can't move! Help! HELP! Oh, please help m------

__ END OF TRANSMISSION __

CHAPTER 13 - Washington Press Conference

When Hughes time landed by himself inside Bay A, confusion and uneasiness spread through the room. Simultaneously, the guide asked the techs where his clients were. A technician jokingly asked him if he'd finally managed to leave his attendees behind.

"Never on purpose. What the hell?"

Things looked awry. First, the mysterious apparition of a lady throughout the time events, and now, the disappearance of guests. What was going on?!

"Get Washington on the line now. Right now!" exclaimed a nervous button-pusher.

Graves wasn't one to be talked to that way, but his hand was already on the phone, dialing his boss' extension.

"Washington," he replied after the second ring.

"Sir, you asked to be notified whenever something strange happened. Well... it did."

"Go on," Richard encouraged, bracing for what was to come.

"Well, you see, Hughes came back from FRA-1223."

"Yes?"

"But the four men accompanying him... did not."

Richard covered the mouthpiece and swore loudly. To make matters worse, someone else was trying to reach him on the other line, workers from one of the other bays. *Fuuuuuuu*—"Hold on a second—Washington."

"Sir, something weird just happened!"

"Guests didn't come back?"

"That's right, the Olympians. How did you know?"

"I'll call you back," and hung up without waiting for an answer. *What to do now?*

On the outside, Richard looked calm and collected. The demeanor of someone who knew what he was doing, someone in control. But on the inside, he was fuming. His plan hadn't gone as expected, and now journalists were gathered out on the front lawn, waiting for comments.

"Thank you all for coming. About thirty minutes ago, FRA-1223 was scheduled to come back to Bay A from its time trip. A bachelor party consisting of four men and their guide were headed to medieval France to catch up on some jousting action and good times. I regretfully have to inform you that only Mr. Hughes made it back to our timeline." A slew of hands went up. *Christ, let me finish.* "Ladies and gentlemen, please. I would appreciate it if you could keep your inquiries to the end. Time is of the essence." A few audible grumbles filled the air. Richard continued. "At the moment, we can confirm that those who have not made it back here have not been left stranded behind. This is good news. Our computers are still tracking their Chronos-issued bracelets. They are alive and on their way back to our timeline. Although this situation may be stressful for our clients and their families, I would like to share with you our optimism and our hope. Presently, Chronos' best physicists and computer engineers are tirelessly working together to bring our customers back, to understand what has happened, and to make sure situations of this sort never happen again. We're doing everything we can to ensure these people get back home to their families. I will now take your questions".

"Robert Grant, *Pena Paper*," said a reporter, half-raising his hand.

"Yes, sir."

"What do you think caused the Chronos to 'forget' people behind?"

"We are not sure." This answer naturally did not please Robert, so Richard added, "But a theory is that all four men, returning clients, were using outdated bracelets. As you may know, our travelers are allowed to keep their bracelets and use them on future trips." He seemed satisfied with the constructed truth. "Next? Yes."

"Alexis Nedry, *Sunrise Daily*. Besides the physicists and the engineers, what else is Chronos doing to make sure it gets its castaways back?"

"We have sent two of our best time guides inside Chronos. This rescue mission had been ordered the moment the four men failed to come back. We were able to make an upgrade to their bracelet, sending them midway to FRA-1223's signal while keeping them tethered to Departure Bay C. Hudson and Douglas will slowly and carefully, but surely, get the job done."

This statement was not exactly truthful. Chalk it down as a mishmash of facts, like a kid who says he drew an elephant when really, it looked more like a hat. Both are drawings, yet the interpretation is vastly different. Did he or did he not send Hudson and Douglas to the past? Yes, he did, just not halfway to FRA-1223. There were no ways, at least known to Richard, to send a manned mission halfway through time inside Chronos. Instead, he had sent his men to another destination, a destination he knew to have already been infected, where scheduled guests hadn't departed yet. Were they, in fact, time guides? No. Time police was the appropriate term, and as soon as this press conference was over, Richard would check on their progress.

Richard should have ended things there. Nothing he could have added would have helped his case. But a reporter from the back raised her hand. She was surrounded by seven or eight other people who looked angry. It smelled too much like STL for his liking. Preemptively, he thanked them all for coming and turned to leave.

"Hey, I've got a question," the lady from the back said. "Is it true that you've known about a problem in your systems since early this morning? That you've decided against preemptive actions? And now you have eighteen clients, not four, stuck in there." Murmurs progressively grew louder from the crowd.

"I'm afraid you might be mistaken." *How in the hell did she know about all this?* "We've only encountered this problem—" he glanced at his watch, twenty-two past eleven "—less than an hour ago. We have done everything we could so far and will continue to work to bring the four men back."

"Well, that's not what my contact said," explained the lady matter-of-factly, crossing her arms as if to challenge Richard's comment and credibility. The grin expanding on her lips irritated Washington to the core.

Just then, Miss Ellis walked up behind Richard and whispered something in his ear. She waited a short moment before running back in. His facial features must have betrayed him because the lady in the back snickered. "What is it, Mr. Washington? A new problem?"

Richard could not believe it. Chronos was on lockdown—from the inside. No one could get in. Even the *wave* had completely disappeared from the codes. To make matters worse, Richard's phone started buzzing. He felt cold sweat drip down his back. *Marsh.* He let it go to voicemail.

Mentally regrouping, he took a subtle breath, put on a fake smile, the one he'd mastered working in this unforgiving business, and called to the ensemble of journalists and reporters. He was playing it cool. "On the contrary, I am happy to let you know that Hudson and Douglas have reached the group. Miss Ellis was just informing me that it shouldn't be too long before—" SPLASH! Something had flown over what was now a mob of raucous newsmen and newswomen before hitting Richard on the left breast, exploding and leaving a stain. A tomato!? *What the h—*

"Shut Chronos down! You had it coming! The timelines are fighting back!" The lady and her goons were chanting loudly and proudly. *STL, I knew it!*

Richard's bodyguard ran in to cover him. Fruits and vegetables flew over the laughing mass. If they hadn't before, they would certainly have something to write about now.

Although under the cover of his chief of security, Washington kept getting hit in the back by fresh produce, and just as he was making his way inside the building's front doors, a rolling apple found its way under his foot. It was already too late by the time he'd seen it. The entertainment tycoon stepped on the fruit and twisted his ankle, awkwardly falling to the ground, his chief of security tumbling over him. All to the rousing approval of the crowd, naturally. He heard the sound of a few more snapshots being taken behind him. Miss Ellis ran up from her front desk to help him. She glared at the cheering throng outside, an expression of disgust on her face. Richard gently pushed off the apologetic man who had momentarily crushed him. He took Sadie's arm and awkwardly rose to his aching feet. As his secretary rushed to close and lock the gaping doors, Washington brushed off his dusty pants with a hand, took a deep breath to recollect himself, and confidently limped to the elevator alone.

He could hear his private line faintly ringing through the door before he'd even made it back to his office. Washington walked in and picked up the phone. *Please, let it not be Marsh*, he prayed. It wasn't.

"What the hell was that!" yelled the man on the other side of the line.

"Good morning to you too, Mr. Strone."

"I demand answers," the older man on the other line continued. "As a senior partner, I should be made aware of those types of problems first, not reading about them online, Richard."

"It's nothing to worry about," Richard absent-mindedly replied, pulling a piece of lettuce out of his hair. "Just another protest from the STL."

"Is that what you're calling it? Just another protest—" he stopped himself. "You better figure out a way to get rid of these people, Washington." Was that a hint of a threat in his voice? "I would regret pulling my funds from your company." And on those words, he hung up.

Richard continued to pull chunks of food of all sizes out of his hair when the phone rang again. He'd clearly made a mistake picking up Old Man Strone's call. Naturally, angry and worried board members were about to give him an earful. But what he did next was probably best for his mental psyche; remorseless, in the middle of an extremely heated and unpleasant yelling match, he unplugged the damned thing in one quick yank. Silence filled the room. The protesters had been pushed back, and interns were presently clearing out busted fruits and veggies from the front lawn. Go composting!

Washington took a moment for himself. Sitting down, he closed his eyes.

"A tomato," he sighed out loud after a long, silent while. "Who does that?"

Richard languidly stood up from his chair. He unbuttoned his ruined shirt and pants and fully undressed before jumping in the shower. Warm strings of water hit his back, leftover tomato juices streaking down his body. Steam filled the room, covering the mirror and glass doors. He took two deep breaths and then sat on the wet floor. Slightly hunched over, he cupped his knees, letting the jet hit his already-soaked hair. He stayed like this, vulnerable, he knew not how long. Finally, refreshed, he got out and enveloped himself in a clean, dry towel.

With a hand, he wiped the mist off the mirror, then froze, staring at his reflection. He looked older than he remembered. The face looking back was not one he recognized. Features elongated, tired, beaten. How did he get there, to this point? When did his dream become the ultimate nightmare? If it were to be done again, would he have left the relative safety of his car for this? Would he be able to quit now? Who knew playing god would have its consequences?

His cell phone buzzed again. Marsh, always Marsh. His name floated like a storm cloud above Richard's head wherever he went. An ominous reminder, a foreboding warning. His naked arm threw the device across the room.

Richard knew there was only one way out of this now. However, he wasn't sure he felt brave enough to take it... yet.

⟨∿⟩

0 day(s): 2 hour(s): 55 minute(s): 31 second(s)

CHAPTER 14 - Washington
Master of Illusion

"You sure? Try again," James Hudson was saying, almost pleading as he fingered the side of his bracelet.

"I swear to God," his partner replied angrily. "You ask me one more time, and I'll shove this thing so far up your—"

"Fine, fine. What do we do now?"

"Follow orders, soldier," Charlie Douglas said matter-of-factly. "Find her and neutralize her."

But where to start? Without a trained time guide, Hudson and Douglas were just two tourists who had next to no knowledge of the time and place they were in. They'd memorized the picture of the woman they were to find, at least, but it was the extent of their intel.

Notes she'd previously clandestinely acquired mentioned the couple had traveled from England to celebrate their fiftieth wedding anniversary. The hypothetical thought of having lived half a century married to Pete, her jerk of an ex-husband, made her sick. Still, she recomposed herself, weaving her metaphorical web, ready to snatch the last of her pawns.

To say she was surprised when she saw two robust-looking gentlemen wearing seventeenth-century constable attire would be an understatement. Yet, she relished the challenge. *So you've come to play? Let LETO teach you the rules.* Slowly, as if hovering, she went and met them.

꩜

The wheels had fallen off the wagon. Figuratively, of course.

Richard's first dreadful move after taking his shower was replugging the landline. Within a few seconds, IT called with dark news, mainly confirming that Hudson and Douglas were now also stuck in the program, but worse still: Chronos had been locked up. No one going in, no one coming out.

Over the phone, the head engineer also confirmed that the locking of the system hadn't been generated by anyone from HQ. Was that positive or negative news? Nobody knew where to start after that.

No one in, no one out. Needless to say, safely returning the eighteen patrons and employees back to this timeline appeared even more impossible by the minute.

"What if we just, you know, reboot the system?" Richard heard someone tentatively say in the background.

"We can't," replied the head computer engineer, Graves, clearly irritated. His tie hung loose around his neck. "There is no way to know whether they'd be stuck halfway, come back safely, or be completely erased from reality."

Way to paint a grim picture. He fidgeted with the phone. "Any sign of the wave?" inquired Richard.

"Nothing, sir. We haven't seen it since it disappeared in the lockdown."

"Alright, keep up the good work." He pinched the bridge of his nose and gently put the receiver down.

His second regrettable move had been to check his social media account. One should not do that, like ever, especially this soon after a massive blunder of this magnitude. His name was trending—and not for any of the right reasons, as expected. An article titled *Rotten Businessman – Master of Illusion* was at the top of the list and was getting exponentially shared faster than he would have liked. There were also pictures and videos of him dodging, but mostly getting hit by, flying tomatoes, cucumbers, and bananas. *Savages! What is this? The Dark Ages?* For a moment, Richard found solace in knowing that his dear mother was not keeping up with any of those online social applications and that she would not come across those pictures. His brother, on the other hand, was probably laughing his head off and sharing every single compromising post. And it was fair to say that anybody who was anyone was following him nowadays.

How did they drift apart, himself and Victor? Brothers were meant to carry each other and be there for one another in good and bad times. At least, that's how Richard thought the world was supposed to go. The Washington brothers had slowly stopped keeping in touch about a decade ago when Richard had just recently started working for the secret organization run by Marsh. He could not tell his family about the specifics for obvious reasons. His parents had understood that and were supportive, but Victor was suspicious and, as might be expected, a tad jealous.

The younger brother had always felt selfish pride in knowing that he was more successful than his older brother. He had a family with a kid on the way, a nice house on the outskirts of the city, walking distance from a five-star golf course. Despite his young age, he'd skyrocketed up the political ladder and was on track to acquire serious ministerial power, maybe even a seat in near-future elections, whereas his sibling's situation was less than enviable. Broke, homeless, with no prospects whatsoever. But then, almost overnight, Richard's shadow and fame grew, and Victor's ego despised it.

A few weeks before Thanksgiving one year, Richard had invited his parents and brother's family over to his new house. Victor had been skeptical. Someone who had recently been living out of his car could not possibly nor reasonably be able to out-host him, could he? But then he pulled into the arching driveway. That's when he knew his brother could and did. Victor did not like that and felt sour the whole day long. He tried prying information out of his brother, who would answer the same thing every time, "Don't worry about it. You'll know soon enough." If only patience had triumphed.

Victor saw his brother's secret activities as a threat to his political career. Unfortunately, the Washington brothers had a falling out, which did not sit well with their father. He'd tried to reconcile his sons, inviting them to a football game, a round of golf, something. The attempts were getting fewer and fewer, with no resolution to the brotherly feud in sight. Then one day, the invitations stopped altogether. The phone rang. Helena, their mother, was crying on the other line.

The last time the brothers saw each other was at their father's funeral, a month before Chronos' grand opening. Not a word had been spoken between the two of them since.

Richard was hungry. It was well past noon, and he hadn't had anything decent to eat since lunch the day before, a few hours before the interview. He got up and grabbed a jacket intending to go out and get food somewhere. Ultimately, he decided against it, standing still, frozen behind his office door, making arguments in his head. He would send someone. Being seen in public was probably not a good idea at the moment.

The tired CEO called Sadie, asking if she could order him a bite to eat. She joked, "Anything fresh? A tomato sandwich, perhaps?" Richard did not answer. "Too soon?" she replied, a note of pity in her voice. He snickered to humour her, maybe. *Brownie points for trying to lighten the mood, I guess.* Shortly after he'd hung up, Genero, Chronos' treasurer, called him.

"I can't say I'm surprised you called," he said, answering the phone in a semi-defeated voice. "To be honest with you, I was expecting to hear your voice much earlier."

"Believe me, I tried. Must have been a problem with the phones."

"Ah," *right.* "Okay, then. Let's have it. How bad is it?"

"Stocks dropped -6.4% in the past hour. We are projecting around -14.3% by the end of the day."

"Anything we can do about it?"

"Getting the clients out would be a start," he replied in a genuine voice. "But then again, the damage has already been done. Unless you have a new invention or project to unveil soon, like tomorrow, stocks will continue to fall well into the weekend."

Richard thought about the MiChronos. To his knowledge, five copies had already been made with no problem. The prototype was working and could be mass-produced and a first batch could be sent to retirement homes as early as next week. That could get them a six to eight-point increase. Naturally, he would have to get clearance from Marsh. *Tough love.* The portable device was still "officially" in the research phase. Unveiling a product that was supposedly in the blueprint stage would raise unwanted questions and inquiries. Plus, the military would continue to dish out serious moola, no matter how disastrous the market got. "No, nothing miraculous to save our corporate asses at the moment. We'll just have to ride it out."

"Personally, Rich, and this is your friend talking; it might be time to get back to the drawing board."

"Will do." *Vulture. Yes, I'll come up with another billion-dollar idea so that you and the others can keep your house in Malibu and send your less-than-deserving kids to an Ivy League.*

It wasn't the end of high-brow moneybag calls. A half-dozen investors contacted him, worried and panicked about the future of their investments. Richard gave them all the same answer. "Yes, we are doing everything we can and more." "Yes, I have a plan." "No, no need to worry."

During one of those calls, Sadie walked in with a brown bag. Food had finally arrived. Richard was grateful, his growling stomach too. But then she quietly gestured at the window, a worried expression on her face. Puzzled, he raised his shoulders. His secretary mouthed something, still pointing. "I'll call you right back, Simon." He put the phone down before the man named Simon could reply. He followed Miss Ellis' finger. Getting closer, he could hear the chants of an angry mob, one that must have recently amassed. Peering out the window, he saw the lady and her Cro-Magnon, food-chucking goons from earlier. To his dismay, she'd brought reinforcement with her. Family members of the semi-local missing people, friends, and sympathizers of the Society of Timeline Liberation littered his lawn. They had hastily created protest signs, one of them even held a bullhorn. Their intentions reached Richard's ears loud and clear.

"FREE THE STRAYS!"

"SHUT CHRONOS DOWN!"

"PROTECT THE TIMELINES!"

Heatedly, Richard called his head of security. Sharply, he said, "Get those hooligans off my lawn! We don't need more publicity as it is." That's when the news copter showed up. "Great."

A few seconds later, he got another call. This one coming from the mysterious Site B. *I really should have left it unplugged*, he thought to himself. *Will this day ever end?*

"Washington."

"Sir, this is Officer CP458."

"Sure, what's going on?"

"We wanted to inform you that we are in a bit of a situation."

Looking outside at the crowd. "You and me both, pal. Why are you calling me? I thought Marsh wanted to be made aware of every little thing that was going on inside Site B."

"He is, sir. In fact, it was at his request that I am talking to you now."

Tag, you're it. Thanks, Marsh. "Okay, what's up?"

"The STL is out front."

No shit, Sherlock. "I know. They hijacked my press conference."
He glanced toward the window.

"No, sir. I mean *here*. The STL is here at Site B."

"What did you just say?" That new piece of information had truly surprised him. "That can't be! Marsh made sure you guys were operating from a secure, and I quote, 'very secret location'. Hell, even I was not allowed to know where you guys are now." Site B's existence, for that matter, was supposed to be top secret, classified. An urban legend made up by tinfoil-hat-wearing conspiracy theorists. Richard was getting extremely nervous. "How did they find out?"

"We don't know, sir."

Washington could not handle it anymore. He slammed the phone down. An attack on two fronts. *How did this all go downhill so quickly?* He could not wrap his head around it. He wondered, was it too late for a career change?

Yesterday, they celebrated their fifth year. Today felt like a really bad hangover.

⟿

0 day(s): 1 hour(s): 18 minute(s): 35 second(s)

CHAPTER 15 - Washington
Lady Time's Apostle: A Request

The IT room was packed. A warzone. Men and women, geniuses in their own technological fields, were working feverishly around the clock, trying to find a way to bring all time stranded, unfortunate souls back. Shirt buttons were loose, and the air smelled of strong coffee. They must have tried everything! *Not everything*, they kept telling themselves. They held onto hope that a solution, something they hadn't thought of before, would arise. Every big entertainment company has had its *Oops* moment in history. And if that resort off the coast of Costa Rica was able to bounce back from *that*... Well, they were far from being undone.

Suddenly, the giant screen hanging at the front of the room flickered once before going dark. The buzzing of voices abruptly stopped. All eyes converged on the blank wall-sized TV where, not a moment ago, vital signs of Misters Grover, Roberts, Conway, Barnaby, and the others were showing. Some held their breath in anticipation of the unknown.

Lightning—

Thunder—

"Good afternoon." Complete silence hovered in the room as the digital face of a woman slowly constructed itself, pixel by pixel. "I am Lady Time's apostle, and I am here to bring an end to her suffering."

Chatter grew softly at first, then louder. As Anne shared her knowledge of the timelines with the crew, as she had done with Jeremy Wilson a mere seventeen hours before, a fast-thinking technician worked her way inside the system, presently trying to pinpoint the virtual provenance of this unwelcomed hacker.

"Clever girl," ejaculated Anne with a smile in her robotic voice, before turning off all of the monitors in the room. "As I was saying—" she continued before being unceremoniously interrupted, this time, by someone who'd kicked open the door to the laboratory center.

The man, who was followed by Mr. Wilson close behind him, had a sour look on his face. The virtual visage seemed pleased.

"Mr. Washington. How nice to finally make your acquaintance."

Richard sat pensively in his office, reminiscing. He'd ripped out the phone wires from the wall to escape from the noise as much as possible. Sitting on the ground, head and back against the wall, he thought about how *his* invention had changed the world of entertainment. He, Richard Washington, had provided millions with a chance. A chance to relive a moment. A chance to do away with the regret of missing out. A chance to dream.

Then doubt started to creep up his back. *Am I the bad guy in this story?* An alarm sounded from his computer. Richard stood and hobbled over to see what the matter was. His live stream of the IT room had just gone dark. Something was wrong.

He left his office in a hurry, adrenaline kicking in, numbing his sore ankle. He took the emergency fire escape to his right. Jumping stairs four by four and sometimes clearing full flights, he made his way to the main floor with astounding speed. On his way to the basement, he saw Jeremy speaking with Sadie. The Father of

Chronos grabbed his young protégé by the collar, insisting non-verbally that he followed him.

"Mr. Washington, Sir. There's something weird going on with Chronos," he was saying, trying to keep up with his boss. "I called Dr. Stone after I'd left you a message, you know, and—" He realized they were running toward the IT room. "She swears she didn't get my voicemail or my email from last night. I'm sorry, sir, this is all my fault."

Don't worry about it, Richard replied inwardly as he kicked open the door to the mainframe room. Lightning spread through his leg.

"Mr. Washington. How nice to finally make your acquaintance."

The nervousness in the atmosphere was almost palpable. Heads were on a swivel, like at a tennis match, going from their boss to the A.I. and back. Advantage A.I., no love.

"What do you want?" Richard ventured himself. "You're that *thing*, aren't you? We saw you looking at one of our cameras. Dammit! I knew—"

"Do not blame yourself, Mr. Washington. You were playing a game you were always meant to lose. Nothing but a pawn in the grander scheme of things." *A pawn*, he thought as Jeremy hopelessly tried to turn something, anything, back on. *Could she be referring to my being Chronos' pawn, a slave to fame, or to my situation with Colonel Marsh?* He calmed himself and relaxed his face.

"What do you want?" he repeated in a much calmer voice. "Money? Information? To make a statement, maybe?"

"All I want is for the timelines to stop bleeding. Although you call yourself a visionary, you are blind to what has, is, and will happen. That is why I set upon you an ultimatum."

Anne's digital visage was replaced with ominous, glowing red numbers.

01:00:00

Gasps exploded in the room. Panic seemed to have seized every soul. Some bolted out by way of the opened door while the rest helped Jeremy in rebooting their systems. Only Richard stood motionless.

"Hear my demands," she continued with a slight hint of pleading in her synthesized voice. "In one hour, I will destroy Chronos and kill all those stuck in my web. That is unless you shut down 'Site B'—"

"But Site B doesn't exist!" a few techs whimpered in unison.

"It's only a myth," others interjected.

"Shut down 'Site B,'" she repeated, a little bit louder, "and arrange for someone to be delivered inside TimeRoom C before the clock runs out. Those are my conditions. Follow them, and I shall return you my hostages. Follow them not..." Anne let the sound of her unfinished sentence carry dreadfully over horrified listeners.

"Very well," Richard was the first to speak, keeping his head down. "I agree to your terms. We will have someone brought in and ready for you in TimeRoom C in the next fifteen minutes."

Not a bad deal, after all. The wheels in his head were turning. On the one hand: to sacrifice one for the needs of his company's future. He could offer a million dollars to whoever was willing to participate in a "revolutionary experiment"—that's what he would call it. And when the poor goof had disappeared—rest his soul—after signing a legal contract indemnifying Chronos' people, he would be free to continue as if nothing had happened. The public would forget about this troublesome event; he would unveil the MiChronos in a couple of years, stocks would climb back up, and during their tenth anniversary, they would celebrate by retelling the story of how they overcame adversity. He would play the long game. Everything was going to work out.

No, no, it would not.

"And as for Site B—"

"NO!" Her voice was loud, like a roar coming through the speakers.

"Pardon me?"

"You will not send me 'anyone.' I demand someone in particular."

Uh oh, that changes things. Whom might it be? Can't say I'd be too sad if it were Marsh. But what if... What if it's me she wants in exchange?

Richard straightened, "Yes, of course. And who might they be?"

The silence was excruciating. Richard looked at his watch. It was mere seconds to two. He permitted himself a glance around. They were all looking at him, their boss, the hero of this story, expectantly. He noticed his hands starting to shake. He crossed his arms. *Get on with it, will you?*

"Willa Watson."

After speaking the name, all of the room's computers came back to life, but more importantly, in a "get things going" type of way, the countdown on the big board had started. Richard peeked at his wrist again. It was two o'clock on the dot. Jeremy hesitantly snuck up behind him.

"So, who's this *Willa Watson?*"

With a glint of fear in his eyes, for himself, for the company, who knew, he replied, "Son, I seriously have no idea."

〰

0 day(s): 0 hour(s): 58 minute(s): 19 second(s)

PART TWO

OF HEROES AND STRAYS

"What's your name?"

— Alex

CHAPTER 16 - Stray

Who Am I?

Seventeen days ago, there was a blinding light, and then a teenage girl appeared out of thin air. At least, that's what the couple picnicking said—no—yelled, as they ran away. *Stray!* Stray, they screamed. *Is that my name?* She thought it might as well be, for she had no memory of her life before that.

The first thing she remembered was an emotion: fear. She didn't know where she was, and she didn't know who she was. Then, out from behind a bunch of trees, three people wearing identical uniforms, dark blue, started running towards her. Their facial traits were deformed by anger. As soon as she saw them, her legs moved on their own. Survival instinct was kicking in. She ran. She ran far and fast and didn't stop until the dark-coloured uniforms of her hunters were naught but a vivid, scary image branded in her mind. Why did she run away anyway? Could they have helped? Nah. Her gut was telling her she'd made the right decision.

That night, it rained. The amnesiac's clothes were drenched, and her hair was dirty. She walked aimlessly, following the sound of her wet, soaked feet. At one point, she willed herself to a stop. Sitting down, head between her knees, she tried, but failed miserably, to remember how she'd gotten here. How!? She had a pounding headache. Pictures in her mind were fuzzy and dark, like an intense light was shining from behind and hiding important, finer details.

There, on the cold asphalt of an alleyway, sleep overtook her. Dreamless. Clueless.

The first six days and nights since her arrival were much of the same: confusion, fear, and exhaustion. The nameless teen grew exceptionally hungry. Water wasn't a problem. There were water fountains all over the place. The problem was the food. She'd been able to get by, somewhat, by stealing bits and scraps from here and there. Not the most appetizing-looking stuff, but hey, beggars can't be picky—or something like that. *Gimme a break, okay?*

One morning, she woke up with a newfound optimism. Her hazy dream had gifted her the picture of a smile. Well, it was more like a flicker than an actual picture. It seemed so warm and inviting. She couldn't shake the feeling that she had known those lips at some point in her life, however long it might have been. Weirdly enough, that was sufficient enough to give her the proverbial kick in the rear.

That morning, at dawn, she decided she would not live by those three emotions anymore. Confusion, fear, and exhaustion would be replaced by confidence, optimism, and excitement. Rubbing the sleep out of her eyes, the newly made teen stood up and stretched a bit before making her way back to where she had supposedly magically appeared. *Time to find out where I'm from. Let's find some clues.*

Well, there weren't any. There were no clues whatsoever. But there was a stream nearby, so it was not a total loss. Scooping her hand in the water, she poured some of it on her neck, letting it drip back into the stream below her. The cold seemed to ease the pain of her amnesia. Refreshed, she lay on the grass, the base of her hair still wet. Birds were singing, and the sun warmed her skin. That was when another memory popped up in her brain. Eyes this time. Bright blue eyes. She leaned over the water's edge to confirm her suspicions. Hers were brown. She smiled. Just as she thought she was going to have a good day, something she had not had in over a week, three shadows blocked the sun behind her. With a start, the young girl stood and ran. But such was her luck that she tripped and fell backward into the shallow water, hitting her head hard at the bottom. Everything went black for what felt like an instant.

The next second, the semi-conscious teen heard voices discussing her presence. She heard soft as well as hard ones. She heard singing. And she heard a voice as sweet as honey. *Wake up, Honey*, it said. *Wake up—*

"You've finally decided to wake up," said someone. Not the same soothing voice that had implored her to rise from her slumber.

Amnesiac and now dumb, she remained quiet, not finding the words to answer the tanned boy, half-standing, half-sitting in front of her. Laying in a small bed, she looked around the room, taking it in. A nightstand, a dresser, a desk. Clean clothes, definitely not hers, folded nicely on an office chair. Wary of her host, of this room, of this situation in which she was, she slowly sat up. Head pounding, she felt a headache coming, but not from amnesia this time. Small victory?

The kid, who will later be known as John, yelled out towards the door, "Yo, someone go get Alex. Our guest is finally awake. They're gonna want to talk to them."

A second later, someone walked in. They waved to the shivering girl in the bed and introduced themselves as Alex. They could not have been much older than the Stray from what she made of their facial traits, but they were at least five inches taller. The new arrival asked if they could examine the back of her head. The amnesiac instinctively reached behind her head and felt a large bump between her fingers. The patient did not move after that. Too shocked to even try to flee. Gently, Alex moved the silent girl's head from side to side. They were examining it minutely.

"What's your name?" they suddenly asked.

She hadn't replied, couldn't. The caretaker waited a polite amount of time, then, with a sigh and nod, they said a few things to John and shuffled their way out of the room. They knew there was no need to push.

As apprehensive as she felt, little did the amnesiac know that she had just met the person who would become her greatest friend and ally.

A couple of days later, she eventually came out of her shell. When Alex asked her what her name was for what seemed like the eighteenth time in forty-eight hours, she had mouthed the word, *Stray*. They were silent for a moment before bringing a chair closer to the bed and, in doing so, removing the clothes that were still untouched. They sat.

"Well, well, well. I should've known. I mean, I had guessed as much, but..." They fixed their glasses upon the bridge of their nose. Deep in thoughts. They were staring at her. "I'll ask you a few more questions. You can answer by shaking your head. Understood?" After a second, she nodded. "Great. Do you know what city we're in?" She shook her head no. The thought had not even occurred to her. "Do you know what year we're in?" Again, no. *I can't even remember my own name!* Alex paused, thinking about their next question. "Wait here a second." They left the room. Footsteps were heard getting further and further away.

The patient had just closed her eyes when they came back through the door. They sat down again, holding a piece of paper to their chest.

"I'll show you a picture. Let me know if it means anything to you." They flipped the paper, and all of a sudden, the girl in the bed acted as though she had been hit by two invisible punches. One to the head, knocking it backward, and the other to the stomach, leaving her searching for her breath. As quickly as they had shown her the picture, Alex threw it across the room and hurried over to make sure she would not fall off the bed.

It took the Stray a minute or two for her breathing to come back to normal. Alex had brought her a glass of water. The person crouching in front of her now looked as uneasy as the amnesiac felt. Gathering her strength and opening her mouth, she finally vocalized words for the first time in a very long time.

"What... was... that? What did... you show me?"

"Bear with me. What I'm going to tell you might sound ridiculous, but it's the truth." Alex waited for their guest to acquiesce. "I showed you a picture of what a Chronos client sees right before coming back to this timeline. There are two possible reasons to explain your reaction. One: you went on a time trip and lost your C-issued bracelet," they continued while pointing at the girl's naked wrist. "Subsequently, your memory got wiped out, and, without the homing device, you time landed near that stream outside of Chronos' building. That's where we found you, after all."

"And the... second?"

"You're a Stray. An unlucky passerby who got trapped in a time vortex when a nearby group of time travelers came back from their excursion."

She contemplated what Alex had just said. *Is he making fun of me?* She thought she would play along. "And what do you think?"

"Sorry?"

"Who do you think I am? One or two?"

Alex pondered the question before answering it. "If you were a Chronos client, we'd know if people were looking for you." A sudden twinge in her chest had seemingly reacted to those words. "And Chronos would've put your face on their 'Missing People' page. I checked, and you're not. So you must be a—"

"A Stray."

"You know what? I dislike the word 'Stray.' It's a little pejorative if you want my opinion. How about we call you... I don't know," they looked around, searching for inspiration when finally, the girl's eyes landed on a diploma hung on the far wall. She pointed at it, and Alex glanced behind. "Roxanne? How about Roxy?"

"Roxy," she repeated, shrugging. Although it did not feel quite right, she agreed to the new moniker. *Having a name, even if it's not really mine, is better than not having one at all.*

The two of them stayed quiet for a while after that. Silence filled the room. Later, the patient asked her nurse about Chronos. What was it? What did they do? If she truly was a teen out of her time, a time escapee as some called them, wouldn't the ones responsible for her—condition, situation—be able to send her back?

"I'll just walk right up through those front doors and ask to be sent back to whenever I am from."

Alex was taken aback. "Actually, that would be a no-go. The TPF, Time Police Force, would be all over you in a matter of seconds, and they'd send you to Site B. And even if you managed, somehow, to get past them, well..." They showed her an article published the previous year. Stories about con artists trying to exploit the time machine's abilities in original ways to make the big bucks or simply to escape their present-day lives.

∽

Roxanne Nash - Chronology of an
Inter-Timeline Catburglar Extraordinaire

Year 1BC (Before Chronos) -

Miss Nash was in her final year of undergrad at MSU in a Classical Studies program prior to working part-time with the time traveling company known as Chronos. Her main areas of study were the Latin language as well as Roman Art and Archeology. During her time with the Spartans, fellow classmates and faculty members would have described her as driven, resourceful, and highly intelligent. A month before receiving her BA, Nash, who was dropping off a request form to return to Italy to be part of an archeological team, noticed an ad on the Classical Studies Job Board: "Welcome to Chronos - Where the Future is a Thing of the Past."

Year 1AC (After Chronos) -

With her credentials, but principally her extensive knowledge of Latin, Miss Nash was offered a part-time position with this new up-and-coming entertainment business. In her job description, it was written that she was to accompany small groups to ancient times and serve as a sort of tour guide. The hourly wage (hourly inside Chronos) was more than agreeable for someone fresh out of college, and the experiences she had and the things she saw were second to none. In our conversation with Miss Nash, she assured us the first year of her employment went well, and nothing illegal took place.

Year 2AC -

The second contractual year, however, was a different story. Chronos' fame and demand grew exponentially over the first twelve months. She insists that instead of giving senior guides more shifts or simply promoting part-timers to full-time, the brass hired more and more entry-level beginners. She was told that it was for safety precautions because spending extended periods of time in a multitude of timelines in a short amount of time would have negative effects on a person's body and psyche. "They used cheap labor. An easy way to save a few bucks." That is when she started collecting items during her tours: coins, jewelry, and small statuettes. "They only searched guests on their way out. Guides were free to go. I can't be the only one who did stuff like this." At first, Miss Nash stole as a way to rebel against her employer, to show her discontent. It did not take long for her to notice that she was easily getting away with it—and the thrill found in the illegality of her actions was something for which she learned to yearn.

Year 3AC -

By the time her third year started, she was finally promoted to full-time guide with access to a wider array of time destinations. She could have stopped her thieving ways, but she was hooked. Rings became pendants. Tiny sculptures moved to mid-size busts. She was good at it, and she knew it. In her early days, she had heard of a certain group of people who were willing to pay a pretty sum for antique relics. Miss Nash quickly became a rising star on the black market, bringing them very rare items in mint condition. "All this fame made me want to do it even more." She admits to having snuck in the time traveling machine plenty of times after hours to sneak out bigger, more lucrative souvenirs. Amongst her gravest achievements, she does not deny having transported through time Vivaldi's violin, an obsidian Templar chalice, and the Magna Carta, to name a few.

Year 4AC -

But her schemes were not meant to last. While trying to sell off an original Pompeian painting to an undercover stolen art officer, she was recognized and was immediately fired from Chronos. In all, Miss Roxanne Nash's transactions are estimated at over five hundred million USD. To this day, the stolen artifacts have yet to be found. She remains free as she has yet to be found guilty in a court of law because her lawyer claims: "She has not stolen anything belonging to anyone in this timeline."

〜

Roxy put the paper away, happy in a way. *Hey! I remember how to read. Go me!* But ultimately, her luck seemed to have run out. She had no memory and even less chance of going back to her time, whenever that was.

Suddenly, something clicked in her mind. She reread parts of the article and then looked back at the diploma that had inspired her new name. Alex must have understood what she was thinking. They re-introduced themselves.

"Hi, I'm Alex Nash. And yes, Roxanne Nash is my mom."

〜

8 day(s): 2 hour(s): 41 minute(s): 13 second(s)

CHAPTER 17 - Stray
Heroes of Ancient Times

Alex was born in Detroit, Michigan when their mom was only seventeen years old. They'd never really asked for details, but the way they understood it, they were a "prom night baby." Roxanne, a junior, had been asked out by her then-boyfriend, 'the senior with the prettiest eyes,' she would always say when describing her old flame. They were only kids and knew next to nothing of the world. They fooled around that one night, and nine months later, little Alex was born. By that time, Mark, the biological father, had moved across state on a lacrosse scholarship, never to be seen or heard of again. Keeping the baby had put Roxanne's plans on the back burner, but she was adamant about raising her child in the same loving way her own mother had done when she grew up, God rest her soul.

Finally, when Alex was ready to go to school full-time, Roxanne took this opportunity to enroll in the program she had planned on attending half a decade ago. Times were rough, to be sure, but the duo battled through all the hurdles that were unceremoniously thrown at them. At a very young age, Alex learned to be a critical thinker, resourceful, and a quiet force to be reckoned with—much like their mother.

A few weeks before her child turned ten, Roxanne announced she received this job offer from a *pretty cool company*. Alex was skeptical of their mom entering this new line of work. As had been said before, Alex was a keen observer, an intelligent and inquisitive youth who had learned to battle adversity more than once in their young life. Mom should have listened, for although she took the job with the best of intentions, it was the beginning of the end in the Nash household.

It was true, however, that there were perks associated with this new position. Financially, things were slow at first, but steady. When Alex turned thirteen, they were surprised by their mom with a new house. The both of them had been dreaming about getting out of their derelict one-and-a-half-bedroom apartment for as long as Alex could remember.

The new place was perfect. Large and outdoorsy, no houses around for hundreds of feet. The small forest surrounding it filled the air with fresh pine smells and cut down on the winds. The house itself had two levels. The upper front side had three large windows facing East. In the morning, natural light shone through, gradually warming up three individual rooms: Alex's bedroom, Roxanne's office, and the master bedroom, respectively, from left to right. From the inside, if one were to leave any of these rooms, they would see a guarded hallway in a U-shape. A railing prevented the walker from falling to the main level.

The upper West side had a single patio door that opened onto a massive balcony. Early in the evenings, Roxanne and Alex would sometimes sit on lounge chairs or lean on the wooden railing and simply watch the sunset. One spring, a family of finches, one with a brownish coat, the other with beautiful red feathers, had elected to build a wiry nest near the northern part of the balcony. Alex had noticed them one cool April afternoon. They were elated to witness such pretty birds this close to them. To be frank, ever since moving to the woods, Alex had not been able to see much of their friends. Therefore, it's safe to say that when they found three white eggs in the nest and subsequently told their mom, they were devastated to find everything gone the next day except for a few dry blades of grass.

The balcony was held up by six large oak columns. One in the middle of each side of the patio, four more equally divided on the longest side. The main floor, facing the western vista, sported a similar kind of door as the upper homolog. The front of the house, although quite new, looked as rustic as a home built over a hundred years ago.

Inside, the foyer was bigger than Alex's bedroom and, one could have easily thought, larger than their previous apartment. Alex had joked with their mom that they could hang a crystal chandelier and host a ball. Roxanne had laughed at the idea. Yet, not three weeks later, Alex woke up one morning to the chiming sound of their mom affixing a luster with dangling crystals to the ceiling. *That thing looked like it came straight from the eighteen hundreds,* Alex had thought. And right they were because Roxanne had brought it in, five or six pieces at a time, from one of her time trip destinations.

Although Alex never brought it up with their mom, they knew the timing as well as the financial commitment were suspicious. One day, on their way back from school, Alex came home to Roxanne being escorted out of the front door by two police officers. She was handcuffed and had an air of shame on her face when she crossed eyes with her child.

For a reason Alex never quite understood, they were told they could stay in and keep the house, albeit being sixteen and alone. On the day of the trial, they had expected to lose everything. Not only the house, of course, but their mom as well. To almost everyone's surprise and Chronos' team's lamentation, Roxanne was proven not guilty due to lack of evidence and something that came to be known in court as *Temporal Properties*. Her lawyer had struck an important point in asking the judge, the jury, and the crown if a timeline was subject to another's jurisprudence. It was, amongst other points made, the proverbial finger to push the dominoes in a loud and ethical cascade of rights and wrongs.

Although Roxanne had been acquitted, she was never able to look at her child the same way she had when they had been a little and innocent kid. Was it this guilt that pushed her to infiltrate Chronos one last time? What did she have to prove? Either way, whatever happened that night had left Alex all alone. Roxanne never came back, leaving Alex to wonder where in the worlds their mom had gone.

This had been some six months before Chronos' fifth anniversary. By that time, Alex had heard of and noticed strange things happening in the park just outside of Chronos Headquarters. Their mom had told them about reports of people appearing out of thin air in those parts. One afternoon, a month following their mom's disappearance, curiosity got the best of Alex, and they bravely made their way there.

They never thought anything would come out of their little escapade, yet, a few hours into their stroll, Alex came face to face with a boy who looked as confused and scared as a deer stuck in headlights. Using their most soothing voice, Alex reassured him that he would be okay. Although, thinking back, they probably did not have to slowly raise their arms, it was not a feral animal after all. The gesture seemed to have calmed the kid. An instant trust bloomed between them.

"What's your name?" Alex had asked. But the boy did not answer. "It's okay," they continued. "We'll figure it out together."

Since then, Alex's home housed four Strays, five if you were to include Roxy. Although not a Stray themself, Alex was unanimously elected Leader of the Strays. In that position, and now having a better understanding regarding how these kids got here, Alex had been trying to make the most of it all by correcting some of the wrongs their mom might have committed to other Strays who had not had the same luck as John, Kary, Max, Akiro and, most recently, Roxy.

〜

After the story was told, someone knocked on the door. It was John.

"Hey Alex," said the boy, apologetically walking in, sorry to interrupt. "Kary's just come back. She's downstairs."

"I'll be right there," Alex replied, gently tapping Roxy on the back before making their way out of the room, leaving her alone with her thoughts and an old newspaper.

In the following days, Alex had told her about the other members of the *Heroes of Ancient Times*, a name they had agreed on as a sort of jest. If the villain in the story was to be Chronos, an ancient Greek entity, they might as well consider themselves heroes of their time in a land far, far away.

Alex was to represent Odysseus. They were the architect and mastermind behind everything their little group of rascals was ever up to. John was Ajax the Greater. Although his facial features could have identified him as being no more than fifteen years old, the rest of his body was something entirely different. Not only was he a head taller than Alex, who themself were second in height, but his physical strength was unparalleled. In his time, he probably was the son of a farmer or land-clearer because, and this is the truth, not a single teenager from Alex's timeline ever had a physique so naturally built as his. Despite the fact he could not remember a thing about his past life, John's hands never faltered when it came to manual labor around the house.

Kary was a young girl of probably thirteen or fourteen. She was a person of very few words, but what she lacked in terms of vocabulary, she made up for it with her tracking skills and forestry senses. Just like Teucer in the *Iliad*. She was also adept at the bow. It was only by pure luck and chance that she was found by Alex and John. It looked as though she had survived in the park thanks to her instincts. How long had she been there with no memories? Five days? A week? She was absolutely filthy. Her long dark braided hair was full of twigs and what Alex believed to be animal droppings. Her indigenous hunting gear was cut in many places, but it was her expertly handcrafted bow that drew eyes to her. It was clear she had come to this timeline holding that weapon, and even clearer, she was no neophyte when it came to using it.

Max, a.k.a Nestor, was the third Stray to be rescued and sheltered by Alex. Max was the physical opposite of John, being thin and short, as well as the polar opposite of Akiro's personality. Where he was quiet and preferred to be alone, Max delighted in sharing his thoughts and being surrounded by others. It was he, in a long-winded speech, who suggested they call themselves the *Heroes*. More than once, Alex had come to him for advice on different points: food, lodgings, chores, etc. Although no one in the group was certain of his background (it had become sort of a game once they were comfortable with each other), Alex had found a photo online that bore an uncanny resemblance to Max. But truly, would this scrawny kid have grown up to be King Louis XIV?

Akiro was the most recent kid to join the fray. To tell the truth, it did not take too much convincing to get him to join this little group of misfits. To say he did not speak English was still to be determined. For as long as he had lived with them Akiro had not uttered a word. But he did not get the moniker Phoenix for no reason. Like his *Iliad* counterpart, Akiro was a talented mediator. The young boy had a way of understanding and soothing emotions and feelings. Without a single word, he would douse flaring tempers with a gentle touch or a look. Needless to say, the camaraderie had bloomed exponentially since his arrival.

For the next week or so, Roxy stayed and helped Alex and the *Heroes* around the house. She would contribute to cleaning the rooms, making food, and shadowing the other kids. She quickly learned things about herself. For example, she couldn't sweep the floor properly. "It's not a hockey stick," John would say. But on the other hand, she played the piano at night for the other kids. Roxy had noticed the shiny black instrument the first time she willed herself down the stairs to the main floor. It was hard to miss, as it occupied a large portion of the foyer. Roxy had asked Alex about it.

"My mom always wanted me to play the piano," they replied.

"Well, do you?"

"Used to. Not anymore. How 'bout you?"

"I... I don't know," she had answered, covering a chuckle.

"No time like the present. Here," Alex had said, lifting the key lid. "Why don't you give it a try?"

Hesitantly, she sat on the hard, dusty stool. Her hands hovered over the keys for an awkward instant before finally deciding to strike them. As soon as her fingers touched the keys, they danced and created a beautiful melody. She had no idea what she had played. Talk about muscle memory!

"Not bad, Roxy!" It was John who had congratulated her. He had snuck inside once he had heard the music. The others had done the same. Roxy suddenly felt self-conscious and felt heat rising in her cheeks. Alex put a hand on her shoulder. Roxy looked up shyly.

"I can't remember if there were any musically inclined *Heroes* in the *Iliad*," Alex stated for the whole group to hear. "But until we figure that out, I think you've earned yourself the name of the Muse. Welcome to the Heroes of the Timeline."

The other kids cheered. Roxy, the Muse, gave them a bashful smile.

A lot of things happened during those seventeen days since her time landing. In her mind, Roxy believed she had finally accepted her lot. Conceded to the hand she had been dealt. But one morning, thoughts and sounds invaded her sleep. It also marked the return of the sweet, honeyed voice. *It won't be long now—*

I'm coming for you—

⌇

2 day(s): 1 hour(s): 23 minute(s): 52 second(s)

CHAPTER 18 - Stray

No Shoes

She played the last note on Alex's old piano, a left-handed G. Again, the pianist struggled to remember the name of the song she'd just played, but judging by the applause coming from the *Heroes*, she must have played it right. Shyly, the young girl out of time stood and curtsied awkwardly. Her new friends returned to their plates while John pulled a chair out for her. Did he have to smile at her the way he did? She felt her cheeks flush a bit at the gesture. Roxy ignored this feeling building in her stomach—for now, at least.

Supper time with this gang of teens and tweens was never the same two nights in a row. One night, Max would *educate* his fellow listeners on his newest topic of interest—he'd been reading nonfiction work every free moment he had ever since Alex had taught him about the Internet. One such soliloquy happened no later than two nights ago when he enlightened his peers on the merits and drawbacks of philanthrocapitalism. Needless to say, more than one listener was utterly lost.

On this night, however, the mood seemed off. Max, who was usually so loquacious, hadn't said a word all evening, nor had he touched his food. It was duck, hunted and prepared by their in-house hunter, Kary. Roxy hadn't been seated fifteen minutes before Max excused himself, sulkingly making his way to his room.

"What's up with him?" Roxy asked Alex in a whisper.

"You really don't know, do you?" they only replied.

It was John's turn to melt in front of his food. His face had turned a shade darker than the tomato-based sauce covering his food. Kary only giggled knowingly. Alex was about to tell Roxy why Max was suddenly acting this way, that is until they crossed eyes with Akiro. His facial expression seemed to say *Maybe not everything. Let her work for it.*

"He's... Ummm..." they ventured before being cut off by Kary.

"He's a jealous boy. That's all."

Akiro rolled his eyes.

"Jealous? Of what?" Roxy pondered. "If it's the piano, I can teach him, I think."

"It's not the piano," John finally said after keeping quiet for some time.

Roxy looked from him to Alex, then from Kary to Akiro. They knew something she did not and it annoyed her.

"Tell me," she asked in an even voice.

Unfortunately, Roxy did not get the result she'd expected. Alex sighed and picked up their half-eaten plate before making their way toward the kitchen. Kary soon followed after them, yet not before squeezing out another smirk. Akiro was the last to leave the table. He half-bowed, grabbed his plate, and put a hand on John's shoulder as he exited the room. The camaraderie motion looked to be one of consolation as if to say *Be brave. I wouldn't want to be in your shoes right about now.*

John fidgeted with the bottom of his shirt. Roxy was so confused. Never had she seen him so sheepish. The hulking young man seemed to be shrinking in front of her questioning eyes by the second. Eventually, after what felt like an eternity, he turned his head towards Roxy and met her gaze.

"Well, you see, the thing is... Max," he pointed in Max's general direction upstairs. "He's a great guy, right? And so are you, by the way; you're awesome, in fact." He kept blabbering like this for a while and was using way too many hand gestures. Roxy could have sworn she felt the back of her head burning by the intensity with which Kary was ogling them from the kitchen doorway. John continued, ignoring, or was it oblivious to, his housemate. "I know you haven't been with us for long. How long has it been anyway? A week?"

"Ten days," she finally added to the conversation.

"Right! And you've made such an impression on the group. And I... I was wondering..."

Oh no! Roxy realized, a tad too late, what was happening. *He can't be. Sure, he's cute, but... No way. What the hell are you doing, John!?*

Coincidentally, John had thought those exact words at precisely the same moment. *What the hell are you doing, John!? Here goes nothing!* He took a deep breath, and for the first time since embarking on his rambling pursuit, he uttered a complete sentence using his normal, rich, and suave voice.

"Would you like to go out with me?"

I can't believe he did that! Roxy was at a loss for words. It would be a lie to say she was not attracted to him. But the emotions she felt for John were still so confusing. *Wait a second! The reason why Max left... It can't be. OMG, he's jealous of John!? Cause he likes me too?*

"Roxy?" he gently asked, bringing her back from her inner monologue.

"You're a great guy, John, really great." *Am I really going there right now?* "And I appreciate you telling me how you feel. Truly, I do." *But—* "I… I need a second." Without another word or waiting for a reply, Roxy bolted out of the house barefoot.

John was left there, alone with his thoughts and completely deflated.

"Well, that could have gone worse." Kary had snuck behind John.

"Go to hell," he simply said before picking up his plate.

How long did she run? How far? She did not know. Roxy did, however, feel a pain in her foot and a knot in her stomach. The teenage girl slowed to a light jog before huffing and puffing at the foot of a great big oak tree.

Suddenly, the sound of ruffling leaves under shoes made Roxy prop her head up. *I swear to God, if it's John who came to declare his love to me again, I'll punch him in the face.* It wasn't John. Nor was it Max, who was, unbeknownst to Roxy, still sulking in his room.

It was dark by the time Miss Heartbreaker stopped running. So it wasn't until Alex was ten feet away that Roxy finally realized who had been following her.

"You startled me," was all Roxy could say.

"Why'd you run away?" It was Alex's turn to catch their breath.

"I'm sorry. I know it was stupid."

"Don't apologize. That's on John and Max. We knew it was coming. We just didn't know when."

"Akiro did warn you guys, I guess." She couldn't help but chuckle a little.

"Ha, I guess he did." Alex crossed their arms. "Here," they said, motioning to a park bench with a movement of their chin. "Let's sit down."

"Thanks," she said as she sat down. "Did you run after me?"

"Yeah, I did," they replied with a slight note of embarrassment. Alex continued combing through their hair with a hand. "I couldn't let our newest recruit run off in the dark, right?" They looked around. Remembering something. "It's funny, though."

"What's so funny?" Roxy replied, intrigued.

"This is where we found you."

Now that they mentioned it, Roxy did recognize the area. She could hear the little stream in which she had fallen, could somewhat make out the shadowy outline of the large trees, and, ominously, could feel the danger looming from being so close to Chronos' headquarters. Alex picked up on what Roxy was probably thinking.

"Don't worry," they reassured her. "The TPF won't come. At least, not for us."

The thought of the Time Police Force chasing after her again made her shiver.

"You must be cold," they said, putting an arm around Roxy.

Although she was not freezing, she appreciated the gesture. They smelled of pine. Roxy liked that. *How come I never noticed?* Alex's warmth spread to her. She could feel their heart beat fast against her body.

"Your heart is beating so fast," she commented in a half-whisper. "I thought you were an athlete. No way that little run tired you that much."

"I am. And... it didn't."

By now, their eyes were locked onto each other's. Roxy slid a little closer to Alex. She could feel their chest moving rapidly against her hand. *When did that happen?* Still, she kept it there.

"Alex, I..." Roxy was about to say something before their fingers touched her cheek. What was it that changed between them to make her feel this way? It was so easy to reject John, yet she felt it would be harder to resist should Alex decide to lean in closer. No, why kid herself? It had been there all along. Nothing had changed. Roxy had simply started listening to herself. She gently grabbed the collar of their shirt, but before she could do anything, a scream pierced the night air.

"Gotcha, bloody Stray!"

The voice came from very nearby, beyond the trees. The words were not aimed at Roxy, thankfully, but they had broken a magical moment between her and Alex. Speaking of, they were on their feet faster than Roxy had a chance to react. They were saying something about having to go help whoever was in trouble.

"And you need to get back home." It wasn't an order, but didn't feel like a suggestion either. They took off their shoes, offering them to Roxy. "Put these on." She did. They were maybe a size too big, but she didn't care. Her adrenaline was pumping. Alex continued, "When you get home, tell Kary. She'll know what to do."

They started toward the sound.

"What are you gonna do?" Roxy asked, a hint of concern in her voice.

"Don't worry about me," they said with a smile. "Just get home safe."

That was it. She wouldn't see them again that night, or the night after for that matter.

As quickly as she could, in slightly oversized runners, Roxy dashed through the naked trees, crunching yellow and red leaves as she went. Maybe it was because she was making too much noise, or simply a bad place, bad time kind of thing. But the very last thing Roxy remembered from that night was a sequence of high-pitched sounds, followed by an acute pain in the neck. She felt herself falling to the ground. In her mind, she knew she should have been worried about what was to come, but a part of her focused on the fact that she regretted not having kissed Alex when she'd had the chance. Now, her vision was getting blurry, like clouds cast over a pair of sad eyes. Closing them, because they felt so heavy, she thought she saw three shapes. Not long after she hit the ground, three shadows lifted her from nature's mossy floor. To carry her to who knows where.

〰

0 day(s): 18 hour(s): 36 minute(s): 02 second(s)

CHAPTER 19 - Stray Answers

Roxy woke up to the sound of screeching iron. Her small frame was weak. Her back was aching. But the pain was belittled by what came next. As she shakily erected herself from what felt like a cold, wet, concrete floor, a forceful jet of water hit her in the stomach, knocking the wind out of her and propelling her backward, falling once more to the ground.

Her eyes were open now. Breathing heavily while on all fours, Roxy looked around. She wasn't in the forest anymore. Metal bars surrounded her on three sides, a solid grey wall to her back. She was a prisoner of some sort. The man with the hose backed away from the cell door, and immediately after, four people dressed in dark blue uniforms rushed in. Tactical, swift, rehearsed. *The Time*

Police Force. She tried to wriggle free, but hers was too weak compared to their combined herculean strength.

Leaving her cell, not knowing where she was led, the drenched girl never touched the ground. She was being carried, dragged unceremoniously through a long, dark corridor. At the end of it, an obsidian metal door. They opened it. At that point, Roxy was too scared to move. The new room in which they brought the teen was alien, to say the least. Electrical wires hung from the ceiling. Light reflected off the walls, black as the door she was dragged through. But where did that light come from? She did not know or begin to comprehend. There were no windows. A giant screen was mounted on the wall opposite the door. The weirdest thing, though, was the single piece of furniture set dead in the middle of the Square Room. Like an iron throne surrounded by blood, there stood her destination. A semi-inclined surgical bed.

The guards strapped the girl to it, tight, very tight. She would have liked to say she gave them a good fight, but there was no kidding anyone. Her clothes, still wet from the surprise attack, were like an anchor pulling Roxy's will further and further down the darkest pits of her soul. Who cared anyway? She was just a Stray. There was nothing for her here, no one waiting. Nothing to fight for.

Is that so?

A voice made itself heard somewhere deep in the broken youth's subconscious. A sweet, honeyed voice. A voice that seemed all too familiar. One she was sure she knew.

"No," she said weakly.

"What was that?" replied one of the shades.

"No, no, no, NO!"

With every word getting louder, Roxy's thrashing intensified. She had seemed so subdued a moment ago. The sudden change had taken them by surprise. She was going berserk, certain to make it out of here!

In her attempt to free herself, although her arms and legs were fastened to the bed, she successfully bit someone and headbutted another. The punch she subsequently received to the jaw was somewhat warranted. She shook the dizziness and the pain off her face. A new life coursed through the fighter's veins. A goal for happiness. Roxy spat blood at the feet of an upcoming assailant.

"Come at me!" she roared in a rough voice, disheveled hair clinging to her forehead.

At once, the man who'd struck her slowly backed away, unsure of what to do anymore. He looked around at his mates. They shrugged their shoulders as if to say *What's wrong with you? Why did he stop?*

It is to be said that most, over ninety-eight percent of Strays, who were brought to Site B by the TPF were adults. To have this fifteen- or sixteen-year-old teen fight back was something this specific guard had never encountered before. It had always been so easy to think of them as rabid animals needing to be put down for the good of his world. So what had changed? Why now? To his colleagues, he mouthed the words, *I can't.* Whether they were at war or not, there needed to be limits, and some lines should never be crossed. *She's a child, for Christ's sake.* As if on cue, sent from the Devil himself, Marsh barged in.

"How are things going in here?"

They all looked at the gigantic man, but no one said a word. His eyes laid on the struggling youth.

"Whatya waiting for, son? Calm her down," he said to the guard nearest Roxy.

When he made to back away from the inclined examination table as if to refuse the order, the Colonel simply sighed.

"Well, shit. They sure don't make them like they used to."

On those words, he pulled a gun out of its holster and blew the insubordinate soldier's kneecap out. Blood splattered all over the console, the black wall, and a now very quiet Roxy.

"Look at whatcha made me do. You," the authoritarian brute ordered over the wailing man's screams of agony, "clean this shit up. And you," Marsh instructed another, "strap that Stray properly and start the sequence. There's not a minute to lose, folks!"

And that was it. Just as suddenly as he had appeared, Colonel Maxon Marsh was about to leave the room through the obsidian door behind Roxy. As he passed by her, however, she could have sworn he stopped for a fraction of a heartbeat to look at her. His eyes flashed with a hint of recognition. *What the hell?*

Not willing to face their superior's wrath furthermore, the remaining employees continued with the Frankensteinian procedure. A silicone cap was produced out of the corner of Roxy's eye. All she could muster was a wheezy, half-hearted, "Is that all you got?", but she sounded less than convincing. The fight she once had inside of her was gone.

One of them affixed the headpiece to the teen's head and subsequently secured a leather strap under her already bruising chin. She sensed someone else attaching something to the top of it.

Roxy saw a thumbs-up flash near her. What happened next was pure white-light-agonizing pain surging through her broken body. Bile came up to her throat. She felt herself slowly blacking out.

So this is how it ends—

"I hate it when he does that," murmured the cleaning guard to no one in particular. She was presently scrubbing the wall, away from her colleagues. "Much longer there, doc?" she asked, louder, to the person manning the electrical contraception.

"The Helmet was accepted by the host's neuropathways. Shouldn't take too long now."

As if on cue, the screen flickered, and the words FEBRUARY 1988 appeared in large white and bold letters and numbers in the middle of a black background. Soon after, the word and year transitioned to the bottom right, reducing in size.

Music started playing. The sound came from the screen's speakers. A projection of Roxy's memories. From a time before her abduction.

"Edge of Seventeen" was blaring in the background. She could not help but wonder why her mom always took her brother's side and, for that matter, would not stand up to Dad. Sitting on her bed, she looked around at all the useless stuff her parents had bought her in an attempt to *buy* her these past few years since the divorce: the keyboard, the radio station, the Walkman, and even the lava lamp. She felt anger rise within her. She had to leave. Looking out the window, the girl saw the sun setting. The remaining rays hit the snow-covered ground in such a way that lit up the upper left side of her windowsill, and near it hung a china dove, suspended a foot or two from the popcorn ceiling. A dove, a symbol of love and peace, but also freedom. *Well, if that ain't a sign.*

Willa Watson, sixteen, had been in the midst of this rebellious phase for a while, but tonight, she felt especially mischievous and particularly angry at her mom. She'd made up her mind. The teenage girl picked up her yellow Walkman and black handbag. The second time the chorus came along on her radio, she turned the volume up a bit more and opened her bedroom window. The chilly evening air quickly filled the room, or was it the heat that escaped it? No matter, already wearing a cozy sweater and tattered runnings (for she conveniently never seemed to take them off), she hopped out and slowly slid the pane back down. It wasn't the first time Willa had pulled such a stunt, but it would be the last. Only she did not know it yet.

She had already made up her mind on the course of her next actions. Feet crunching the dry snow in a slow rhythm, little Miss Watson clipped the cassette player to her waist belt. Subsequently, she put on the headphones, adjusting the flimsy metal part so both ears could have equal snugness and sound. Once this ritual was complete, she pushed the big triangle without looking at it; her thumb knew the positioning of the different buttons by heart. Right away, a song, midway done, started playing. And just like that, she hummed along as she walked down Crichton Street.

It only took the length of a song and a half for Willa to arrive at Stacy's house, her BFF. It was a tall brick building with a washed-up yellow door. She got herself up a couple of snowed stairs and knocked at the door a few times. Mrs. Wayne, Stacy's mom, was the one to open it.

"Why, hi there, Willa. How are you doing?" she said in her most motherly tone.

"Hello, Mrs. Wayne. I'm fine, thanks. Is Stacy home?" the teen had said while removing her headphones. The music coming out of them could faintly still be heard.

"Yes, she's watching the closing ceremony with Marty. I'll get her for you."

On that note, she left down a narrow hallway.

"Yo, what's up, homegirl?" asked the redheaded teen, a big smile on her face.

"You know me, just chillin'." They embraced and talked for a bit until Willa said, "Wanna get out of here?"

"I got you." She picked up her keys and hollered at her parents, saying she would be back later.

To that, Stacy's dad only replied, "Not too late, please. There's school tomorrow."

The two teenagers drove to their favourite coffee shop on Fifth, ordered a drink, and kept talking about all and nothing. Their conversation ranged from the most recent English novel assignment to that new action movie with Stacy's TV crush from *Moonlighting*. They talked about that Jamaican bobsled team and that British guy with the glasses, the Eagle he was called; after all, why would they not, since both historical moments had happened a few days ago right here in their Albertian backyard. Yet, of all the things they discussed, never once did Stacy bring up Willa's mother, father, or twin brother into it. There was an understanding, an unwritten rule between the two young women. Some might say it is not healthy to not talk about such things and that it is better to vent. But did they know that back in February of 1988? In any case, had Stacy pushed her friend to talk about her mom, maybe her best friend would still belong to this timeline. Who knows?

In the late hours of that fateful night, Willa and Stacy were on their way back to the car when, suddenly, a group of four people ran past them. They were wearing Canadian Olympic gear from head to toe, but it was clear to the ladies they were not Olympic athletes. *Must have come from the closing ceremony*, Willa thought. *Is it already over?* She looked up at the massive street clock. Indeed, it was definitely past her bedtime.

The four people continued running until they turned into an alley, one between the coffee shop she and her friend had just exited and a music shop. *That was weird.* Her friend's car was in sight when two more runners came up behind them.

"Wait for us!" one shouted, a tall man with a beard and long hair tied in a bun above his head.

"I told you!" the woman said in an angry voice. She was about to say something else, something about *leaving without us*, whatever that meant; however, mid-sentence, she tripped on an elevated cobblestone piece on the sidewalk and fell into the amassing snow.

It looked like it had hurt. She got up in a hurry and kept racing, albeit limping, after her friend who had just disappeared into that same alleyway. That was when Willa noticed it, a running shoe. The woman had lost it in her tumble. Hadn't she realized the fact? Willa gave Stacy her purse and Walkman, asking her to wait for her by the car.

"I'll be right back," she said, picking up the shoe off the ground and chasing after the shoeless lady.

And then she was gone. Vanished. Did Stacy know it was to be the last time she would ever see her best friend?

As Willa turned the corner, she saw that the woman had reached her group. They were waiting in an awkward semi-circle, looking at their wrist, their backs to her. She quickened her pace. When she was but a metre or two behind the group, a bright blue light flashed out of nowhere, blinding the teenage girl.

She dropped the running shoe.

The light was so bright.

She closed her eyes.

〰

When she opened them again, she was surrounded by fuzzy black shapes. Her body was aching. Bad! It was as if someone had taken a hammer to her brain and nailed it non-stop. As she twisted her head around, she remembered where she was, but most importantly, the girl out of time remembered *who* she was.

Willa Watson. That was her name, but at this moment, she was nothing but the living embodiment of pain. Pure hot agony rushed through her body, a mere vessel of drenched flesh. Her senses were in overdrive, and everything hit her at once. One second, the youth was tearing up, teeth grinding inside her bruised mouth. The next, she was in a hallway, dragged by strong merciless arms. But although every instant was physical torture, one shining beacon kept her mind from going haywire. A feeling of guilt and shame.

"I'm sorry," Willa, not Roxy, muttered between two breaths before blacking out. "I'm so sorry, mom!"

〰

0 day(s): 2 hour(s): 56 minute(s): 49 second(s)

CHAPTER 20 - Stray

The Silver Door

With as little care as one could possibly muster—it was a recurring theme she noticed—they threw Willa onto the floor of a cold cell. At least this one was dry. She looked at her hand, her wrist was already purple and swollen. She must have sprained it when she hit the ground, trying to protect her body. Quickly, the guards shut the barred door. The noise sent sparks of pain through her throbbing head. Everything just hurt so much.

A few moments later, their footsteps faded in the distance before completely disappearing. That was when she realized she wasn't the only one stuck in this joint. As she massaged her temples with scraped hands, Willa became aware of the sounds of breathing coming from her left. The girl risked a look at the adjacent cell. As they locked eyes, the other prisoner said, "You a'ight?" There was concern in the woman's voice.

Blame it on the electroshock therapy or what have you, but Willa remained quiet, a daft expression glued to her face. All little Watson could muster was a half-hearted, pain-grinning nod. She kind of looked like Stacy, Willa thought briefly.

"So when you from, home skillet?" the other girl inquired as she repositioned herself, her back against the stiff grey wall. Funny accent she had. Willa could not place it at the moment.

"Calgary, it seems," she replied after a short pause, trying to reassemble the scrambled words in her fragile mind.

The dark red-haired girl snickered, "Didn't ask where you from, bruh. I asked when."

The words took a second to compute in her head. Whatever these people in uniform had done to her had probably done more than just give her a splitting headache. She kneaded at her forehead with her most able hand before correcting herself.

"Yea, sorry. I think I'm from the eighties. Name's Willa."

"'Sup, Eighties Willa? I'm Nineties Clara." She did a peace sign with her left hand.

Despite all her aches and pains, Clara's demeanor sure brought a smile to her lips.

She looked a tad older than Willa was. In her early twenties, maybe. She wore a flannel shirt under jeans overalls, which was an interesting combination. *Canadian, too?* Willa thought. She presently busied herself with small arm movements, a quick flick of the wrist here and there, seemingly carving something into her cell's concrete wall.

"How long have you been here?" Willa continued.

"Depends what you mean. 'Here' locked up or 'here' out of my time?"

"Both, I guess."

She considered her answer an instant before telling her new cellmate. As it turned out, Clara's stopover to this timeline was very much unlike Willa's. Barely one hour she was on the run before getting caught by those guards in dark uniforms. (Contrary to Alex and the others, when talking about the time police, she referred to them as *the fuzz*.) She went through the electro show just over three days ago.

When the fuzz brought her to her cell, seventy-two excruciatingly long hours ago, the place was apparently jam-packed with other Strays.

"Something weird is going on. The first day, I swear they brought like two or three guys through those doors." She pointed to the shiny, silver metal thing with the letters D-H etched an inch above the frame. "And then, more of us started leaving. I got hella scared, man! I told myself, 'Clara, we's gots to bounce.'"

Willa liked the way she talked. She didn't understand half the things she was saying, but the new girl's fiery attitude kept her focus off of the mysterious, slightly unnerving, one-way door. *Don't worry about it, Willa. It'll be fine.*

In the short time she'd been stuck in here, Clara seemed to have gathered a solid understanding of this place, or at the very least, of her situation. The nineties girl had heard two guards discussing late one night when she was pretending to sleep. "It's always better to pretend you're asleep," she added in a whisper as if it was a well-kept secret. After getting their brains fried by that wired helmet, Strays were divided into two groups. The *useful ones*, doctors, scientists, engineers, and cooks, entered the Blue Door and were put to work in specific wings. Their knowledge and practical skills were secretly being held hostage, all for the benefit and advancement of Chronos. "Talk about free labour, right!"

"So what do they do with us, the 'expendables'?" Willa asked after having kept quiet for the better part of ten minutes.

"That's the thing, though, ain't it? No one knows for sure. Artists like me," she motioned to herself. "I heard they're being experimented on. Bad stuff! And no one ever seems to come back. The Evil Empire doesn't care for beauty, I guess." She shrugged.

The eighties girl glanced around the empty room. It was bleak. This was the place where art came to wither, and so would she, apparently. To be sixteen and to have no other skill than playing the piano, what a drag. Lost in her thoughts, she snapped back into focus, realizing Clara was still chatting away.

"That's why they plug us into that machine, you know? The one with the wires and the big TV? That's how they triage us. They watch parts of our life as if it were a VHS to them, and then figure out how best to use the skills we have." She suddenly stopped drawing on the wall. Looking down, sullen-faced, she added. "When I got here, some old *hombre* with white whiskers, the guy who used to be in your cell, in fact, he said he had a pretty good idea of what was going on here."

The man's name was Theodore, Ted for short. According to her fellow *illegal*, Ted had been imprisoned here for about two weeks before being dragged like a rag doll through the shiny doors.

✺

The Countess of Santa Clara

Three days ago

What her crime was, she did not know. But at least she remembered her name. Clara. Those people in uniforms had thrown her in jail, discarded her like you would a bad draft. She was a writer, or at least an aspiring one, according to a series of images pulled from her mind. Unlike her heroine from The Final Frost, there was no freezing of the bars to escape and probably no members of the A.R.C. coming to her rescue.

Once her breathing came back to normal, she took a moment to survey her surroundings. Clara was not alone. Half a dozen prisoners sat quietly, awaiting uncertainty. Then she made accidental eye contact with one of them, an old guy sitting cross-legged in the cell next to hers. The writer was not sure where she was exactly, but she was certain that locking eyes with a stranger in a place such as this one would only lead to an awkward situation. The old man smiled. There it is, she thought. He reached into his pants pocket and pulled something out. It was crudely wrapped, about three inches wide.

"Cookie?" he asked, handing her the wrapping.

Clara would have politely declined had it not been for her grumbling stomach answering first. The old man chuckled quietly.

"Name's Theodore, Ted for short," he continued as Clara nibbled on a stale wafer. "Everything will be okay. You'll see," then he turned around, lay down on the hard floor, and started snoring.

And the best part was, she believed him. Yes, we'll be fine.

Two days ago

Clara woke up, shivering from cold, to the sounds of struggling. In one of the furthest cells, someone was about to be dragged through The Door. Still confused from having just woken up from a dreamless rest, Clara felt herself panic, but out of the corner of her eye, she saw Ted subtly motioning to her to slow her breathing. Clara willed herself to close her mind to the atrocities that were happening around her and quietly counted to ten in her head.

One... Two... Three... Four... Five... Six... Seven... Eight... Nine... Ten...

The door slammed shut.

Everything became quiet.

Clara unclenched her fists. Wet streaks rolled down her face.

"Don't do that to yourself," Ted had told her. "The earlier you realize we are nothing to them, the easier it'll be when your turn comes." Clara froze. "Sorry, I didn't mean it like that."

The old man half-crawled, half-dragged himself to the bars separating his and Clara's cells. He leaned against them, letting his head rest there, and, with a wave of his hand, pushed dirty hair out of his face.

"Here's how it is," he continued in a hush-hush tone. "This place, I have a feeling no one on the outside knows about it, or at least knows what's going on in here. I've been here for a while, you know, and I've learned that if you shut up, comply, but keep your ears open, you'll pick up bits and pieces of knowledge here and there. For instance," he continued in his soft monotone voice, "I suppose we were sent, voluntold really, to participate in time traveling-related projects: cutting edge and dangerous, new updates to the time bracelets, a portable time traveling device, new destinations—"

Old man Ted had to stop himself for a moment. The sound of a metal door scratching at the floor was soon followed by the boom of heavy boots. This time, Clara kept still but also preserved her cool.

Eyes low, she dialed in on what the guards were saying. Strays... Another... Tighter schedule... The future.

A few minutes later, silence crept back into the cell block. Clara was happy she was not the one to have gone through those doors. However, a frightening feeling enveloped her: she did not like how fast it took her to become numb to all of this.

"You see now? The race for the future is in full swing. They used to bring one of us through every two to three days. At this rate," Ted looked around at the remaining five prisoners, "we'll all be goners in three."

With nothing else to do, Clara crossed her arms and propped her head against the concrete wall, soon drifting to sleep.

When she finally came to, which felt only like a few minutes to her, she examined her surroundings. Something did not add up. Her eyes met Ted's. He simply said: "And then there were four."

Yesterday

The day started in the same fashion as the morning before. Like a rooster announcing the dawn of a brand new day, an unkempt, skinny Stray was hastily dragged through The Door. However, this time, Clara did not have to count to ten to calm herself down. The captors had a job to do, and they were frantic, almost as if they were running out of time. She was no idiot either; with only three prisoners remaining, she knew it was only a matter of time before she was the one to be carried through.

To be frank, the last few people to have been taken away had disgusted her. Sure, the fuzz acted like those Aryan bastards from the forties, but what had put her off was the way the prisoners were going to their presumed deaths. Hijos de putas, she swore inwardly. They will not get the satisfaction of breaking me. When her time came, she promised to no one in particular, she would meet her maker with dignity.

But was she ready for what was to come?

The old man in the cell next to hers hadn't said a thing since the night before. His head rested against the wall, eyes closed. Ted's turn was coming. She knew it, and so did he. Clara would have liked to reassure him; tell him everything was going to be okay the way he had when she was on the brink of breaking down.

"You alright there, Ted?"

He did not reply with his words but lifted a thumb and drew a frail smile on his lips. But even that seemed to take a monumental amount of effort. His breathing was shallow, chest barely rising. Was it Clara's imagination or did he look paler than the first time they met? Now that she was paying attention, she caught sight of beads of sweat trickling down the old Stray's forehead.

"Ted?"

He coughed once. That was the last noise he'd ever make.

Far over to Clara's left, the other remaining prisoner hummed a song that reverberated over the cell's walls. She guessed, at first, that it was intended to be heard only by the singer himself, but as the minutes passed, the emptiness of her world filled with the words of who, she guessed, had been a time displaced minstrel.

M'lord, M'lady, such a tale needs being told
I've been stuck in this world, most unpleasant and cold
Would you care to hear it, be entertained for a bit
For a ballad of time, let me shed some light
On what will be known as the Dead of Night

They broke my lyre, who would have thought
That the future, for beauty, could care not
They splintered the wood, ripped out the strings
And all through the while, not a bird did sing
So it begins, in the Dead of Night

M'lord, M'lady, my account is biased

My hate for them, truly the driest

In the dead of the night, no music rang

But I'll break down these walls, that is why I sang

What will you do

When it's your turn to venture

In the Dead of Night

Let it burn or quencher

For no help is coming, there is no white knight

When you're stuck, all alone, in the Dead of Night

Should these be my final words

A message of hope, as fragile as sherds

Dead of Night

Dead of Night

M'lord, M'lady, I bid you goodbye

For in the Dead of Night, my end is nigh

Upon the last spoken word, like a melodic clang, the door swung open, and men in uniform came to drag the singer away. He did not fight much, as though his will to live had left his body the second the last note left his throat.

Clara sat alone in the dark, singing to herself. "In the Dead of Night."

⟨∿⟩

"But here's the kicker!" she said after finishing her story. "Nobody can get by that time barrier unscathed. Ask me how I know that."

Willa obliged. "How do you know?"

"Glad you asked. Two reasons." She lifted a finger. "One. I heard one of them mention it a couple of hours ago. And two." She halfheartedly raised another finger. "The smell."

"The smell of what?" she asked, half curious, half-scared of the answer. But Clara never replied. Some questions were better kept unanswered.

Her eyes were fixed on the silver door when they heard them. Footsteps. Clara slowly exhaled before looking the younger woman in the eye.

"It was nice chatting with you, Eighties Willa. See you on the other side, okay?"

To say she was at a loss for words would be an understatement. Everything happened in slow motion. Three time police officers in dark uniforms entered the corridor. The one with the key grinned at Willa as he opened Clara's door. *You're next*, he mouthed at her. The other two rushed in, batons raised, expecting resistance. But she never flinched. It looked as though she knew there was no point in fighting back.

As they carried her toward, what? The future? Willa swore she caught a glimpse of a wink from her new friend. A sort of playful *see you later*, knowing full well where—rather when—she was going. They went through the silver door and closed it behind them. Leaving only a resonating echo to keep her company.

This show of serenity was exactly the boost she needed to take control of her emotions. Then she realized—Willa had to escape, although she knew not how.

Frantically looking around, she noticed something. In their robust haste, they didn't bother examining the writing Clara had left on her wall.

"Well then. Maybe art *can* survive in a place like this after all," Willa mumbled as she read Clara's poem. A testament to her strength. One last hurrah.

Where am I from?
They ask.
From somewhen, I answer

But still.

Bonds of yesteryears?

A time long gone.

Though I reside here

Somewhere in this timeline.

I fight for the future

As much as for the past

A shiny door, my salvation,

Or my end.

Where are you from?

No one knows here,

All I know

Is where I'm going.

〰

0 day(s): 2 hour(s): 27 minute(s): 36 second(s)

CHAPTER 21 - Bill & Stray

Lights Out

A few hours before Chronos' press conference.

The next morning after his little trip through the World's Wonders, at approximately seven thirty, Bill sat at a chair surrounded by the Society's second in command as well as the other members who usually got called in when a big mission was afoot. Leader One, who was most than likely awaiting divorce papers, had called in this emergency meeting to address LETO's most recent message: What to do with Site B. The email he'd sent his small strike team contained the same information and schematics LETO had sent him. The thought was for them to be properly briefed and ready to produce ideas and plans.

Bill was of no help. With a cup of strong black tea in one hand, the other cradling his bruised ribs. He was so tired he felt hungover, like that hazy state of mind people often get into when sleep has eluded them. He'd tried going to bed after having sent his message to the Society, truly, but Ginny's perfume clung to the sheets and had kept him awake.

Carmen, who had vanished before he came back to his current timeline, had been texting him non-stop since past midnight. He'd been ignoring her, part resentment, part guilt, but all of it ate at him, and before he knew it, the sun was up.

Following the Monaco mission, the Society of Timeline Liberation elected to expand its guerilla branch to counter more efficiently against Washington and his attacks on Lady Time. A referendum voted with a majority for a cell to work out of a "secret" basement of a local grocery store located near Chronos' headquarters. Although the location was questioned at length, it was undeniable to all that the site proposed had superior tactical advantages. And here they were, Wednesday morning, on the twenty-third of October, devising plans to infiltrate an until-now mythical building that housed horrors worse than the bleeding of timelines: Site B.

Despite the early morning hour, the meeting was already in full swing. "Yes, I saw the plans," someone to the left of Bill exclaimed.

"Doesn't mean I understand them. How the hell are we supposed to get in?"

"I got you, Sherm," replied a big guy with comically small round glasses. "What we need is a diversion. This place is probably full of that Time Police Force. We need to flush 'em out."

"Easier said than done, Mike," commented a blond woman in red slacks. "Got any ideas?"

"Nope, ain't that why you're here, H?" asked the glasses guy.

"I mean, we could drag them out and bring them to HQ." Hilda was taking notes, biting the tip of her pen as thoughts popped into her head. "Yo, Bill. LETO is supposed to hold a couple of clients hostage, right?" She waited. Then seeing he wasn't listening, she repeated herself. "Bill. LETO's got herself hostages, right?"

"Ummm... Yeah. Sixteen or something like that. LETO's been in their system since last night." He took a small sip of his too-hot tea and winced.

"Right," Hilda continued. "So there you have it, that's our diversion. Washington is bound to call a press conference when the public finds out about this certain situation."

"How would they find out? Who's gonna tell 'em?" asked Sherm with a childish smile on his face.

"Leave that to me. Who knew social media could have such devastating powers?" And on that note, she took out her phone and started drafting something.

"While you're at it," thought Dorian out loud, Bill's 2IC. "Let's really shake the world."

"Announcing that a bunch of people are stuck in a time machine isn't enough?" asked Mike.

"I'm thinking bigger. We've finally got solid proof of how crooked they are," Dorian continued while pointing at the schematics. "Let's reveal them to the world. Expose to everyone this Site B and let the people have their say."

"I don't know, D," replied Sherm, who always seemed to be the most pacifist of the bunch. "Seems pretty drastic. Sure, we want to see them close down and all, but... heck, I don't wanna see anybody hurt, is all. Bill?"

They all looked at him. He was, after all, Leader One. With such a position came the added responsibility to have the final say on such things. He sat up straighter, caressing his side as he did so. In short breaths, he told them exactly what was about to unfold.

↞↠

A few moments after the Chronos' press conference.

Alex woke up with a massive headache. They kept replaying the scene in their head from last night, where they left Roxy to go rescue whoever was in trouble. They'd gotten there too late. A group of time police was already all over the poor person, their arms handcuffed behind their back. The Stray looked to have no more fight in them. Had they been drugged? Begrudgingly, powerless (and shoeless, for Alex had given their shoes to Roxy), they returned to the house by themself. The first thing Kari said when Alex walked in was a tad confusing, to say the least.

"What do you mean 'where's Roxy'?" they inquired. "She didn't make it back?"

Kari only shook her head "No," and, just like that, Alex bolted right back where they'd come from, leaving the front door wide open behind them.

Someone knocked on Alex's bedroom door softly.

"Come in," they replied in a grumbly voice.

It was John. "Good morning, fearless leader," he said with a smile.

"Shut up," they replied in the same way.

"I got you some to eat," John approached Alex with a tray of toast, fruits, and OJ. "What time did you get back in anyway?"

"I don't even know." They sat back up, rubbing the sleep out of their eyes. "What time is it?"

"Eleven-forty-five," he answered, glancing at his watch. "You know, we went looking too."

Alex looked up from their improvised brunch.

"You left so quickly. We knew something was wrong. And, umm..."

"Go on," Alex said encouragingly.

"I didn't know you felt that strongly about her."

Alex cocked their head sideways, confused. "What do you mean? I would have done the same thing had any of you gone missing too. You know that."

"That's not what I meant," he let the words hang over them for a second.

"Oh!" Alex replied once they'd finally clued in. "Right. I wouldn't worry about that too much."

"No?" John replied, a little too hopeful.

"Nah, not really our choice anyway, right?"

After that little heart-to-heart moment, which truly made John feel better, Kari barged in with a tablet in her hands. She looked significantly too excited.

"You guys are never going to believe what the Society just found."

They both waited for her to continue.

"Site B!"

"What?!" Alex shot up, their migraine suddenly mysteriously gone. "Show me that."

Kari handed them the tablet. Alex browsed the text, John reading over his friend's shoulder.

"You can't be serious," John ejaculated after having read most of the message.

"The Society is calling for help. This is our chance to do more than what we've been doing thus far." Then she added, "A chance to maybe get Roxy back."

"You know Alex had made up their mind to go even before you brought up the Muse, right?" said Max from the doorway. Akiro was standing behind him, grinning.

Alex finally put down the tablet.

"Gear up, Heroes. Time to storm the enemy's base."

Willa must have been at it for an hour before the pain became too much to handle. She admitted that trying to kick down a cell door and punch through a concrete wall were no clever ideas. She leaned against the unscathed wall, her back to it. Slowly, she slid to the floor. Using her sweat-soaked shirt, Willa wiped the blood that was needlessly spilling from her mauled knuckles. But she was not giving up, far from it. Not yet, at least.

One moment after another, she charged at her cell door. Although this action produced the same result every time: Willa, falling to her ass, her shoulder throbbing, and her head ringing. She did not stop. *I will not stop.*

It was strange, though. She noticed no one was coming to stop her. Did they know something she didn't? Did the guards understand how futile her attempt at escaping was? And yet, these attempts and the energy it took to sustain the assault lessened every time she fell to the cold, hard ground. Was she about to give up?

Then something caught her ear. A commotion outside her tiny, barred window made itself heard. In the beginning, she figured it was only cars or something like that. Then the noise had gotten louder. She didn't believe it at first but the sound never subsided, and now, the uproar of an angry mob gathered at the foot of her tower. The crowd, she could not see them, but from their voices, the girl could have guessed hundreds had milled nearby. The words *Freedom*, *Stray*, and *Chronos* manifested loudly on everybody's lips. She wondered if John was among them, the same was true for Kari, Max, and Akiro—the Heroes of Ancient Times! What about Alex? Were they given a chance, Willa was certain Alex would be at the forefront of the group of agitators outside. For some unexplained reason, the energy of the gathered mass was invigorating. The prisoner stood up, determined to run through those bars.

Thank you, Alex, she thought. *I'm coming.*

Willa jumped up and down, gearing herself up. She planted her feet firmly into the ground. Then she ran, four quick, powerful steps. That was it! She was mere milliseconds away from freedom. Her shoulder made contact with the bars first—the head hit second. Then, total darkness.

When she finally came to, Willa had no idea how much time had passed between the blackout and the resurgence of lights. However, she was sure of three things: first, she was concussed. Second, her shoulder was dislocated, and third, her ego was badly bruised. She lay there, motionless for a while, trying hopelessly to redistribute the pain by biting down hard on her tongue. It occurred to the young woman that, maybe, she should just stop thinking for a moment and not come up with ridiculous plans. She just lay where she had fallen, motionless. What was the point anyway? Nothing was working.

"Goddamn, don't tell me it's dead. Come on, get up!" suddenly said an irate voice.

Willa opened an eye. The lone guard opened the door and then knelt at her feet. He looked relieved to see the prisoner alive. Why was there only one of them? Did he come to free her? Thoughts were running free through her mind. *Oh! Maybe he works for that Timeline Liberation Society thing Alex had talked about.*

"Oh good, you're alive," he seemed relieved.

She smiled at him. The man in the dark uniform proceeded to grab her by the ankles and dragged her out of the cell towards the shiny death door. *Nope*, she concluded, *not a friend*. This did not bode well at all.

Soon after, Willa, still unwilling to move her own body, felt her legs dropping to the ground. The time police reached at his side, picking up his ID badge. After swiping it, making a little red light turn green, he let it go, and the card swiftly retracted, bungeeing back at the man's side. Then he hurriedly yelled something, and two pairs of hands lifted the inert body back to a standing position. As much as she would have preferred not to be touched by these people, Willa was confident she would have fallen flat on her face were they not still holding on to her.

They shuffled into the *Future Room*, the one where Clara and countless others before her had very likely encountered an unfortunate fate. She could smell it now, the horrendous odour of burned hair. Where were they taking her? This room was gigantic! The size of half a football field at the very least and nearly as high. Then, the guinea pig's gaze fell on the structure in front of her, the one she was inevitably being led to.

There, in the middle of this mysterious mind-torture chamber, were mirror panels reflecting the darkest of lights Willa had ever seen in her life. As they, the girl and her handlers, neared it, the glass walls, five in all, pivoted on themselves, revealing a bright, almost too-white center.

At one point, soon after the revelation of the blinding light, she hadn't even realized that the guards holding her had stepped away. Willa was petrified, to say the least. Muscles unmoving, mind racing. *Willa, you've got to do something!*

A lady wearing a dark blue lab coat approached the adolescent and started explaining the procedure she was about to experience. But the subject wasn't listening. Her mind raced back to that man who had dared question the humane aspect of these procedures. Was her life worth this little to them? *I guess conscience is a thing that isn't meant for everyone.* As she thought those words, the lady affixed a metallic bracelet to the youth's wrist. It felt bulky on her slim forearm. Was it made of copper? The scientist then stepped back as if to let Willa walk to her doom on her own. Someone else put a big hand on her shoulder and said, "You're going to be a hero," before shoving her forward.

Awkwardly, Willa advanced at a snail's pace toward the white light. *Think, damnit! Think!* Inching, unhurriedly, forward. *I'm not ready.* Before she knew it, she'd passed the mirrored panels and was standing on the pentagon-shaped floor. The smell wasn't too bad here, weirdly. Suddenly, an odd whirring sound was launched. The portal to the future had been activated, and the doors were closing slowly. As the panels closed, Willa saw a little cloud form in front of her, voices and sounds faintly coming out of it. She took a final look at the panels, which were almost completely closed. *If you are going to do something, anything, now is the time.*

Deus Ex Machina.

Everything went black. This one was different from her earlier blackout. The lights had gone out, but her mind was fired up. The protesters outside must have done something. Not wasting a second, she quietly snuck out of the BBQ. The backup generators brought the power back online a few seconds later. Still, those five seconds were all Willa needed.

Confusion was easily readable on her captors' faces when they noticed her disappearance. And confusion quickly turned to anger when she elbowed the nearest guard in the ribs with her good arm, stealing his swipe card. They had not expected this. The element of surprise was unquestionably on the girl's side.

Trying to escape, adrenaline pumping through her, she rugby-tackled one assailant and clotheslined another. At the exit, with a time police and a scientist closing in behind her, Willa awkwardly swiped the badge. To her immense relief, the door slid open. She did not know where she was going, but she started running down a long corridor like her hair was on fire.

〜

Sometime before the blackout.

Shortly after Richard Washington's press conference, STL sympathizers had gathered in front of Site B, and they were loud!

Leader One and his team had effectively revealed the location of this supposedly nonexistent building, and within minutes, the spark sent social media ablaze. With everything that was going on at Chronos HQ, the masses did not need much more convincing to gather and show their disagreement. With megaphones, protest signs, and face masks, for some, the less-than-happy mob was doing exactly what Leader One had expected: providing an effective distraction.

With his small unit, he marched to where the underground tunnel was supposedly situated. Knee-deep in muck, they slowly advanced toward their target. And there it was, an old sewage tunnel covered in vines but readily accessible. Crawling inside the concrete passage, the small group noticed how the noise was getting fainter with every step.

"Something's not right," said a female Liberator, her voice cutting through the semi-darkness. "Where are the guards? We should have seen someone by now. No way they don't monitor this exit."

"Careful what you wish for," replied someone behind her half-jokingly.

They were armed and ready to protect themselves had the situation demanded it, but Leader One was relieved that no bullets were flying his way. After what had happened last night, the fewer lives lost were for the best. The mission would surely go much more smoothly if this lack of resistance persisted.

"Here," said the GPS guy, pointing to a ladder. "This one should get us within a few feet of the electrical room."

Bill was first to climb the metal rungs, one by one. When he finally arrived at the top, he noticed an orange handle. There was always a chance for someone, an enemy, to be waiting topside. He took his pistol out of his belt and, with the other hand, slowly turned the handle clockwise. *Here goes nothing.* It went 'click.' Carefully, excruciatingly slowly, he lifted the lid open, holding his breath. Nothing happened; he wasn't getting shot at. *That's a good sign.* With a little bit more gusto, he finished opening the hatch, looked around, and whispered to his comrades below: "Clear."

One after the other, the team entered what looked like a bigger-than-average closet-size room. With an ear to the door, they waited to hear whether the coast was clear.

"It's just in the other room, like right there," the tech guy murmured as he motioned to the dark wall in front of him.

"Shhh!" someone exclaimed.

"Sorry."

"Seems empty. On your command, Leader One."

"Go for it," he replied after considering it for an instant.

They swung the door and, as advertised, the corridor was empty. Not a single TP or scientist in view. As relieved as he was, the situation also made Leader One uneasy. *Where the bloody hell are they?* In single file, weapons at the ready, they moved on to the following door—ELECTRICAL CONTROL ROOM. With two Liberators guarding the entrance, it gave the tech guy some time and ease of mind to focus on his part of the mission.

"Blue wire... here. Green... there," he whispered to himself.

"How's it going, Sherm?"

"Almost there, Leader One." He hooked up a couple of recently spliced wires to a device resembling a smartphone. "It's up to you guys now. Get ready. In three, two, one—"

Lights out.

〰

0 day(s): 1 hour(s): 33 minute(s): 27 second(s)

CHAPTER 22 - Washington

Let the Chase Begin

After a careful game of *finding a needle in the digital haystack*, Chronos' system was back online. Well, sort of. Richard's team could finally see the destinations in the computer's lines of code. They could also, technically, send more parties to the past if they wanted to. But Mr. Washington, with so much at stake, did not dare entertain the idea of losing more guests inside his creation.

"They're somewhere in our system, for crying out loud. Find them!"

Stone-faced, with a chilly demeanor, he told his employees very clearly that not a word of this was to leave this room. Fruits and veggies were flying around his head quite enough as it was. He did not need the feds to barge in and assume a fake sense of control. Wreckage, that's what they would bring. And what of the Colonel? Richard was sure to get an earful, something referencing the fact that civilian enterprises were weakly managed and always doomed to fail. *I created Chronos,* he thought. *No one will take it away from me. Especially not Marsh and his little experiments at—* Richard stopped mid-thought. Site B!

What if *she*, the virus that was grounding everything, was looking for someone from *her* time? If this *Willa Watson* was a Stray, maybe Marsh's goons caught up to her and, with any luck, she was still in their custody.

Richard moved with renewed positivity toward the back office, a small windowless area attached to the tech room. He didn't even bother sitting down. Richard got to the phone and dialed an unregistered number. After a couple of rings, a suave male voice answered.

"IndigoSun Tech, Sylvain speaking. How may I direct your call?"

IST was a covert, secret name for Site B. Richard gave the man on the other line his credentials and was immediately transferred to the time police office.

"Mitchell," said a no-nonsense, rough voice.

"Washington here. Looking for a Stray. Need location ASAP."

"Name?"

"Watson, Willa."

Clicking noises could be heard over the receptor. A few seconds later, the man on the other side confirmed that he had found Watson in the system. She was brought in early this very morning. Richard couldn't help but sigh in relief. He let himself fall to a chair, it squeaked under his weight. With a smile on his face, Richard combed through his greying hair with his free hand. *Everything will be alright now.* He glanced at his watch, two-twenty-nine.

"How soon can you guys arrange a transfer?"

"With the crowd outside, ten to fifteen minutes, sir."

With all the commotion down here at Chronos HQ, the Society of Timeline Liberation's riots at Site B had momentarily escaped his mind. *Right, not ideal, but doable.*

"One more thing." *Uh-oh.* "The Stray, Watson, was categorized as 'expendable' following Memory Shock Therapy."

"Christ." Richard, unfortunately, knew what that meant. She'd probably been vaporized like the others who were bound for the future.

"It... escaped, sir," Mitchell continued.

"What!?"

"The STL managed to cut the power line, and, during that time, all hell broke loose. It took this opportunity to sneak out amongst the rioters."

Richard was about to throw the phone to the wall but restrained himself, arm in midair. He honestly did not know how to feel. Angry, because an asset was on the loose? Elated, because he still had a chance to keep his company alive? The problem now was finding her. Where would they start? He checked the time again. Was his watch running fast? Less than thirty minutes before Chronos was to go belly-up.

"Sir?" the man inquired after an uncomfortable airwave silence.

"Where was she picked up?" Washington mumbled.

"Checking now," more keyboarding sounds. "By a small creek, near a house registered to an ex-Chronos employee."

"That's where we'll start."

"Sir?" replied the man, clearly confused.

"You will assemble a team, find her, and bring her here to Chronos HQ." Richard was very assertive in his tone.

"With all due respect, sir, only Colonel Marsh has the authority to deploy the Force."

"To hell with Marsh!" answered Washington, irritated. "Let me use lingo you'll understand. We're at war, son! And the enemy is right up our asses. She has civilian hostages and won't hesitate to kill. If we don't deliver Watson by fifteen hundred hours, everything we have done will be exposed to the public. And we all know the fires of a civil war are less douseable than an all-out war's." Silence on the other side. "Have I made myself clear, soldier?"

"Sir, yes, sir!"

〰

It took less than five minutes for what was left of the Force to assemble downstairs in an underground garage. Decked out in their dark uniform, dark helmet, and face coverings, they looked ready for any type of mission. And this particular one would be especially important.

"Alright, listen up," announced the commanding officer. "This is a high-priority operation. We are to find the Stray known as Willa Watson and bring it home to Chronos HQ before fifteen hundred hours. It escaped Site B less than an hour ago and is presumed to be working alone. Should we fail this, lives will be lost... and prison time will most likely be in our future."

Normal humans would have grumbled or felt uneasy even. But not these hardened GIs. Although they knew what was at stake, they were here for one reason and one purpose. The Time Police Force was elite, and this mission had to succeed.

"Alpha group," he pointed to three men. "For your assignment, you will search the woods where Watson was found. It is not much of a lead, but that is all the intel we have for now." The trio nodded. "Beta group, you're with me. We will investigate the perimeter surrounding those woods. More specifically, houses and buildings that might have harbored the Stray before its arrest." The small militia of men and women standing in front of him didn't budge, waiting obediently for their dismissal. *Well-trained dogs*, the commander thought.

"Let's break."

And with that, the Sevens entered their vehicle, a nondescript inconspicuous sedan. As they emerged from the garage, some six hundred metres from the horde of STL rioters, the Alpha group veered west, whereas the Beta group continued north. This was a manhunt, pure and simple. In twenty minutes, they would either be heroes—or criminals.

Let the chase begin!

～

0 day(s): 0 hour(s): 20 minute(s): 18 second(s)

From: leaderone@timeserver.net

To: LETO@timeserver.net

Subject: Site B

LETO,

Site B is no longer operational. The machine, which you had requested should be our number one priority, was a prototype of some sort meant to send people into the Future. We know this from other blueprints and notes left scattered across the floor as well as testimonies from less than willing participants—

You'll be glad to know we C-4ed the damn thing to hell.

CONSIDERATION

Site B was eerily empty. We walked through with little to no opposition. Most computers had already been wiped, and filing cabinets cleared of the most important stuff.

Although Site B will no longer be of use to the Scythe, I fear they might have been up to something for a while. With your permission, we will look into it right away.

P.S. We rescued a few time displaced folks, those who had been put to work by the Scythe in a wing far away from the machine. They told us there might be others in the prisons, but none were found.

CHAPTER 23 - Stray

The Big House

Willa did not exactly remember how, but she did it! She escaped that hellish place, this Site B. There were so many people outside, screaming and chanting. None of them minded her, leaving the bloodied, crazy-looking person to her own devices. Oh well, freedom was freedom, and it felt good. But the girl knew she wasn't out of the woods yet. Where could she go? It wasn't like she could jump on a plane and return to Canada, could she? Were her mom, brother, and Lacy waiting for her? Did they exist in this timeline? *Do I exist in this timeline?*

She had to have a plan, a good plan, a well-thought-out plan. In other words, everything was to be improvised.

Running down the street, holding her dislocated arm, the escapee followed her feet until the pain was too much to handle. Her breathing was heavy when she stopped walking. As she raised her eyes, taking in her surroundings, she realized she was *back*. Not exactly sure back where, but the grass, the trees, and the path seemed familiar. She continued walking, at crawling speeds, for another minute or so before hearing rhythmic footsteps hitting the forest ground hard. As fast as she could manage, Willa shuffled toward the nearest bush, planning to hide herself.

She wasn't fast enough.

"Roxy?"

The jogger's voice surprised her.

"Alex?!" she said, turning around, and going in for a hug. She was so happy to see them. Tears swelled in her eyes. It was only when she pulled away from Alex's arm that she realized they were not alone. Akiro, Kari, Max, and John were all breathing hard a few steps behind them.

"What the hell happened to you?" Kari questioned, looking her friend up and down.

"Roxy, let's get you outta here first," Alex replied in a hushed voice. Almost as if they were only talking to her.

"By the way," Willa said, wincing. "I'm really Willa."

The group nodded and said nothing else, as if it were the simplest of statements in the world.

By that point, Alex and Akiro carried most of the broken girl's body weight. She was so tired; she couldn't even put two words together. How long before she fell asleep in their arms?

What were the chances of her friends almost literally running into her? The one and only group of people she had ever trusted in this timeline. After everything that had happened to her, dark thoughts invaded her fragile mind. *What if it was not a coincidence?* Willa turned her head and looked at Alex intently. Their mom used to work for Chronos, didn't she? What if they were one of them? And just as easily as the thought came, it disappeared. *Nah, that's impossible.*

When all six teens arrived at Alex's house, which was probably only a fifteen-minute walk, but felt excruciatingly much longer, Alex single-handedly brought her up the stairs and into her old room. Her friend—she had never truly realized how strong they were—deposited her broken body on the mattress as gently as they could and promptly directed their attention to her swollen wrist. Willa closed her eyes a second, and a moment later, when she reopened them, Alex had a medic bag opened beside them. As Alex tended to her hand and shoulder, they tried to keep her out of unconsciousness by talking to her, asking her where she'd been and who had done this. A shiver went down Willa's spine when they brushed a strand of her hair to take a closer look at her bleeding forehead.

After a while, she finally said, "I know." Her voice was weak.

"What's that?" they replied, gently tightening a sling around her neck.

"Who I am. They did something to me. Gave me back my memories, I guess."

"That's great, Rox—Willa! I'm sorry you had to go through... Whatever you went through. But you must be glad to finally know."

She shrugged. Was there a good answer to that question?

"What were you doing?" Willa asked. "I mean, where did you come from?"

"Believe it or not," they started, "we took part in a riot. Site B is real. Once we got there, we tried to sneak in, but the time police were keeping everyone out of the front gate. Is that where you were?"

She nodded.

"I'm so sorry," Alex replied in a broken voice.

Willa put her good hand on their shoulder. They looked at her. There was something in their eyes. A mix of pain and anger. The sort of fire that fills people's eyes when they're about to do something utterly reckless.

"Hey, Alex." It was John, and from the shake in his voice, whatever he came to say probably wasn't good. "You better come downstairs."

"What is it?" they replied in a tone much different than the soft one they'd used with Willa—a much, much more vicious one. Their eyes had stayed locked on Willa's.

John took a step back, startled. "There's someone here."

Alex had turned their head so fast toward John. Their facial traits looked more beast than human.

"Looks like time police," John finally said, half-hiding behind the door frame.

At those words, Alex sprung up. They reached the bedroom door in a few steps and would have pushed John out of the way had he not moved in time.

No one had ever seen Alex Nash so pissed.

Years of pent-up feelings finally boiled over. They were mad at Chronos for compromising their mom, mad at Chronos for stealing her away from them, and mad at Chronos for hurting their friend. And now, of all things, one of them was in the house Roxanne Nash and her child had called home. Alex would have none of it.

John stared at Alex stumping down the stairs before slowly turning his head toward Willa. "Should I go with him?"

Willa nodded.

"Alright, stay put, don't go anywhere."

Willa rolled her eyes. *Do I look like someone who wants to and/or can move?* He left the room, leaving the door ajar.

The person at the front door must have been impatient, for it seemed like the conversation, oral jousting between Alex and the unknown man in uniform, was reverberating through the entire house. Both of them were exchanging heated words, not one yielding to the other. Alex wanted him and his comrades to leave this property immediately. The other meant no harm, so he said, only looking for a lost child, a runaway teen named Willa Watson.

At the sound of her own name, she couldn't resist it any longer. Curiosity pushed her to more intently eavesdrop on the conversation. As much as possible, in her current state, she arched her neck to see if she could maybe make out the face of who Alex was talking to. Slowly, she got out of bed and slowly snuck to the door. She peeked out. Although Willa was not able to recognize the face, the sight of the dark uniform sent her heart racing. Presently standing behind the wooden door, it was much easier to hear what was being said.

"—not what I've been told," the man from Site B continued. "Have you watched the news recently? Eighteen people are currently being held hostage by some psycho-hacker. And you, with your cooperation, could be a hero. What is more important to you? Protecting it? A Stray? Or saving the lives of our fellow citizens who are actually from this timeline?"

It? It wasn't the first time Willa had heard someone referencing Strays as nothing but things. To him, she was nothing more than an object. A misplaced thing, an inconvenience, a bargaining chip. From her vantage point, Willa only saw Alex's back. They were unmoving, a strong oak in a windstorm. Nothing could make them bend. Except maybe lightning.

"Say, that's a mighty nice house," the agent said while crossing his arms across his chest. "Used to belong to a Chronos employee until, you know, she disappeared." A smirk appeared on his face.

"You're not her kid, are you? Damn, what a legacy she left you. A criminal."

Alex's face twitched ever so slightly, but the man noticed how uncomfortable he was making them. To make matters worse, three other time police soldiers closed in behind the first one. The evil leader kept going.

"A coward, really. Who just goes and hides like this? Leaving her kid behind to fend for themselves."

Breathe, Alex. But breathing didn't help. Both hands were clenched into fists, making knuckles whiter by the second. As much as they condemned their mom for what she had done, Roxanne Nash was still the one who'd raised and cared for them when very few others had even tried. Alex would not stand there and let this low-life, albeit massively built, goon spit on their mother's name.

"For the last time," Alex asked in a most polite voice, "please leave the premises."

"Ha-ha, or what?"

Alex was not sure what they could do against four grown and trained adults. But then, a hand rested on their shoulder. It was John. He simply nodded at them as if to say, *got your back*. Not long after, Kari, Max, and Akiro also shouldered Alex in an effort to show solidarity.

"I see how it is. Sorry for intruding." The big man turned and took a couple of steps away from the house.

Willa could barely believe it. Her friends, people she'd met only a few weeks ago and who owed her nothing, stood up against metaphorical tyranny to save one of their own. Suddenly, the large officer turned his head around and looked directly at Willa. In her excitement, she'd made her way to the upstairs railing. What a blunder!

"Why, hello there." The military squad had turned and walked toward the door as a unit, toward Willa.

The Heroes assumed a fighter's stance. The physical comparison between the two groups was laughable. Other than John, everyone looked like a wet stick. On the other team, every member of the TPF resembled a large black bear.

With a beastly smile and still advancing, the leader said, "Alright, kids, nobody needs to get hurt. She needs to come with—"

He did not have time to complete his sentence, for he was rudely interrupted by John's mighty fist squarely connecting with his big ugly mug. The man in command was knocked straight down to his arse. Alex looked from the felled man to their friend, who was shaking his hand, and then to Willa.

"What are you waiting for?" they asked, a hint of fear in their eyes. "Run!"

Alex was right. The fight was not won yet. Although the agent was caught by surprise the first time, he stood right back up and tackled John with villainous ferocity. Both of them went flying right in the middle of the hallway.

That was how the clash started. The Battle of the Strays. Alex had their hands busy with an officer wielding a baton a few feet from the doorway. Max and Akiro, out on the veranda, double-teamed a blond-haired dude with fists the size of watermelons. Kari had been able to grab her bow and her quiver before jumping out of the window and heading to the tree line. As expected, the fourth and last member of the TPF followed at a run with what looked like a taser stick in one hand and a riot shield in the other.

The exit was right there in front of Willa. Freedom was within her reach!

She ran past John and Alex and jumped off the porch, stumbling a bit as she landed. *Alright, where to next?* Willa chanced a look behind, making sure no one in a dark suit was following. She took three or four steps in the direction of the woods, and then something pulled her hard from behind, choking her and knocking her flat on her back. The watermelon-fist guy had her tattered shirt collar in one hand. Gasping for air and wheezing, the young girl searched for the face responsible for her misfortune. But all she saw was a knee pinning her head sideways, digging into the grassy nature floor.

"I got it," he said, speaking into his radio. "Bring the car 'round and let the boss know."

In the distance, Willa saw the one that had chased Kari run away from her, an arrow stuck in the shield. Shortly thereafter, Big-Fist rolled Willa over on her stomach, handcuffing both wrists behind her back. She screamed in agony when her messed-up arm was hastily swung backward. As she was getting her face pushed deeper into the turf, muffling any further attempts at wailing or sobbing on her part, Max and Akiro both jumped on the goon's back, hitting him with bare hands and sticks they'd found lying nearby on the ground. Their effort was fruitless.

By the time the car showed up, all of the Heroes had been neutralized. Kari had no more arrows to shoot, and Max and Akiro were easily pinned down by the blond officer. John was lying unconscious on the porch's railing, and Alex, bloody-faced, had a foot digging into their back and their hair pulled roughly.

Willa was thrown headfirst into the backseat of the black sedan. Whilst her cheek hit the interior door handle on the other side, all she could think about was *Gosh. I hope they'll be okay.* And just like that, with a driver and Willa in the back, the car pulled away from the house, leaving the rest to an uncertain future. What would happen to her friends?

On their way to HQ, the agent explained the situation to an extremely quiet Willa. It was not to be friendly or anything of the sort. If anything, it sounded more like a scolding, a sentence being read to a juvenile delinquent. When the car finally arrived at Chronos Corp., hundreds of protesters made it hard for the driver to get through. She honked incessantly. Clearly, the sign-wielding people did not know what was being transported. Or did they? Willa had heard how the STL's main purpose was to shut Chronos down. What better way to do so than by preventing the exchange? For Chronos' people, in trading the young girl, they would save eighteen lives. But for the Society, it was more like sacrificing eighteen for the sake of countless *future* casualties.

The teenager had to admit she was morally torn. Either way, her illegal presence in this timeline directly impacted the lives of many. If the STL protected her and she lived, people would die. If Chronos delivered her to the hacker, she would most likely die, and so would other Strays. It was, generally speaking, a no-win situation.

They ultimately made it to the front of this big building. After parking, a narrow path was created to bring her inside. Some people were yelling at the guards to let her go free, appalled at the bruteness directed toward the girl. But it would only come to that, a clear case of a bark being worse than the bite. Willa was essentially on her own.

Walking through the fancy front doors, the girl glanced at the clock on the wall, seven minutes to three. They would be getting their patrons back after all.

⟨∿⟩

0 day(s): 0 hour(s): 06 minute(s): 54 second(s)

CHAPTER 24 - Washington
The Exchange

Soon, Willa. Soon.

A strange voice rang in Willa's head, coming from who knows where. *That's it*, she thought. She'd lost her marbles.

With four armed members of the Time Police Force guiding her, the Stray felt quite nervous. She'd given up all hopes of escaping or even being rescued. Why were the walls so grey?

Down a corridor, they marched past a museum-like room. The echo of her captors' boots hammered through her throbbing brain. She could not go very fast but the woman behind her was sure to help the broken teen keep the pace. After what felt like an eternity, the small procession finally stopped. Willa looked up and thought she saw, through her puffed-up swollen eyes, a familiar machine, similar to the one she'd barely escaped at Site B.

Everything, except for its size, was identical. White revolving panels, reflective mirror floor. Suddenly, a voice came from the time gadget.

"Leave her," it said.

No one moved. Then a man in a dress shirt advanced from the shadows of the machine. He repeated his order, with more force this time. The arms that were holding the Stray finally loosened their hold. A second later, they freed her hands from the cuffs. Then they left the room. Gingerly, Willa brought her arm back to her chest, cradling it as if it were a newborn, fragile, and scared little thing. She was alone with the man. An uncomfortable silence grew. What now?

"You were not an easy young lady to find, Ms. Watson." There was no smile or emotion in his voice. "My name is Richard Washington, and I... am sorry for what happened to you."

In TimeRoom C, Richard Washington had been anxiously waiting for Willa's arrival. When he got the call from the commander, saying the prisoner was on its way, Richard exhaled a sigh of relief. He'd tried to contact the hacker to let her know that the person she'd requested was on her way. But when she didn't answer or even acknowledge his update, he swore and made his way to the appropriate TimeRoom.

Richard was mad. He was angry at the hacker, at the STL, and all of the Strays that had, at one point or another, directly and indirectly threatened what he'd worked so hard to accomplish. Chronos was his life's achievement, the one thing that would ensure immortality for his name, his legacy. But just as quickly as those red thoughts had been racing and growing in his mind, they disappeared when he, Richard Washington, the Father of Chronos, laid eyes on the shattered, bloodied teenage girl the TPF had dragged toward him. At that moment, he knew something needed to be done. He remembered why he had created an entertainment business in the first place.

"This is not right," the CEO whispered to himself. "We can do better. I *will* do better."

Willa was still standing there, shivering, not knowing what was to become of her. Richard approached the frightened youth, leaned in, and, with a heartfelt apology, asked again for forgiveness.

"Why?" Willa breathed.

"Beg your pardon?"

"Why were you keeping us? Strays. Exploiting us?"

"I have no excuse," he said, looking down at his designer shoes in shame. "Some men are weaker than others, I guess." Was he talking about himself? He looked at his watch, one minute to three.

"I need to go, don't I?"

Richard could not bring himself to say the words. He felt a hand touch his shoulder. It was small and bruised. It was Willa's.

"Let's just get this over with."

With a smile, and a sad but resolved expression, the one who'd been called "it" and "Stray" staggered onto the mirrored floor of TimeRoom C. She then turned around to give Richard, who had been called "entrepreneur" and "visionary," a shaky thumbs up.

Then his watch beeped, time had run out. Hoping it wasn't too late, the sorrowful CEO wiped a tear away and pushed the *start* button. A soft whirring sound filled the room, followed by the panels turning on themselves in unison, enclosing Willa in a high-tech tomb.

Inside, Willa felt a breeze caress her bruised cheek. The light was getting brighter and brighter. She had no choice but to close her eyes. Then a feeling of weightlessness coursed through her body. It felt fantastic to someone who could have crumbled under the weight of their body at a moment's notice.

In a few seconds, she would be transported inside a tunnel of lights.

Then silence.

↤↝

0 day(s): 0 hour(s): 00 minute(s): 00 second(s)

EPILOGUE
TWO MONTHS LATER

"That certainly explains a few things."
— Bill

LETO, we haven't been in touch in quite some time, so I dearly hope this message finds you well.

Two months have passed, in our time, since the storming of Site B. We were able to cripple the beast, but something is stirring. An informant recently made the Society aware of another Black Site. One hidden deep in the Sahara Desert. They call it Tartarus. Unfortunately, even she did not know precisely where it was located.

Although Washington has come out publicly and revealed everything he knew to the press, which turned out wasn't much at all in retrospect, Marsh, the real mastermind, is still on the loose—and very active.

A friend of mine successfully sent the intel I am about to share with you. But in a nutshell, Marsh has done it. Someone came back.

She was the last one to have gone through the Silver Door at Site B. I was told her name was Clara. She reappeared at Tartarus about a week ago, five years older than she was when she left—and eight months pregnant.

The file says that no one really knows how Clara got back or even why she had aged so rapidly. She was unconscious when the medics brought her to the Memory Room, plugging her in to find out what had happened in her time in the future.

The details from the brain scans were hazy, but I can tell you that a lot of people got excited. Even Colonel Marsh was called in to personally "deal" with the situation.

He is not quite ready to send his own men to the future yet, but seeing as the number of missing people in northern Africa is rising, it can't be a coincidence. He also wants to monitor the pregnancy. The child's DNA will be of major interest and breakthrough to him.

I fear for the mother.

You have been of great help to the Society and our timeline in the past. We are, again, in need of your skills. Let's bring Marsh and Tartarus down once and for all before the collective futures meet their end.

Leader One

After clicking *Send* he turned the computer off and stared at the dark screen for an eternity. Bill did not know what to do with himself anymore. Ever since Ginny left him, deciding to stay at her sister's place, he'd been living in a constant mental fog, as if his life was nothing more than a second-rate video game with nothing but linear quests.

He had not even tried to fight to get her back. He just stood there and took his wife's words and insecurities in full force. Hers was a storm that had been brewing for years, kept at bay dangerously close yet still in the distance. Until it was no more. It rained on metaphorical roofs, and all that could help Bill deal with the leaks was the bottom of a bottle.

When his feet could finally no longer support him, he headed back to his room. He turned the wooden door's handle and stumbled in. As he cracked it open, the smell of her perfume, even though she had been gone close to two months, hit him square in the nose.

For the first time since her abrupt departure, Bill cried. Sitting on the bed, his head turning here and there, wiping tears off of his face and out of his beard. He sat there for a while, unmoving, staring into nothingness, when eventually the moonlight shining in through his window invited him to get up and join her. Who was he to refuse an invite from such a celestial being? But first, something needed doing.

Noiselessly, he made his way to the closet room, which had looked utterly empty since she left. There, against the wall on the left-hand side, were his shirts and pants. Burned out-Bill rummaged through the lot, looking for something he hadn't worn in ages. He sloppily unhooked a bag, the one at the very end, and opened it. His wedding suit was exactly as he remembered: slick black-looking pants and jacket, white silk shirt, silver-grey vest, and charcoal tie. Even the socks, dark grey wool, were there. He would be dressed to the nines.

It took him some time to button up the shirt, and even longer to tie the tie. He could decorate a cake with his eyes closed, but to link together a silky neck accessory was beyond his current weary capacities, apparently. The thought made him chuckle. *Oh hell!* Having had enough of choking himself, he left the apparatus in the bag before parading in front of a mirror. Although it was tighter around the belly than the last time he'd put it on, the moonlight shone over his face in satisfaction. The time had come. *Let's party!*

Although every neighbour and their dog were sound asleep, for it was probably close to three a.m., jazzed up and rhythmic music began playing in Bill's head. Wide awake now, a second wind as they call it, he headed toward the basement. There was no stopping his dance moves. When he walked in, all the lights turned on, and a jukebox played his favourite song.

Moving to the beat, he walked up to the bar and liquor cabinet he had put together a few years back and called for the bartender.

"Hey, Jack, my man, whisky neat. Put it on my tab. And two Tequila Sunrise for the ladies," he said to the imaginary bartender, pointing in the direction of two empty bar stools.

Once served, he made his way to the dance floor (his home gym floor), showing off his slightly ridiculous and near inexistent dancing skills. Shortly thereafter, the two girls—albeit pretty figments of his imagination—from the bar joined him, and the three of them continued to live their best lives, moving in harmony to the beat of their favourite tunes. No one knew how long he spent pirouetting by himself, but one thing was for sure, he was as intoxicated as a freshman on his first night out. Rosy-cheeked and panting, he went to sit at the bar.

"Man! Are we having fun? Aren't we, Jack?"

"Absolutely, sir," he replied absent-mindedly, cleaning a glass. Bill noticed a hint of a British accent.

"You're alright, Jack. You're a cool chap. Pour me another, will you."

"Right away, sir," he reached behind him and grabbed a whisky from the shelf.

"Thank you. Cheers," he swallowed. The liquid burned his throat whilst going down and hit him hard. "So, is it always this fun to work at night?"

"I've no idea."

"Come again? Is this your first shift?"

"Not sure."

He looked puzzled. Then, after a moment, the server asked Bill. "Where's Ginny?"

At these words, it was as if someone had pulled the plug on the jukebox. The music stopped in Bill's head, the girls disappeared, and a more serious, almost ominous phase of intoxication took hold of his mental capacities.

"Where's Ginny?" the ghostly voice of the bartender repeated.

"Not here," Bill replied.

"You know it's your fault, right?"

"Go to hell, Jack!"

He chuckled, then, in a transition as smooth as water, Jack's face transformed and took Bill's traits. "We're already there."

Total blackout—

He woke up to the sound of the doorbell ringing. He was lying on the couch in the basement, still wearing the wedding suit, a half-drank bottle of whisky balancing in the crook of his elbow. The bell rang again, sending needle-like pain all around his head. What time was it anyway? Just after noon. Bill's stomach hurt, but he was not ready to bet it was because he was hungry. He tried getting up. The first time he tried, the room had spun at such a speed he fell to his knees. *Ding dong* again. The drunken man willed himself up, eyes half-closed, one hand on his belly, the other against the wall.

The door finally swung open.

"Can I help you?" Bill had asked a tad rudely. He was putting on sunglasses he'd picked up on his way through the kitchen.

"It took us some time to figure out who you were, Bill the baker," replied the man at the door.

Bill didn't even try to hide it; yes, he was Bill the baker. He did, however, make an effort to look at the man who had called on him. Surprise was easily read on his tired face when Bill ultimately realized who was standing there. He took a step back and invited the man inside. "What brings you here, Mr. Washington?"

"I wanted to share information with you. The extraction didn't work. The girl did not return home." Washington waited for a reaction, but the baker did not oblige. "There's one more thing. Marsh has her, as well as the one the Society calls LETO."

That certainly explains a few things. "And why would that matter to me? Why are you telling me this?"

It was Richard's turn to look confused. "Because they're your sister and your mother. Are they not, William Watson?"

TO BE CONTINUED IN TIME—

ANNEXES

Getco Just saw something weird! Was hiking in this privit spot and for real I heard voices. Went to check on it then their was this green light and then people just GONE! I swear. Stuff is happening and They dont wanna tell us what's it.
4 hours ago

MafiaFinest Where R U?
4 hours ago

Getco Fiordland in the Southland.
4 hours ago

RockerAnarky Ain't' that where they shooting that movie? Prob nothing. Just a trick. U crazy Getco.
2 hours ago

IMjfk Was clearing out my mom's attic. Found this. Wth am I looking at? Plz help.
8 hours ago

IMjfk *Attachment.jpeg*
7 hours ago

LaoSpin Thise be futurefolks. Im telling ya. Be carfull out there. Day be dangerous, have thise gagets wit dem.
7 hours ago

TimesBauer So glad I found this group. I thought I was going nuts. You have no idea how much clearer this is making things now.
23 hours ago

Bazarix Nous sommes là pour toi TimesBauer. Qu'est-ce est arrivé?
21 hours ago

Ceutious English, mf, do you speak it?!
15 hours ago

LeHistoryTeacher So many treasures have been lost to the history of mankind. What if these futuremen are responsible for it? I wonder, are there such things as time traveling thieves? Maybe even a guild. Let's not forget the confirmed disappearances of the Honjō Masamune and the Amber Room in 1945. Have we been blaming the wrong people for over 50 years?!
Saturday at 11:23 pm

Bill's Original Turnover

Many of Bill's clients make the extra detour in the morning just to get his extra delicious Apple Turnovers. Baked fresh every day, made from hand-kneaded dough and apples picked from local orchards, now you too can impress friends and family with these not-to-be-missed flaky delicacies.

Steps (Makes 12 turnovers)

1 Preheat the oven to 400°F.

2 In a two-inch deep non-stick pan, boil together apples (5 medium sweet apples cut lengthwise—peel first), butter (1 TBSP), brown sugar (½ cup - or ¾ cup coconut sugar), cinnamon (2 TSP), and vanilla extract (1 TBSP). Simmer for exactly 7 minutes, then take off the heat. Set aside.

3 On a cookie sheet, add parchment paper which will be sprinkled with flour. Take the dough out of the fridge and roll it flat onto the workstation. Cut into 12 squares. Place each square onto the parchment paper.

4 Add cooled-down apple mixture to each square (about 3 ½ TBSP). Fold each square in half in the form of a triangle. Brush egg wash (1) concoction on top of each turnover. Poke 8 holes/vents into each turnover using a thick toothpick (a fork may also be used). Finally, sprinkle the sugar of choice on each freshly egg-washed square.

5 Bake for 23 minutes. Take those flaky goodies out and let them sit for 5 minutes.

6 Enjoy!

Site B's very own "Bomb Shelter" experiment.

When Marsh and his associates came to learn of the excess of "return visitors," an executive team was put together to fix it. One of the first solutions put forth was meant to be the most humane: simply sending them back to their own timeline. However, after some tests, it was determined that it was not something that could be achieved, at least from this side of the timeline. Then someone suggested they should simply send them back to whichever timeline with no care of the actual "when": out of sight, out of mind.

Although Marsh insists it was he who came up with the idea of Site B, and no one was crazy enough to doubt him, it was an older lady by the name of Edlyn Oliver. Before joining Chronos and Marsh, Mrs. Oliver was a Professor of Ethics and morals who would lecture at top Universities across the world. From her came the real-life application of the "Bomb Shelter" experiment, where psychology and philosophy students are asked to fill up their bunker with a small number of people from a list of made-up people of different ages, professions, and other criteria. Thus began the division of *useful Strays* and *expendable ones*.

To be deemed useful was not a problem; they were put to work right away. The question was, what to do with the other ones? Sooner rather than later, the race for the future took a significantly important step forward.

A CHRONOS EXCLUSIVE

7 WONDERS

A NEW ARRIVAL

AGRA, 1653 - Taj Mahal
YUCÁTAN, 998 - Chichén Itzá
ROME, 82 - Colosseum
RIO DE JANEIRO, 1931 - Christ the Redeemer
WADI MUSA, 1284 - Petra
SHANGHAI, 1644 - Great Wall
ANDES MOUNTAINS, 1450 - Machu Picchu

Will you be part of history?

Coming August 2

ConEX, in partnership with Chronos,
Presents
<u>Time Travel Convention</u> - *press release*

Come celebrate Chronos' fifth anniversary in style. Join us on April 5th, 6th, and 7th of next year for the first-ever installment of the *Time Travel Convention* - an event truly out of this world.

This one-of-a-kind event, sponsored by arguably one of the biggest entertainment businesses of the twenty-first century, will offer a wide range of exhibits and activities for patrons of all ages. Come to *Vermont GC Center* to meet with local artists, collectors, and fellow genre-loving aficionados and cosplayers. Whether you are a fan of *Dr. Who*, *Star Trek*, or *Timeline*, there is something for the whole family.

Looking for something more? You will not want to miss our guest panels and workshops. Let legendary author Yasutaka Tsutsui (*The Girl Who Leapt Through Time*) tell you about his life. Experience what it must have been like to relive the Groundhog Days with actress Andie MacDowell (*Groundhog Day*). Test drive a DeLorean inspired by the minds of Robert Zemeckis and Bob Gale (*we might run out of plutonium—time traveling not guaranteed*). Special appearance by Dr. Emmett Brown himself, Christopher Lloyd (*Back to the Future*), on the sixth of April only.

Other notable guest appearances:
- *Hugh Jackman (X-Men: Days of Future Past)*
- *Linda Hamilton (Terminator)*
- *Amy Smart (The Butterfly Effect)*
- *Derek Gagnon (Out of Time)*
- *Audrey Niffenegger (The Time Traveler's Wife)*

Professional photo sessions and guests meet-and-greets can also be purchased as part of a package.

For more information, please visit our website: *www.timetravelconvention/ConEX.com*

Forman Weekly - Retrocognition vs. Timeline displacement
Vol. 4 No. 27

Retrocognition vs. Timeline Displacement: A Psychoanalysis of the Mind

Have you ever felt this moment of *déjà-vu*? A feeling you have had about a place or a person even before having been there or met them?

In the last five years, more and more people have come forward with multiple cases of retrocognition. This trend is to be expected, according to a pocket of experts, ever since the giant entertainment business Chronos came online.

To begin, what is "retrocognition"? The term was coined by one Frederic W. H. Myers in the late eighteen hundreds, who was, at the time, the father of the "subliminal self." Since then, the idea of "backward knowing" has greatly evolved to the point today that it is calling for Mr. Washington to slow down with his business' temporal visits.

What was once regarded as an untestable field, retrocognition is gradually gaining ground among a group of researchers in eastern New York. According to their statistics, forty to sixty-eight clients had experienced retrocognition each year in the past fifteen years. However, since Chronos opened its doors five years ago, the numbers have skyrocketed to one hundred and twenty in the first year, two hundred and eleven in the second, and three hundred and forty-four during the most recent census.

"I was walking down the reflecting pool in DC with my dad," says Jonah Eckler, a New England senior visiting the capital city, "when suddenly, images of MLK's speech popped into my mind. I knew about his 'I Have a Dream' speech, of course, but I'd never heard it, I swear. So it was strange for me, in the span of walking between the Lincoln Memorial to the Washington Monument, that I could recite most of the address word for word. I was so confused. I didn't know what had just happened."

Although researchers have yet to prove the connection between retrocognition and Chronos, many are calling it a sort of time displacement syndrome, a side-effect someone might come across if they were exposed to intertemporal particles.

18

BRAINstorm

Is time thieving illegal? A thread in response to Roxanne Nash's non-guilty verdict.

Lawless Dude, if I was working at Chronos, I'd be running back in there and coming out with my arms loaded with treasures. What do you think I should hit first? The Queen's coronation jewels and crown or the Romanovs Faberge eggs?
7 hours ago

StillStanding Why would you even joke about that?
7 hours ago

Echo I'm a Chronos employee, and I can tell you right now that there's no way they're gonna let us just walk out with stuff from different timelines. If anything, because of Nash's verdict, restrictions are gonna be even tighter.
5 hours ago

OwlBearing In Canada they have this thing called the Criminal Code. In article 354.1 it states that anyone who has in his possession any property or thing knowing that all or part of the property was obtained by an act, <u>if it had occurred in Canada</u>, would have constituted an offense punishable by indictment. Don't you see?
12 hours ago

Standards18 What's your point? Nash wasn't tried in Canada.
9 hours ago

OwlBearing I know, but it clearly says that if, for example, she stole something in England, she could not be tried in Canada. Couldn't it be the same with inter-timeline laws? She "allegedly" stole stuff from a "different" country. Short of sending her back to that timeline, I don't see why they'd put her on trial here.
9 hours ago

TextbookHero TY Supreme court. Now look at what you've done. Heck of a precedent to set. It won't be long before protesters crowd Natural History Museums around the word demanding they give back every last bit of physical archeological findings. Smithsonian 'bout to get emptied!
21 hours ago

XvsY world*
18 hours ago

Bigwig As much as I agree with you in saying there's a fine line between owning and forcefully taking objects and treasures from a cultural group, this Chronos thing is different. I mean, does Chronos actually own what was stolen from those timelines? Why would they have any say in this?
13 hours ago

Time Displaced: A Tell All
by Herbert Wells

"I had no one. I remembered nothing. I was being chased like an animal, no, like something less than that, because animals have rights. I had nothing, and I was no one. That was three years ago. Today, I have a life. I matter to a lot of people, to my wife and our one-year-old boy. All thanks to the Society and everything they do for all of us."

– Carmen Stehc, a victim of time displacement

Herbert Wells is one of the founding members of the Society of Timeline Liberation and a vocal advocate for time displaced victims' rights. In his book, he invites the readers to join the fight against the enemy: Ignorance. Each chapter develops on the ideas promoted by the STL's manifesto with testimonies, picture evidence, and—warnings.

"Too many people are in the dark. It is high time that someone shines some light."

– Ghemma Drake, author of The Power of Knowledge

A soon-to-be international bestseller, Mr. Wells' account looks to make noise and exact most needed change against the twenty-first century's newest darling and high-tech entertainment business Chronos.

"It's all true. More people are getting ripped out of their lives than you think."

– an anonymous Chronos employee

What will it take for the masses to finally realize just how many lives have been stolen? And when, not if, Chronos shuts down, what happens then? How do we go about the fallout? Herbert Wells has an idea. Who will listen?

COMING OUT NEXT FALL

Acknowledgement

Not unlike Washington's reason for creating Chronos, I too began thinking about this novel after having missed out on the type of spectacle where the orchestra would play on stage, and scenes from the movies would be projected on a large screen above the musicians: one night only, the last show on the tour. It was Star Wars in Concert, hosted by the amazingly talented Anthony Daniels. So, although I have not been able to see it, I first want to thank the people responsible for putting the show together.

Secondly, I would like to thank the master of technothriller, the late Michael Crichton, for being such an important inspiration, especially in the early days of the first few drafts. In a way, Out of Time began as a sort of homage to the brilliance of Mr. Crichton's work. Without Jurassic Park, Timeline, Next, and many more, I don't think I would have had the discipline or the drive to research the many aspects found in my novel. Like Mr. Crichton, I wanted to inject as much truth as possible into the fiction, even if I knew that an entertainment business that used time travel was well beyond the scope of our reality... for now.

Next, I would like to thank the people who have inspired and encouraged me throughout this whirlwind of a journey. First of all, to my wife, Nancy. Thank you for your patience and understanding as you had to deal with the chaos and craziness that accompanied my creative process. To my children, Lily and JJ, who inspired me and showed me that I would do anything and everything for them. To my parents, Luc and Kyna, who were the first to believe in my writing and who laid the foundation for my storytelling. To my siblings, Yanik, Kim, and Zoé for your thoughts and immeasurable insights. To my first readers, Nicholas, Aaron, and Katya. I appreciate your willingness to dive into those early drafts. I'm sorry you had to go through some of the earlier ideas. To my students and the members of the Turnbull Writers' Club. Seeing your enthusiasm for writing has fueled my own passion. To the entire AOS Publishing Team. To Michael, especially, for being the first person to believe in Out of Time enough to give it a chance. To Julia, for the many insightful editorial notes.

My novel would not be where it is today if it wasn't for all of you.

Finally, there is special thanks to be given to you, the reader, for picking up this book and embarking on this crazy journey. Out of Time would be nothing without you and for that, you have my heartfelt gratitude.

Thank you,
Derek Gagnon